Tainted Too

Tainted Too

Blacc Topp

www.urbanbooks.net

Urban Books, LLC
300 Farmingdale Road, NY-Route 109
Farmingdale, NY 11735

ISBN 13: 978-1-64556-659-5

First Mass Market Printing October 2024
First Trade Paperback Printing April 2024
Printed in the United States of America

10 9 8 7 6 5 4 3 2 1

*This is a work of fiction. Any references or similar-
ities to actual events, real people, living or dead, or
to real locales are intended to give the novel a sense
of reality. Any similarity in other names, characters,
places, and incidents is entirely coincidental.*

Distributed by Kensington Publishing Corp.
Submit Orders to:
Customer Service
400 Hahn Road
Westminster, MD 21157-4627
Phone: 1-800-733-3000
Fax: 1-800-659-2436

Chapter 1

CHANGE IN CURRENT

Monica smiled as she signed the card that she'd addressed to Bird. He'd made good on his promise to leave the game and travel the straight and narrow. She was proud of Bird. He'd opened a restaurant called Bird's Burgers, and he was having the grand opening of his third location. Monica giggled. She was happy that she'd remained friends with Bird after all they'd been through. He'd hit on her relentlessly until she finally sat him down and explained to him all the reasons why they could never be. As a DEA agent, she had been bound by her duties and she'd simply been doing her job. Kochese had not only been the case of a lifetime, but unfortunately, he had become a casualty in the war on drugs. She still felt a twinge of guilt about him committing suicide, but it was his choice to die rather than serve time. She'd also explained that her main priorities were Jasmine and

Noisy Boy. Bird had been somewhat surprised and hurt, but he'd understood and reluctantly moved on. Either Bird had been trying to be a playboy or he had moved incredibly fast, because not even a month later, Bird had called Monica, hardly able to contain himself.

"Guess what, Monkey?" Bird had said excitedly.

She hated when he called her Monkey, but she understood that it was his way of establishing a familiar connection. "What, Bird? What's got you so excited?"

"I'm in love, Monkey! I know what you're going to say: 'Bird, you're moving too fast,'" he said, mimicking Monica's voice. "I'm telling you, though, she's the one. My little sister loves her."

"Okay, okay, calm down ol' super-duper-in-love-ass dude. Noisy Boy, Uncle Bird has a new girlfriend. What do you think about that?" Monica said.

Noisy Boy lifted his head from the floor and gave two quick yelps.

"I'm excited for you, Bird, and so is Noisy Boy. We can't wait to meet her."

"I love this feeling! Shit, I don't know which one I love the most, her or this feeling that I'm feeling right now. But, Monica?"

"Yes, Bird?"

"Don't interrogate her when you meet her, because she's shy."

"What makes you think I'm going to interrogate her?"

"Because I know you."

"What's her name?"

"Bridgette."

"Where's she from?"

"She's from here."

"How old is she?"

"She's twenty-six."

"What does she do for a living?"

"She owns a bookstore/coffee house."

"Any kids?"

"None I know of. See what I mean? You're interrogating me about her and you haven't even met her yet."

"Yeah, yeah, yeah. So how'd you guys meet?" Monica asked, continuing with her barrage of questions.

"Well, we were both taking an entrepreneurial course at East Lake College, we got to rappin', and that's how it happened. Seriously, we just found that we had a lot in common, and we've been inseparable since."

"Well, I'm happy for you. You deserve it, Bird."

"Yeah, well, you had your chance, and you blew it, shawty! Now *all* this chunk of lovin' is going to somebody else!" Bird teased.

"What the hell ever, boy, bye! Get off of my phone!" Monica laughed.

That had been almost nine months earlier. Now Bird was a married man, and he and Bridgette were expecting their first child.

Monica sealed the envelope and placed it beneath a dozen roses that she'd bought for Bird and Bridgette. She looked down at Noisy Boy, who lay lazily at her feet. He stared back at her, bewildered. Monica grew sad as she looked at her puppy. Well, he wasn't exactly a puppy anymore. At more than fifty pounds, Noisy Boy was full-grown and the most beautiful canine she'd ever seen. He made her think of Kochese much too often.

She had allowed herself to fall deeper in love with Kochese than she'd imagined. He haunted her dreams, often turning her dreams into nightmares. She could still feel his touch, oftentimes sending her body into fits of ecstasy-filled convulsions. Even from the grave, Kochese had a hold on her. She hadn't so much as looked at another man since she lost Kochese. She could still see his intense eyes burning through her like freshly blazed embers, but she couldn't remember his voice. When she tried to imagine something that he might say, she only heard her own voice.

Noisy Boy let his blue puppy dog eyes sag sadly. He licked his chops greedily and then whimpered softly. That was his way of letting her know that it was past his feeding time.

"Okay, Mommy's hungry little man. As soon as Jasmine gets out of the shower, we will get something to eat. Okay, baby?" Monica said.

Noisy Boy cocked his head to one side as if to ask, "Are you serious?" He was the alpha dog, and he knew it. He stood and circled the table once and then trotted toward the bathroom.

Monica listened with a knowing smirk on her face. Moments later, she heard Noisy Boy bark and then scratch at the bathroom door. The shower stopped, and Jasmine emerged covered in a lime green bath towel. Her jet-black hair fell in heavy, wet ringlets around her bronzed shoulders.

"Don't rush me, Mr. Meanie," Jasmine said as she knelt to pat Noisy Boy on his head. He whimpered again and wagged his tail feverishly.

Monica smiled to herself. Noisy Boy was over-protective of the sisters who were often mistaken for twins. Their looks seemed to garner too much attention for Noisy Boy's taste, and he'd scared away more than one suitor who'd come calling. They jogged every morning and nobody, man or woman, could get close to them without Noisy Boy going into attack mode.

"Hurry up, Jazzy Bell. The grand opening ceremony starts in an hour," Monica said.

"Okay, I'm hurrying. You're just rushing me so that you can feed your little greedy son!"

***

Less than an hour later, they pulled up in front of Bird's new restaurant. A small crowd of about thirty people started to gather. Bird was expecting a much larger crowd by the end of the evening. This newest location wasn't as large as his other locations, but the building could still hold double that number easily. Monica smiled and nodded at Bird as she made her way to a reserved parking spot in front of the café. As usual, Bird was the center of attention. He was dressed in the finest designer clothing, smiling his immaculately polished smile from ear to ear. He held a grotesquely oversized pair of golden scissors, and a huge red ribbon was stretched across the front entrance of Bird's Burgers. He nodded back in her direction, smiling that same boyish smile. Bridgette stood next to him, glowing. Pregnancy really agreed with her, and even though she complained to Monica about her massive weight increase, she was beyond gorgeous. Monica hadn't noticed any significant weight gain, only the basketball-shaped baby bump of Millicent Bircher, who slumbered peacefully within her mother's womb. Monica liked the name. It was cute, and when she'd asked Bird why they'd chosen the name Millicent, he'd simply shrugged and said, "Because it's pretty."

Bridgette stood between Bird and his sister, Kim, facing the throng of eager spectators.

Bridgette's yellow maternity dress billowed in the slight breeze. She smiled as their potential customers made small talk about how good their burgers were and how beautiful she looked. As Monica, Jasmine, and Noisy Boy made their way to the front of the restaurant, she noticed the white smoke pouring from the roof of the building. It was undoubtedly from the grills inside the eatery, because the smell of freshly grilled beef and chicken wafted through the air.

Bird's imagination and ingenuity were incredible. He was the first person in Dallas, maybe in history, to combine a restaurant catering to both people and their pets. There were two entrances— one for humans and one for pets. As the patrons arrived, they would gladly hand over their pets to handlers who seated the dogs at a long buffet-style table where they could not only mingle with other dogs, but they could also have their fill of dishes ranging from filet mignon to Bird's famous grilled burger smothered in beef bouillon gravy. He'd come up with the idea by seeing that people really loved to eat on the go, but most people in the Thousand Oaks section of Dallas spent a lot of time with their pets. If they were given the chance to take their pets home, then nine times out of ten they wouldn't return to a burger joint, no matter how upscale. By offering to feed their dogs while they in turn were being fed, Bird surmised that most people wouldn't mind paying the slightly higher prices for the convenience of his one-stop shop. His supposition had been correct, and it had paid off in a major way.

"Baby, can we get started? I'm starving, and baby Millie is kicking me. She's hungry too," Bridgette whined.

"Okay, baby. All right, ladies and gentlemen, I want to thank everyone for coming out to join us for yet another grand opening. We plan to open one of these every year until we're old and gray. As long as you wonderful people keep supporting us, we'll keep opening diner after diner," Bird said. He bent underneath the red ribbon and stepped to the front door, opening it and beckoning to his staff.

One by one, they filed out to the sidewalk. Their attire was decidedly elegant for work in an establishment whose main staple was hamburgers. Although they specialized in burgers, Bird wanted to give a different vibe to his restaurant. Patrons were seated and ordered from menus, nothing too drastically different from a Steak 'n Shake or Applebee's. The major difference came with the attire and service. The restaurant-goers were treated more like they were at Ruth's Chris than Burger King, and the entire staff was dressed in black formal wear. The waiters wore black tuxedos, and the waitresses wore black French maid outfits. The cooks wore black also, but not tuxedos. They wore black traditional chef's uniforms. Only the head chef, Rufus, wore chef whites.

"Okay, everyone, now that we're all here, let's get this party started. Kim, since you'll be running this location, why don't you do us the honor of cutting the ribbon?" Bird said, handing Kimberly Bircher the gigantic golden scissors.

She took the scissors and turned to face the crowd. "This is my brother's dream, and although he has given me the privilege of being his restaurant's manager, I'm sure there will come a time when I will be answering to my unborn niece Millicent. Bridgette, come up here and help me cut this so that we can tell Millie she helped cut the ribbon," Kim cooed. Bridgette joined Kim behind the ribbon and took one side of the huge scissors.

"Okay, ladies and gentlemen, count with me!" Bird shouted. "One, two, three!" he screamed with the crowd.

As the scissors sliced through the satin ribbon, an ear-shattering crackle pierced the air, followed by a second bone-chilling snap. Kim's head exploded in a mess of skull fragments and brain matter. Before it registered with anyone that Kim had been assassinated, a third shot rang out and struck Bridgette in her chest, throwing her against the wall. She opened her mouth to scream, but there was only silence. She clawed at her chest as she slid down the red brick wall, leaving a trail of blood as she slumped to the ground. The soft yellow maternity sundress she wore was now a malevolent shade of copper as it mixed with her crimson-colored plasma.

The crowd screamed in disbelief and began scurrying for cover. Bird stood mesmerized, unable to move as Monica screamed at him to get down, but Bird didn't hear her. He had locked eyes with his soulmate, the woman who had believed in him, the woman who had married him, and the woman who would bear his child. He wondered if baby Millicent would make it through this tragedy. He wanted to go to her, to comfort her, but his body felt heavy, and he couldn't move.

A single tear fell from Bridgette's eye as she stared lifelessly back at Bird. Deep within him from his bowels, he began to moan as the realization of what had happened hit him. The entire scenario had unfolded in front of him in slow motion, and he hadn't been able to protect her. The moaning grew louder. His teeth chattered, and his hands shook. He had to be dreaming. He blinked his eyes rapidly, trying to awaken from his horrible nightmare, but every time he closed his eyes and opened them, Bridgette and Kim still lay motionless on the ground in front of him. The moaning had turned into cries of repressed agony as Bird cried out, "God, why?" He dropped to his knees as sobs racked his body.

Monica and Jasmine both looked on in dazed horror as Bird made his way to a spot between his wife and his sister. He took Bridgette in his arms and cradled her.

"Baby, wake up, somebody help me! Bridgette, baby, open your eyes. Monkey, help me please!" he screamed. His tears fell and came to rest atop their puddled blood. He raised his head and looked to the heavens and screamed. His entire body shook uncontrollably as he sent unspeakable curses to heaven, asking God why time and time again. Bird begged God to take him instead, but his deathly reprieve never came, only the shrill whine of the approaching sirens.

Chapter 2

I'M ALL IN

Three blocks from the grisly scene, the gunman drove away undetected. He'd watched the two women and the beautiful puppy arrive, and the time couldn't have been better. A sinister smile spread across his handsome face as the bright lights of fire trucks, ambulances, and police cars blared toward him. As they passed, the deafening sound of their sirens invaded his eardrums. He drove south until he reached I-30 and headed east. The assassin made sure to watch his speed, careful not to draw any attention to himself. The murders had given him a sense of instant gratification, but he wasn't satisfied. He had a blood lust that hadn't been quelled, and he needed more.

The sunlight glimmered and bounced across the dirty brownish blue water of Lake Ray Hubbard as he crossed the bridge into Rockwall, Texas. He owned the plot of land between Lake Ray Hubbard

Road and Rockwall-Forney Dam. It was totally se-
cluded except for a few sparse farmhouses, mostly
abandoned, along Lake Ray Hubbard Road. Dusk
had just begun to fall as he reached the wood line
that encircled his seventy-five acres of property.
He gave a quick glance in his rearview mirror to
make sure that he hadn't been followed before
turning onto the long dirt road that led to his large
lodge-style two-story house.

It was a massive 7,000 square feet, most of
which was unused. It sat back two miles from the
road and was completely surrounded by trees.
He'd chosen this location because trees provided
natural soundproofing and his victims would
never be heard if they decided to scream. From the
outside, the house looked completely abandoned.
A dilapidated pickup truck sat near the driveway.
Closer to the house but off to one side was a barn
that was made from the same termite-infested
wood as the house.

He pulled his car into the barn and made the
one-hundred-foot trek to his house. He walked
into his house and went to a room just to the left of
his kitchen. He turned on an oil lamp on a nearby
desk, and an unstable light flooded the room. It
flickered from wall to wall, casting an eerie glow
against the array of tattered photos that had been
thumbtacked to the drywall. On the wall across
from his unholy shrine were dozens of electronic

monitoring screens that all held different views of spots around Dallas. It was as if he'd gone through the city and installed cameras in random places, but they weren't random. They all held significance to the man. He took the red Magic Marker that sat on the rickety table beneath the photos and put a huge X on the faces of Bridgette and Kimberly Bircher. Next to their pictures was a picture of Bird. The gunman spit on the picture and then circled his face in red. He turned and studied the video screens. On the far-right screen, he studied the women coming through the door. Monica and Jasmine Dietrich both walked through the door of their small brick house with Noisy Boy in tow. He raised the volume just loud enough to hear their conversation.

"I'm glad they were at least able to save the baby, Monica," Jasmine said.

"Yeah, me too. I just don't understand this shit. I mean, Bird doesn't deserve this. He really loved Bridgette, and you already know how he felt about his little sister," Monica said sadly. She sat on the couch and tried to relax. Noisy Boy lay his head on her lap and whined softly. He could feel her sadness, and although he didn't understand death, he knew that something wasn't right.

The gunman had witnessed enough. He turned the screen off and went back to the wall of pictures. He went to a picture of Monica and Jasmine. In the picture, they both looked happy as they sat at an outdoor bistro sipping something from teacups. They looked like twins, but he could see the difference. Monica's eyes shone brightly in the picture as if she didn't have a care in the world. Jasmine, on the other hand, was a different matter altogether. Even though she smiled, her eyes spoke of pain and torment. She was hiding something deep and sinister, a secret that she refused to share. He knew about secrets, and he most certainly knew about pain. Jasmine Dietrich intrigued him, and he stared into her eyes until he felt as though he had some sort of cosmic connection with her. They were kindred spirits, misunderstood souls that craved pain and bloodshed.

Chapter 3

I'LL DIE FIRST

Monica walked into the lobby of Parkland Hospital, afraid of what lay ahead. Jasmine had refused to come because she didn't handle pain well, and Monica completely understood, but someone had to be there for Bird. His mother had blamed Kim's and Bridgette's deaths on his lifestyle. Bird had curtly reminded her that he'd gone straight and left the game behind, but that had been no consolation for his grieving mother. Monica wondered silently why she hadn't walked away from Bird after the case with Kochese had ended. It wasn't that he wasn't a good person. It was that her life was pretty much free of drama except for this tragedy. She'd tried to coordinate with the police department, but they had been less than forthcoming. For whatever reason, the police didn't like Feds and vice versa.

She stepped off the elevator into the halls of the neonatal intensive care unit and went to the nearby nurses' station. "Excuse me, ma'am, I'm looking for the Bircher baby's room," Monica said.

"Are you related?"

"Yes, I'm her aunt," Monica lied.

"She's in room 1050. Visiting hours are over in less than an hour, young lady."

Monica didn't say anything. She knew that they couldn't force a father to leave, and there was no way Bird would let her leave once she was there.

When she walked into the NICU room, Bird was kneeling next to the incubator with his hands clasped in front of his face. He appeared to be praying or deep in thought. She slinked past him and took a seat behind him quietly.

Bird stood and turned to face Monica. Tears streaked his cheeks, and snot ran from his nose. "Hey, Monkey, I didn't hear you come in. How long have you been here?" Bird asked through muffled sadness.

"I just got here. How is Millie?"

"They finally got her stabilized. I think she might come out of intensive care soon. They want her weight to increase a little more. She's only at five pounds, six ounces. I've been here since that bullshit happened. I watched them cut Bridgette open and remove Millie from her tummy," Bird said. He tried to choke back his tears, but to no avail. Between sobs, he kept talking. "She didn't even get a chance to hold her baby. She looks like Bridgette,

I think. What am I supposed to do, Monkey? I don't know shit about being a father," Bird said.

"You have to do the very best that you can. You know Jazzy and I will be there to help. Have you talked to your mother again?"

"Yeah, man, she's really draining me emotionally. She's gotten with Bridgette's family, telling them about my past, and now they are talking about taking Millie from me. I can't lose her too, Monkey. I've been doing what I promised. I've stayed out of trouble and out of the game, but if they try to take my baby, I'm going to kill somebody, I swear on everything."

"None of that killer talk, Bird. Those days are over. Nobody's going to take her from you, so chill," Monica said.

Bird's eyes narrowed to mere slits. "She's all I have left in this world, Monica. She's all I care about, so if I don't have her, I don't have shit. I'd rather be dead than to live without my Millie Bean," he said as he walked to the incubator. He stared down at his baby girl with tubes running into her nose.

"Look at her, Monkey. She's so innocent, so fragile. Her entire childhood will be spent without her mother. Her little life is in my hands, and I'm fucking terrified. I'm afraid to fail. I heard her tiny little voice for the first time last night," Bird said, smiling. "As hurt as I was, when I heard it, it made me

smile, and a weight was lifted from my shoulders,"
he said with his eyes still trained on baby Millicent.
"The police came in asking questions, and the
whole time that they were here, it was more like
an interrogation than an inquiry. They don't care
about solving this murder case, Monica. The fact
that my name is involved automatically makes it
unimportant to them," he said, turning to Monica.
"You need to find the person responsible for this
shit, Monkey."

"I tried to talk to the police, but they aren't giving
me any details, Bird."

"Monica, I need you to find them. I know you
can. Please, I'm begging you. If I know that you're
on this thing, then I can at least get some measure
of peace. Promise me, Monkey," Bird begged.

Monica studied Bird's face for a long time.
There was something in his eyes that let her know
he wouldn't rest unless he knew that she was involved in the case. He looked disheveled and rough
around the edges. Any other time, Monica would
have cracked a funny joke about his appearance,
but under the circumstances she decided against
it. "Bird, you have my word I will do everything in
my power to find the people responsible for this
madness."

"That's all I ask, Monkey," Bird said, turning
back to look at Millicent. "That's all I ask."

Chapter 4

DEITRICH GIRLS

Monica dressed in a hurry. She'd overslept and was behind schedule for her morning run with Jasmine and Noisy Boy. Had it not been for Noisy Boy jumping onto her bed and panting in her face with his hot canine breath, she would have still been fast asleep.

The night before, Monica had come home from the hospital with a heavy heart and a cluttered mind. Bird was heartbroken, and as his friend she wanted to fix it, but her hands were all but tied. As a federal agent, she couldn't supersede the local authorities without permission. She could do some snooping, but that was about it. She'd prayed on it heavily before bed and had finally dozed off, and now she was fully awake and ready for her run.

The smell of freshly brewed Maxwell House coffee pulled her from her thoughts. She examined herself one last time in her full-length mirror before heading to the kitchen. "Even when I'm tacky, I'm still flyer than these bitches," she said to no one in particular. She'd tried to tone down her attire in the hopes of quelling the unwanted attention that she received regularly, but it hadn't worked.

Monica had taken great pride in coordinating her workout gear. She would match her colorful leggings to her Air Max running shoes, but that combination had seemed to drive the men wild, and they'd gotten beside themselves with their lascivious whistles and leers. Jasmine had jokingly explained to her that the men acted like that because her boobs bounced and her butt clapped when she jogged. Monica had turned beet red from embarrassment and had reluctantly switched to heavier sweatpants.

"Good morning, Jazzy," Monica said.

"Morning, sis. How's Bird and the baby?"

"Bird is still a mess, and the baby is stable. Hopefully she'll be moved from intensive care soon. Bird wants me to investigate," Monica said.

"You should."

"It's not that simple. I could get into a lot of trouble for stepping into a local investigation," Monica said as she stirred sugar and creamer into her coffee.

"Trouble shmouble! Bird is family. And since when did you let your right hand know what your left hand is doing? It's not like you're going to barge into different places with guns blazing, announcing to the world that you're a Fed."

"I suppose you're right. I could always just do a little poking around to see what I can come up with," Monica said reflectively.

"Yeah, because you know he'd do the same for you."

Noisy Boy stood by the door whimpering as if to let the ladies know that he was ready to go for his morning walk. He scratched at the door lightly and then walked to Monica and nudged her leg with his head.

"Okay, Noisy Boy, dang. You're a bossy little something, huh?" she said as she knelt to attach his leash to his spiked collar.

The trio exited the home and made the short trek to the park that sat adjacent to their residence. Noisy Boy trotted regally between Monica and Jasmine as he did every morning. The jogging trail was deserted except for a tall runner in the distance headed in their direction. As he got closer Monica still couldn't make out his features. She could, however, make out his chiseled, sweaty, muscular frame. His sinewy pectoral muscles flexed and bounced as he made his way closer to Monica and Jasmine. As he approached, Monica could see his facial features clearly. His cropped bone-straight jet black hair was cut in a perfect

Caesar style and glistened from his perspiration. His stern jawline flinched with every step that he took. Monica's breath caught in her throat as he closed the distance between them. He squinted, and his intense blue eyes burned through her as if trying to recollect a long-lost connection.

"Oh, my God, he's gorgeous!" Jasmine exclaimed.

"Yeah, I guess, if you're into white boys. He looks very familiar though."

"If you're into white boys? Need I remind you that your father was a *white boy?*" Jasmine sneered sarcastically.

As he approached, he stopped just short of the women and doubled over, winded, trying to catch his breath. Noisy Boy broke loose from his leash and ran to the tall, muscular stranger. He barked loudly as he closed the gap between them. Monica panicked because Noisy Boy had always been overly aggressive.

"Noisy Boy, stop! Heel, boy!" Monica screamed.

Noisy Boy kept running, oblivious of his master's pleas. The man stood startled, torn between catching his breath and warding off the approaching pit bull. He stood just in time to catch the canine as he leapt into his arms. Noisy Boy tried to lick the man's face. His tail wagged ferociously as he whimpered playfully.

Monica and Jasmine moved toward the pair in stunned amazement. Noisy Boy had never reacted to a stranger in such a manner, and it startled the sisters. Noisy Boy hated everyone except Monica and Jasmine. Even Bird had found himself cornered by the viciousness of Noisy Boy's advance.

"I'm so sorry, sir! Please forgive my puppy! Bad dog, Noisy Boy!" Monica scolded.

"Oh, he's okay. He's a pretty puppy. He just got a little overly excited," the stranger said. He bent down and scratched the back of Noisy Boy's ear, and then he rubbed his stomach in a circular motion until his leg began to shake uncontrollably. Monica and Jasmine exchanged surprised glances.

"Do I know you?" Monica asked.

"I'm sure, had we met before, my dear, I would remember such an exquisite woman. So I doubt it seriously."

Monica searched his face in earnest deliberation, rifling through her memory bank until it dawned on her. He looked like a younger version of Hayden Cross. She could see remnants of her lost love Kochese in his eyes. They shared the same penetrating azure eyes. He looked like Kochese, only a white version, and his voice was different, more educated and refined, the type of dialect that was often associated with suburban living and expensive boarding schools. "Do you know a Hayden Cross?" Monica asked.

"Actually, I do. He's my father. My name is Khalil, Khalil Cross," he said, extending his hand.

"Pleased to meet you, Khalil. My name is Monica, and this is my kid sister, Jasmine."

"It's my pleasure to meet you both. How do you know my father?" Khalil asked.

"You could say that I am a family friend."

Khalil took Jasmine's hand into his own and kissed it softly. "Are you also a family friend?" he asked and then added, "You two look more like twins than an older and younger sister."

"Well, thank you, Mr. Cross. It was nice to meet you. If you don't mind, we're going to continue our run," Monica said.

"By all means, and please call me Khalil. I apologize for interrupting your morning run. Jasmine, would it be too forward or presumptuous of me to ask for your phone number?" Khalil asked.

Jasmine stood flabbergasted, unable to speak. She searched for the words, but they wouldn't form. Her brain had instructed her lips to consent to Khalil's advances, but her voice was mute. She'd stared at Khalil Cross the entire time that he'd been in their presence, silently rehearsing what she would say in the event that she was afforded the opportunity. She had been given the chance to tell him how utterly beautiful she thought he was in her eyes, and she had been petrified to the point of paralysis. She silently cursed herself for her inability to speak. Jasmine was a Chatty Cathy with Monica and Noisy Boy. Even her classmates at El

Centro College found her to be rather talkative. The truth of the matter was that Jasmine had never really held a conversation with a man outside of Bird and Agent Muldoon, who'd abruptly stopped calling after Monica had switched from the DEA to the FBI.

"She'd be happy to give you her number. Isn't that right, Jasmine?" Monica asked.

"Uh-huh," Jasmine muttered almost inaudibly.

"Let's make this easy. You take my number and call me when you're ready. Do you have your phone with you?" Khalil asked.

Jasmine nodded sheepishly. She handed Khalil her cell phone with trembling hands. He input his number and passed the cellular back to Jasmine.

"I hope you decide to call soon, Jasmine. It was a real pleasure meeting you both," he said. Khalil kneeled and whispered something in Noisy Boy's ear with his eyes still trained on the sisters. He patted the pooch on the head, stood, and then jogged away slowly.

Jasmine glanced at her phone, and a wide grin spread across her face as she turned to watch him jog away. Monica snatched her phone playfully and stared at the screen. Khalil had saved his number under the contact: my future husband.

Chapter 5

MORE OF THE SAME

Jasmine Deitrich sat in the courtyard of the downtown El Centro College campus, staring at her Western Humanities textbook. Her eyes were trained on her chapter of study, but her mind was on Khalil Cross. His chiseled features had etched themselves into her brain, and she couldn't shake the thought of him. She pulled the cell phone from her purse and gazed at it. Hello Kitty gawked back at her with her bright eyes and quick smile. Jasmine scrolled through her phone until she came to Khalil's number. She silently wondered if there was a time limit between when a man gave a woman his number and when it was acceptable to call. The thought of him caused her stomach to quiver. Monica had been a little less than understanding about her reaction to Khalil's advances.

"What was with all the stuttering, Jazzy Bell? You sounded like Porky Pig when he was talking to you. 'Dibbity dibbity dibbity.' I mean, damn, boo," Monica had teased.

"That's fucked up, Moni! It's not like I've ever had a boyfriend or even really talked to a man, for that matter. It's not like men are lining up at your door either, hooker!"

"Hooker, huh? Pull the *Monopoly* game out. Sounds like somebody needs an ass whipping to put that ass back into check," Monica said, trying to ease the tension.

That had been a few days earlier, and Monica had purposely avoided any conversation that had the name Khalil Cross attached to it.

"Hey, Jasmine, a couple of us are going over to Panera for lunch. You want to come?" Farrah asked.

Farrah was in her fourth year at El Centro and much too talkative for Jasmine's tastes. She wasn't an ugly girl, but she wasn't as gorgeous as she believed herself to be. Farrah Harden was slightly overweight and believed that she had been put on God's green earth to bed as many men as possible before she died. Although pudgy, she carried it well and kept the latest in designer clothes, which, according to Farrah, had come courtesy of her many suitors. She spoke of many casual encounters and sexual conquests as if they were nothing more than sharing a recipe.

"No, thank you, Farrah. I have studying to do. Thanks anyway," Jasmine said sweetly. She didn't feel sweet though. She was actually kind of bothered by the fact that Farrah had disturbed her reverie of Khalil.

"Okay, girl, but Donte and Mustafa are going too. You know Donte's fine ass loves him some Jasmine. Toodles."

Jasmine watched as Farrah teetered away in her overpriced name-brand heels, and she smiled to herself. For as whorish as Farrah came across to the average person, Jasmine understood her. She wanted desperately to be a people pleaser. She had daddy issues, and in her twisted psyche, she had convinced herself that by sleeping with countless men, she was somehow getting back at her father for abandoning her when she needed him most.

Jasmine took a deep breath and dialed Khalil's number. Her heart pounded, and she felt hot. Her mouth was dry, and her stomach turned, and then she heard it: his syrupy baritone singing to her through the phone.

"Hello, Jasmine," he said.

"How . . . how did you know it was me?"

"Because nobody else has this number," he said.

"Really?"

"Yes, really. So how are you? I've been waiting by the phone like an impatient teenager for your call," Khalil said.

"I'm sorry. Between school and work, I don't really have a lot of time."

"We'll have to fix that. No wife of mine will be working in the food court of the mall."

"How do you know where I work? Are you stalking me?" Jasmine asked.

"No, I'm not stalking you, Jasmine. I just make it a point to know about the things that are important to me."

"And I'm of importance to you? Listen, don't play with my emotions, because I'm not the one, and besides, you don't even know me!" she snapped.

"I know more about you than you think I do. For instance, I know that you've never really been close to anyone except your sister. I know that when you do get married, you want it to be forever. I know that you decided a long time ago that the man who you gave your life and love to would have to reciprocate that love and loyalty," he said.

"How—"

"Because I've been with you your whole life, Jasmine. When you went to sleep at night dreaming about that knight in shining armor, I was he. Time has a strange sense of humor, Jasmine. It forces us to wait for a perfection that will never come. It allows us to waste precious moments with the wrong people. I'm guilty of loving the wrong women on several occasions, but now that I've found you, I don't want to let you get away. Do you believe in love at first sight?" he asked.

"I couldn't really say one way or another. I mean, I believe that you can be attracted to someone at first sight, but love is a strong word."

"I think it's deeper than that. I think we were destined to meet the way that we did. I mean, not with me sweaty and a mess, but we found each other in the darkness. Look, I'm a mess and I know it, but I think you were sent to save me and I was sent to you to give you the love you've always craved," Khalil said.

Jasmine listened intently, and although she was intrigued and slightly flattered, she couldn't help being somewhat put off by his forwardness. It startled her, but he was in her head. Jasmine's trust for men was all but absent, and she struggled to find the words to properly express herself. "Actions speak louder than words, Khalil." That was all that she was able to conjure.

"So you agree to allow me to show you rather than tell you?"

"We'll see."

"How about I pick you up from school and we can talk about it over dinner?" Khalil asked.

"I have to go to Valley View Mall and pick up my check. Plus, my sister gets worried if it takes me too long to get home."

"I'll take you to get your check, and while we're there, you can turn in your uniform and tell them that you quit. We'll do some shopping, and you can call your sister and let her know that you're having dinner with me," Khalil insisted.

Jasmine shook her head as if he could see her response. She understood Farrah because she, too, was a people pleaser. She found it difficult to say no, especially to Khalil. She wanted to say yes to anything he asked her. "Okay. My last class is over at three forty-five."

"I'll be there with bells on. I can't wait to see you again. See you soon," he said.

She looked at the phone as if it were somehow responsible for Khalil's disconnection. She had never felt as though she needed anyone, but he was a breath of fresh air.

The rest of Jasmine's day was filled with day-dreams and anticipation. Khalil Cross had most definitely made a positive impact on her young, impressionable, fragile mind. Her professor rattled on and on about the British invasion of Africa as Jasmine glanced at her cell phone's clock continuously. The hour-long class seemed to go on interminably with no foreseeable ending in sight.

A shrill, nerd-like voice invaded her daydream and brought her back to the present. "I don't un-derstand why black people are so adamant about being angry with white people. I mean, from what I understand, their own people sold them into slav-ery," Mr. Nerdy Voice reasoned.

Professor Diabo was their humanities professor and a highly respected historian who just happened to consider himself a man of color. He was 100 percent Cherokee and known for his no-nonsense approach to the facts. "Mr. Stewart, you would have us believe that Africans willingly sold their brethren into slavery?" he asked.

"Well, yes, Professor. You should know these things. Aren't you a historian?"

An awkward hush fell over the classroom as the students anxiously awaited their teacher's verbal backlash.

"Actually, I am a historian, and your facts are skewed and slightly tinged with racial undertones. I'll oblige your fancy though, Mr. Stewart. While history suggests that a small percentage—a very small percentage—of tribes in Africa did *business* with the British and sold out their brethren, a vast majority were kidnapped, beaten, maimed, and made to board slave ships with their destination unknown," Professor Diabo explained.

"But you agree that they were sold by their own people, right? So I rest my case."

"There is no case, sir. Let me say this. Slavery in any form we view it is wrong. As far as being sold by their own people, you have to understand that if a larger tribe was tormenting a set of smaller tribes, it was in their best interest to work with the British in order to rid themselves of intra-tribe tyranny. Even if the Africans had come to this country voluntarily and then had been enslaved, would that have then somehow justified slavery?" Professor Diàbo asked.

Silence.

Jasmine couldn't take it anymore. Waiting for class to end so that she could see Mr. Cross had caused her to become irritable and short-tempered. She had studied blacks and Native Americans while in the Buckner Home for Youth. She'd gotten into the study of different races mainly because of her confusion with her own mixed heritage. She wanted to know why black people, her people, were so fascinated with the phrase "I have Indian in my family." On more than one occasion, students at the youth home had uttered of her wavy jet-black hair, "You must have Indian in your family." She'd politely smiled and walked away, not daring to answer for fear of violent consequences. If she'd told them the truth of their fascination, she would have surely been beaten by some of the bully girls in her dorm for being a smart ass. She was an adult now though, with history fully supporting her facts.

"Mr. Diabo, don't you find your argument to be somewhat hypocritical?" she asked.

"How so, Miss Deitrich?"

"Well, history has taught us that among the Indian tribes that thrived and incorporated slavery into their tribes, the Cherokee by far had the largest number of slave laborers. They used the slaves to cultivate the cotton that blanketed their land and other surplus crops. How then, sir, can you denigrate whites for their role in slavery when your people clearly championed their cause? The only saving grace is that Native Americans didn't use violence to keep their slaves tamed and they very seldom separated families, so I guess you guys get a few points for that," she said.

"Well, I'm glad that I was able to restore some of my people's cool points." He laughed, then continued. "Although your point is valid, Jasmine, if you recall the discussion, I only said that slavery in any form is wrong, did I not? Furthermore, the discussion stemmed from Mr. Stewart's belief that Africans sold Africans," Professor Diabo said, glancing at his watch. "Well, that's all for today, class. We will pick up on this discussion tomorrow. Remember, finals are next Tuesday, so study, study, study. Have a great day."

Jasmine snatched up her books and threw them into her backpack. She took the stairs two at a time. The excitement clearly registered across her youthful features. She sprinted through the front doors of the humanities building.

Khalil Cross was leaning against a white Rolls-Royce Phantom. The windows were crystal clear, and the soft camel-colored leather interior only served to make the car look even more expensive.

Nearby, Farrah stood with a band of her merry whores, salivating at the sight of Khalil and his automobile. He knew full well that the young girls were watching him—well, maybe not him, per se, but they were definitely watching his car. Being the son of a billionaire definitely had its perks, and he tried to take full advantage of it.

Jasmine stopped and whirled on her heels in Farrah's direction. Her bright green eyes burned into Farrah's flesh. She seemed to be oblivious to Jasmine's existence. Farrah's eyes were trained on Khalil. Even as Jasmine approached her suitor, it still hadn't registered in her feeble mind that Khalil was there for Jasmine.

Khalil took Jasmine and hugged her tightly. "Damn, that's crazy, I missed you like I've known you forever. I've been out here for like a half hour waiting for you," Khalil said.

It wasn't until Khalil kissed Jasmine deeply that Farrah seemed to get the point. Her face contorted into a ghastly mask of mock horror and envy. She smoothed out the nonexistent wrinkles in her short skirt and walked over to the pair.

"Jasmine! Hey, girl. What are you getting ready to do? A few of us are going down to Deep Ellum to hang out. You guys are more than welcome to come. Girl, you gonna introduce me to your friend?" she cooed.

Jasmine sucked her teeth defiantly and turned toward Khalil, who promptly took the opportunity to explore her mouth with his tongue once again. They ignored Farrah purposely, totally engulfed in their unbridled passion. "Baby, where are we going? You want to hang out with them?" Jasmine asked, motioning toward Farrah.

"Of course not. First, I'm going to take you shopping, and then after that I will take you to my penthouse and let you shower. I've hired one of the finest chefs in Dallas to prepare a fantastic five-star meal, and we will dine on the rooftop of my building."

"Ooooh, that sounds like fun. You guys sure you don't want to have a little threesome?" Farrah asked, half serious.

Khalil shot her a pained glance and sidestepped her lascivious question. He opened the passenger's side door and ushered Jasmine inside. Farrah was still standing curbside with a goofy smile on her face as the Phantom pulled away into the brisk summer breeze.

Chapter 6

WHEN A RICH MAN WANTS YOU

Jasmine looked around in awe. After years of thumbing through *Vogue* magazine, fantasizing about wearing some of the elegant couture displayed in the pages of the magazine, she was now standing in the foyer of one of the most expensive boutiques in Dallas, Texas. Image Boutique was ultrachic and catered to some of the city's wealthiest patrons. She welcomed the smell of fresh cherry wood and money. She was somewhat intimidated by the bourgeois madams who perused the quaint store in search of the latest in designer fashions.

Khalil excused himself but reappeared moments later with a young, swank sales rep in tow. She examined Jasmine curiously, circling her as if she were wounded prey.

"I think I have just the designer for you, Mrs. Cross. Follow me, please," she said.

Jasmine started to correct the woman with the proper name, but then she decided against it. She could see herself as Khalil's wife, and she honored the mistake.

"I'll leave you ladies to get more acquainted. Madison, take good care of my wife. Money is no object, so give her whatever her heart desires," Khalil said. He winked at Jasmine and passed her a black American Express card. He exited the store and walked across the street to Starbucks.

Jasmine had mistaken Madison as just a sales rep, but in truth, she owned the small boutique. She owned much more than that, in all actuality. Image Boutique had more than forty locations from California to Mississippi. She had been one of Trammell S. Crow's many mistresses. He was the son of famous developer Trammell Crow, and he had not only inherited his father's business savvy but his billions of dollars as well. Madison had gone into their relationship knowing full well that she would have to play the side piece, and she'd embraced it. She had decided early on that she wouldn't be like so many other mistresses who had been relegated to living in a paid-for condo, crying herself to sleep at night while her cash cow went home to his wife and kids. She was worth more than a quick fuck and a diamond necklace, and she knew it. She wanted her own money, and she had strategically played her cards. Madison Keagan had convinced Mr. Crow to bankroll one boutique each in the states of her choice and then used the revenue generated from those stores to open more stores. She was totally self-sufficient and could leave whenever she chose to because she wasn't dependent on his money.

"Okay, honey, let's get you into something presentable. You're a very lucky young lady to have landed Mr. Cross. He comes from a long line of clean, quality money," she said sweetly.

"I'm not with him for his money, I'm with him because—"

"You don't owe me an explanation, my love. Just remember that you need to have your own money if he ever decides to upgrade and trade you in for a younger model," Madison said.

By the time Jasmine was finished shopping, she had more bags than she could carry and more information than she cared to remember.

Jasmine met Khalil on the sidewalk, and he loaded her bags into his trunk. The next stop would be his condominium. She wasn't afraid of Khalil but rather afraid of being alone with him. She had never been with a man. Well, at least not willingly.

On the way to his home, they laughed and talked about the future. Khalil painted vivid pictures of his plans for him and Jasmine. She wasn't sure how he was doing it, but he had managed to make her completely comfortable with him.

They pulled into the parking garage of his building and parked. They walked to the elevator hand in hand, and Jasmine wondered silently if it could possibly get any better. Her cell phone rang. It was Monica. "Shit!" she muttered.

"What's wrong, babe?"

"I forgot to call my sister, and now she's calling me. You think I should answer?" she asked.

"Of course. Why wouldn't you? If you don't answer, she'll worry."

Jasmine nodded her agreement. Monica always worried about her, sometimes for no reason. Truthfully, Jasmine understood. She and Monica were all each other had, so she really didn't mind. "Hello? Hey, Monica. I'm with Khalil. Yes, Khalil Cross. We're going to grab dinner. Girl, hush. Bye!" she said, smiling into the phone.

"Is she mad?"

"No, actually, just the opposite. She's happy that I'm happy. She thinks you're cute," Jasmine said.

"Good, good. She has a good eye."

"Listen to you, Mr. Conceited!"

"No, I didn't mean it like that," Khalil said, laughing.

The elevator reached the top floor of Khalil's building. He affectionately called it Billionaire's Row. She'd thought that he was being cocky until she heard a couple on the elevator call it the same. He entered a code into a keypad on the wall, and his doors sprang open.

Jasmine gasped at the sheer beauty of the penthouse. There were no walls, only sheer white curtains hanging from floor to ceiling, dividing the individual spaces. The entire penthouse had been decorated in white and accented in Jasmine's favorite color, jade green, with speckles of gold throughout.

"Feel free to look around. Would you like something to drink? I have merlot, pinot noir, or chardonnay," Khalil offered.

"No, thank you. If it's okay with you, I'd just like to take a shower and change, please."

"Most definitely. I'll show you where it is, and when you're done, you can just meet me on the balcony," he said.

Jasmine smiled and nodded. She was somewhat taken aback that the shower was merely hanging from the ceiling and enclosed by a semi-clear shower curtain. She undressed slowly and stepped into the shower, silently wondering if Khalil could see her naked silhouette through the curtain. The lukewarm water cascaded over her jet-black ringlets and rolled down her slim, curvy body. Jasmine bathed quickly but thoroughly, anxious to get back to Khalil. She let her soapy hands glide over her taut body, and she felt her nether regions quiver. Her nipples were fully erect, and she shivered from the pleasure of washing and fondling her own body.

Jasmine stepped out of the shower feeling refreshed and invigorated but somewhat horny. She had never been with a man voluntarily, but if he asked, she would indeed make love to Khalil Cross. Although it wasn't something that she had planned on, she could definitely see herself doing it. Jasmine giggled at the thought of it. She had no preconceived notions as to what lovemaking should be or how it should feel. She only knew that she was connected to Khalil by a force greater than her comprehension. She not only wanted to be with him. She *needed* to be with him.

After Jasmine was finished bathing, she dressed and joined Khalil on the balcony. As much beauty as his penthouse held, it paled in comparison to the balcony. The floor was white marble with a gold inlay. There was a round table positioned in the center with a snow-white linen tablecloth and a dozen fresh flowers in a crystal vase. The moon rays played tag and bounced brilliantly from the water of the nearby infinity pool that appeared to run over the edge of the building.

Two elderly black men stood nearby dressed in black tuxedos with white linen draped across their forearms. "Right this way, madam," one of them instructed.

Khalil stood as Jasmine approached the table. She was gorgeous, even more so than Khalil had initially thought. The jade green silk kimono-style dress she wore accented her eyes flawlessly. "Wow, you look fantastic, absolutely stunning, Jasmine," Khalil said.

"Thank you, Khalil. Everything looks so beautiful. I'm really impressed. What kind of flowers are those? They are gorgeous."

"They are your eponym, my love. *Jasminum sambac* is the name, but they are known as jasmine flowers. Please, have a seat," he said, motioning for Jasmine to be seated. They sat, and Khalil stared at her for a long time before speaking. "So tell me about Jasmine."

"What is it that you would like to know?" she asked.

"Everything."

"I don't think we have enough time for me to tell you everything," Jasmine said shyly.

Khalil took her hand into his and stared into her eyes. "We have a lifetime, babe. Why don't you start at the beginning?" he said softly.

"I want to, but I don't like putting people in my business. I don't need anyone judging me before they get to know me, you know?"

"Let's get a few things out in the open. What you and I discuss will never leave my lips. All your secrets are safe with me, and I will never violate your trust. I will never judge you either. I only want what's best for you, and if you allow me to, I will be the best thing that has ever happened to you. I only ask for complete loyalty and that you reciprocate this love I am going to give to you freely," Khalil said.

"The only person I talk to is Monica, so you don't have to worry about that."

"Not even her!" Khalil barked.

"Okay! Jeez, Mr. Touchy, no need to bite my head off."

"I'm sorry. I didn't mean to snap at you. I just know from experience that in order to make a relationship work, the only people who need to be involved are the people involved," he said.

Jasmine agreed. She had never kept a secret from Monica, but if that was what Khalil wanted, then she would happily oblige. "I don't know where to begin. I mean, I don't want to sound like a D-list movie, you know?"

"Start from the beginning," he said.

So she did. Jasmine started at the very beginning with her earliest recollection.

Jasmine's earliest memories were of the big house on Ann Arbor Street that she shared with her parents and Monica. Life had seemed so simple then. Back then, she and Monica were her parents' only concern. She could still see her mom standing in the kitchen window watching lovingly as their father pushed her and Monica on the big wooden swing that their grandfather had bought for them. Day after day her mother had stood in that kitchen window, the smell of freshly baked Jiffy mix corn bread and beans filling the air.

On her very first day of kindergarten, she'd been excited until she'd learned that she'd be left alone. Her father had taken a day off from work to sit with her through her entire first day of school. She explained to Khalil how fantastic her parents had been until the drugs had taken control. "I don't know what happened. I mean, one minute they were the greatest parents on earth, and the next minute . . ." Her sentence trailed off, and her eyes were glazed over as if she were somewhere else.

"The next minute what, babe?" Khalil asked.

"The next minute they were selling all our toys, all the nice things that Pop Pop had bought for us, until there was nothing left to sell. So after there was nothing else to sell, they sold me. They promised to come back to get me, but they never showed up. After the dope dealers figured out that my parents weren't coming back with their money, they raped me over and over again," Jasmine cried. "I tried to scream, but every time I opened my mouth to scream, I was punched. They treated my body like their personal rag doll."

"Oh, my God, baby! How did you get away?" Khalil asked, horrified.

"I remember one of them picking me up and putting me in a car. They dropped me off on a dark corner. I was bleeding heavily, and they just left me there to die like an unwanted mutt. I don't really remember much after that. I woke up in the hospital, afraid to speak. I still didn't speak for almost ten years after that, maybe longer."

"That's terrible, Jasmine! I want to find them and kill them!" Khalil said angrily.

"Shit, me too. After it was over and I was in the Buckner Home, I would always whisper their names over and over in my head—Michael Ross, Jappy, Dirt Bag—over and over again until it was embedded in my brain."

"Wow! So if you had the chance to kill them, would you do it?" Khalil asked.

"Can I tell you something without you thinking that I'm crazy?"

"You can tell me anything. No judgment, remember?"

"Well, ever since that happened to me, I've had the urge to hurt people. Not just anybody, but just bad people. I don't know if it makes me crazy, but I just think bad people don't deserve to be here, like they're not worthy to walk among us. Women and men who hurt children: dead. Hurt the elderly: dead. Woman beaters: dead. Rapists: dead. And I've fantasized about killing them all," she said.

"I have a confession to make. I fantasize about killing as well. Maybe that makes me crazy. Sometimes I think it's because of the way that I came up. I barely know my father, and my mother wasn't a mother at all. But enough about our killing fantasies. We should be celebrating our newfound love, right?" he asked.

"Your turn, Khalil."

"My turn for what?" he asked.

"Your turn to tell me about you."

"There's not much to tell, really. I'm young, spoiled, and very rich. I'm a brat with too many zeroes in my bank account, and all I've ever really wanted and needed was true love. I'm a guy who's willing to do anything to find and keep real love," he said. His words had grown soft and reflective. Khalil Cross had deep secrets, dark secrets that plagued him, but he wanted to expose his vulnerability to her.

"If you'll let me love you, Khalil, I promise to never disappoint you. I will spend the rest of my life trying to find ways to make and keep you happy," Jasmine said.

"Those are strong words. Do you promise?"

"I promise," she said.

"Remember that, until death do us part."

"My life belongs to you, Khalil. Until death do us part, my love."

Chapter 7

REVENGE SERVED HOT

Oscar Torres had walked out of the Hutchinson prison unit a free man. He felt fresh and he felt vindicated. He'd served a hard four years for statutory rape. Before he went to prison, he'd been engaged to a portly Mexican woman named Luz. He was only 22 years old, and she was 35, but he'd promised his grandmother that he'd marry Luz to assist in her acquisition of her green card. She had two children who had been born in the States, but the State of Texas didn't care about that. If she didn't get her immigration issues straight, she would be deported, and her children would be placed in foster care. David, at 6 years old, and 14-year-old Gabriella cherished Oscar, and he in turn bestowed upon them all that he knew of fatherhood. Well, at least that was the case for David. Gabriella, in Oscar's opinion, was mature for her age and far better looking than her thick-necked mother.

Oscar had watched her blossom from a 14-year-old tomboy to a 16-year-old woman, and he was smitten. He'd been paying too much attention to Gabby, as they called her, and her mother had taken notice. He refused to sleep with Luz, which only served to infuriate her more. The last straw had been when she'd caught Oscar and Gabby in bed together. She'd sworn to get even with Oscar for choosing Gabby over her, and she'd made good on her promise. Luz had Oscar arrested for raping Gabby. Gabriella had been so distraught, and she swore to the police that it hadn't been rape. Their encounter, as she'd recounted it, was purely consensual.

The State of Texas, however, didn't see it that way. Gabriella wasn't old enough to consent according to Texas law, so Oscar had been convicted of rape and sentenced to eight years in prison. Three days after Gabriella's eighteenth birthday, they were married in a prison ceremony witnessed only by the chaplain and his trustee. Did Oscar love Gabriella? Not even a little bit. But that was the only way he knew for certain that he could hurt Luz. He didn't give a damn about Gabriella. He didn't care about serving the time or about having to register as a sex offender. No sir, Oscar Torres was hell-bent on revenge. He wanted to make Luz pay for interrupting his sexual deviance with Gabby. He'd served four long years, and in order to get parole, he needed a stable address. Luz had reluctantly agreed to let Oscar parole to their address after countless pleas from Gabriella. Now that he was free, he would be living under *her* roof, eating *her* food, sexing *her* daughter in the room right next to *hers*. He would fuck Gabriella so hard that she would scream and cry from a mixture of pain and ecstasy. He would then stroll proudly from his bedroom to the bathroom, right past Luz's door with his dick in plain view to remind her of what she would never have. Yes indeed, that was Oscar's plan. At least, that was his plan if Gabby ever made it to the Dizzy Duck to pick him up.

He'd gotten out of prison at one o'clock in the afternoon, and it was now nine at night. He was drunk, tired, and very horny. Oscar had drunk up the entire $200 that the State of Texas had given him upon his release, and now all he wanted to do was fuck his wife and go to sleep. He stumbled out of the Dizzy Duck onto Atlantic Avenue and into the humid night air. The streets were deserted, save for a few empty cars here and there. He squinted against the myriad of bright lights, trying to make out the figure headed toward him.

"If this is Gabby, I'm going to shove my *pinche* dick in her *culo* for making me wait so fucking long, *pinche puta!*" he slurred. Oscar reached into his shirt pocket and pulled out a Marlboro Red cigarette from the pack. He stopped walking, barely able to stand, and patted his pants pockets frantically, searching for his lighter. He was still patting his pockets when the stranger approached.

"Hey, Oscar, what's up, man?" the voice asked excitedly.

"What's up, *vato*? Do I know you, homes? You got a light?"

"Oscar Torres, man, it's me. Remember me?" he asked.

"Just gimme a fucking light, *puto*. Me who? Who is me, *pendejo*?" Oscar sneered.

"It's me. Death, muh'fucka! This is for Gabriella!" the stranger said. He lifted Oscar's arms and shoved him against the brick wall. He stabbed him repeatedly underneath his left arm until blood leapt and spurted uncontrollably from the gaping wound. The snow-white T-shirt that Gabby had sent him was ruined. It was drenched in blood and looked black against the backdrop of the night sky.

Oscar reached into his shirt pocket and grabbed the crumpled cigarette pack. He slid down the wall, the bent cigarette hanging from his trembling lips. He watched as the murderous stranger disappeared into a blur of blood and pain. His hand trembled irrepressibly. He flicked his lighter, but the blood on his hands made it next to impossible. Silently he cursed. Under his breath, he muttered unimaginable obscenities. Again he tried, this time more feverishly than before. An orange and blue flame sprang from the depths of the BIC lighter. He lit his cigarette and inhaled deeply. Oscar watched the cloud of white smoke ringlets ascend toward heaven. He took another puff and laughed heartily, coughing up blood in the process. He was still smiling as his body gave up the ghost. An eerie calm fell over Oscar, who still held his ghastly and contorted smile. As he slid into eternal darkness, the last sound that he heard was a scream in the distance and the sound of hot ashes being extinguished by his blood-soaked T-shirt.

Chapter 8

DICK DRUNK

Monica watched Jasmine as they jogged through the park. For the past few weeks, she had spent every waking moment with Khalil, and she seemed to be glowing. Monica was glad to see her little sister happy, but she was changing. Whereas before she and Jasmine had shared everything, Jasmine was now selfish, secretive, and withdrawn. On more than one occasion she'd inquired about Khalil, but Jasmine had only brushed her queries aside by saying that she and Khalil were connected. She always said it with such passion and earnestness that Monica had assumed that Jasmine was simply dick drunk, but when she asked whether they'd been intimate, she'd been stifled with a quick no.

"Jasmine, can I ask you something?" Monica asked.

"Sure, you can ask me anything."

"How do you feel about Khalil? I mean, you're with him a lot, but you never really talk about him," Monica said.

Jasmine's features were stern and serious, but when she opened her mouth and began to speak, she sounded like the once-excited child Monica remembered. "I love him! I've never in my life felt like this about anyone. He shows me that he loves me. He knows me and I know him."

"How do you know it's love though?" Monica asked.

"I'm not a child, Moni! I know the difference between lust and love. Khalil and I have shared things that you would never understand."

"Like what?"

There was no answer, only silence. Jasmine sped up her pace with Noisy Boy following close behind. Monica's cell phone rang, and she stopped. "Hello? Good morning, sir. Yes, that's no problem at all. See you then," Monica said. She jogged briskly toward Jasmine, increasing her speed until she caught up with her. Monica grabbed her shoulder to slow her down so that she could speak with her. "Hey, slow down. What's gotten into you lately? You've been very distant," Monica said.

"No, I haven't. You're just always prying, and I don't like it. That's why I'm always with Khalil, because he gets it. No judgment, no prying eyes, just love. He gets *me*. He's the only person who does."

"How can you say that, Jazzy Bell? It's always been us Deitrich girls against the world," Monica said sadly.

"Things change, and if it's always been us Deitrich girls, where were you when those men were raping me? Where were you when I was crying myself to sleep every night? Where were you, Monica, when the older girls at the youth home were using my body for their perverse sexual experimentation? Don't fucking tell me about *us* Deitrich girls, because when this Dietrich girl needed you most, you were nowhere in sight."

"Wow, where's all of this coming from?" Monica asked.

Silence. With no response from Jasmine, Monica took that as a cue to leave. She wasn't sure what Jasmine's issue was, but she had definitely changed. Khalil Cross had a hold on her mentally and emotionally, and Monica wanted to know how.

It would have to wait though. Monica had received a call from a frantic Agent Muldoon. She hadn't heard much from him since her transfer, but she'd chalked it up as him just being busy. His phone call both surprised and startled her. He sounded distraught and somewhat frightened. He'd said that he was afraid to talk on the phone and asked that Monica meet him at the crime scene. She had no idea what was going on, but Muldoon had piqued her interest.

Monica steered her car down the long gravel road leading to Muldoon's crime scene. It had been roped off with yellow tape, and the place was crawling with FBI and DEA agents. In the distance, the sun had just begun to creep up over the horizon with its ominous shades of orange, purple, and blue hues. A team of agents stood guard at the edge of the property to keep the overzealous media from entering the area, probably for fear of them contaminating the scene.

Monica flashed her badge to a young agent who looked more like Harry Potter than a federal agent, and he waved her through. Just ahead, near an abandoned cement factory, she saw Muldoon pacing anxiously as he talked nervously on his cell phone. Monica sat in her car and watched him for a minute. Agent Muldoon's once-cocksure show of strength and bravado had been replaced with a look of frailty. He looked as though he'd been awake all night, and he was puffing a cigarette as if he were trying to suck the life out of it. He looked up and caught Monica's eyes trained on him and managed a weak smile.

"Agent Deitrich, glad you could join us," he said.

"There was a sound of urgency in your voice, sir."

"And for good reason. For the first time in my career, I don't have an answer," he said reflectively.

The same shakiness she'd heard in his voice over the phone was now clearly visible in his features. He fidgeted fretfully, shifting from foot to foot, and he'd begun to sweat profusely. Monica thought that she could see the remnants of dried tears on Muldoon's cheeks, but she dismissed it. Everything she knew of Muldoon dispelled the theory of him crying over a case. She opened her mouth to begin a barrage of questions, but Muldoon waved her to silence.

"Save your questions, Agent Deitrich. This situation warrants no questions. Have you ever heard the saying 'I can show you better than I can tell you'? Well, I believe that this is one of those moments. Follow me, please," Muldoon said.

They walked through the maze of cement silos and dilapidated tin buildings into a large open clearing. Across the clearing sat a rusting tin building with the word CEMEX painted on it. The fog had yet to burn away, and it blanketed the grass and wood line that lay beyond the warehouse. Monica moved forward with trepidation, afraid of what it was that Muldoon wanted to show her. They arrived at the dank, dark opening of the tin structure, and Muldoon stopped, much like a dog that sensed danger ahead.

"Are you okay, sir?" Monica asked.

"I'm fine, Agent. I'm fine."

They continued into the building, and Monica stopped. She tried her hardest to adjust her eyes to the darkness and then she saw it, or rather *him*. Impaled on a sharp metal stake in the center of the warehouse was one of their fellow agents. Monica stood awestruck. She wasn't prepared for the ghastly sight that invaded her vision. From a metal beam extending the length of the warehouse hung a lone figure, stark naked. Although he was hanging by his neck from a chain, his murderer had taken meticulous care in his torture. His hands had been pierced with large hooks and chains and stretched the width of the warehouse. The word "snitch" had been carved into his chest, and as Monica circled the body slowly, she saw that the word "traitor" had been carved into his back as well. Underneath his lifeless and bloody body was a top hat filled with his blood. She removed a penlight from her blazer pocket and examined the body closer. His genitalia had been surgically removed with precision, undoubtedly to aid in the bleeding out of the victim. Monica looked around the area where the body hung for other clues and noticed that his penis and testicles were floating in the blood-filled top hat. She let the light shine in the victim's face, and she gasped in horror. Monica dropped the penlight and stumbled backward, almost trampling Agent Muldoon.

"I told you that you'd have to see it to believe it," he said somberly.

She couldn't believe her eyes. It was Drak! He had been murdered, probably in retaliation or backlash for one of his cases. Monica had become good friends with Drak after King's case, but they'd lost contact after he'd gone undercover again.

"Cut him down! Get a ladder and cut him down!" she screamed.

Chapter 9

GREENHOUSE

Business was booming for the young hustler known only as Toot. He'd come up the hard way with no father to speak of and a drug-addicted mother. His grandmother had done her very best to keep him out of the streets with a steady regimen of church and after-school activities, but it was to no avail. Toot was no saint. In fact, he'd been directly responsible for his grandmother's death. The courts had tried him, and he'd been set free on a technicality. The truth of the matter was that Toot had smothered his grandmother with a pillow in her sleep, and after his trial, he'd told anyone who would listen. That was, after he'd collected the more than $300,000 in life insurance money.

Toot had used the money from murdering his grandmother to start the One Stop Shop. It was a large two-story house on the dead end of Barber Avenue. It sat behind the Stonewood Terrace apartments just off Dixon Circle, and business couldn't have been better. He called it the One Stop Shop because he had everything from $2 crack to whole kilos. Whether a person needed a cigarette lighter or a twelve-ounce can of beer, he had it all, and he sold it all. Toot was even courteous enough to allow the crackheads and meth users to do their dope in the One Stop Shop, not to mention the fact that there seemed to be an endless supply of young, drug-induced girls willing to do any- and everything that Toot asked.

He was by no stretch of the imagination what one might call good-looking. He was a short man, barely five feet five inches, and weighed a rotund 280 pounds. His skin was the color of rusted metal, rather splotchy, with hints of youthful freckles from days past. Toot's short Afro was matted to his head, and although he had money, much of which he spent tricking with the dopeheads, he didn't look the part. He knew that he was ugly, but that didn't bother him. He was of the belief that women liked him for one reason and one reason only: money. And as long as he supplied it, then they would continue to treat him like a king.

Toot stood on the front steps just before dusk and stretched lazily. He'd been asleep since midday after a quick tryst with Candice. She was his on-again/off-again girlfriend who just so happened to be addicted to PCP. She'd been gone for hours, but she had a way of putting him to sleep after her deed was done. The happier he kept her with drugs, the happier she kept him sexually.

He stepped off the porch and looked down the street. Two lone figures wandered down the street toward him. It appeared to be a male and a female. They were obviously new to the One Stop Shop, because anyone who'd been there before knew the rules. Women were to come alone so as to allow Toot first dibs. As they got closer, Toot smiled. He loved it when the white boys came because they would spend their money until the last cent was gone, and then they would send for more. They walked onto the porch and ambled past Toot, who flicked his Black & Mild cigar and followed closely behind.

"What y'all looking to get into today?" Toot asked.

"We want to get high, but we don't like to do it around a lot of people," the woman said as she pulled a large bundle of bills from her purse.

Toot's eyes widened. He loved money, so much so that he always seemed to let it blind him to the obvious. "Well, nobody is here, so y'all can get as high as you want. Hopefully I get a chance to spend some time alone with you, ma," he said lasciviously.

She looked at her companion and then back to Toot. "I'm sure we can work that out. If this dope is good, we can spend as much time together as you want. I have to warn you, though, I'm freaky, and I haven't been fucked good in a long time. Where's your bathroom?" she asked.

Toot could only manage to lift his finger toward the direction of the stairs. "Last door on the left at the top of the stairs," he said. He watched her hips sway seductively as she made her way up the stairs. He turned to the tall white boy in the trench coat. "What's up with you, buddy? I hope you ain't into no kinky shit because I ain't with none of that freaky shit," Toot said.

"No, man, no funny stuff. She's not my property. I mean, I was her first, you know? She was a virgin when I got her, but she hasn't let me touch her in almost six months, so I know you're going to enjoy yourself because her little shaved pussy has got to be tight after six months."

His voice was amusing to Toot. He sounded more like a college professor than a dope user. He reminded Toot of the type of white boy people in the hood made fun of, the kind who walked straight up and down with their asses tight, filled with nerdy swagger. Toot couldn't think. He loved words like "virgin," "shaved," and "tight."

"I'll be right back, playboy. Make yourself at home. As a matter of fact, fire this up," Toot said, tossing him a rolled blunt. He stood and adjusted his Dickies shorts to try to hide his erection. The revelation that Pretty Eyes could potentially have tight pussy was too much to bear.

He climbed the stairs to find the young girl lying naked across his bed. Her taut body writhed sexually against the satin comforter. Her earthy yellow-colored skin shimmered from the glitter-infused lotion she wore, and she smelled like love.

The white man sat on Toot's couch and broke open the blunt. Just as he'd suspected, it had been laced with a substance that was unidentifiable to him. He wasn't sure whether it was crack or meth or something more sinister, but he was nobody's fool. He'd never smoked anything that had been pre-rolled, and he wouldn't start now. He gave one last look up the stairs to make sure that Toot was out of sight. He made his way silently through the house, locking doors as he moved. He came upon a room just to the rear of the kitchen filled with different types of fertilizer and garden tools. Tucked away neatly in a corner of the room was a wheelbarrow filled with freshly cut buds of marijuana. He dumped the homegrown weed from the wheelbarrow and rolled it to the center of the kitchen.

The house was dark except for random slivers of light that managed to slip through the dusty drapes that blanketed the house. Once he'd made his way back to the living room, he removed his trench coat and laid it across the couch with the lining of his coat up. Inside, he had crudely fashioned hooks that held knives of different shapes and sizes. He removed two large meat cleavers from their hooks and headed toward the stairs.

A light knock at the door halted his advance. He turned and cracked the door slightly. "May I help you?" he asked.

A small-framed, brown-skinned girl stood petrified with her head down but with her wide eyes trained on the stranger. "Um, um, um," she stuttered.

"Spit it out, girl. I don't have all day. Do you want to go to jail?" he asked.

"Um, is Toot here? I, um, need to talk to him."

"Toot is being questioned right now by my partner, and unless you want to go to jail, I suggest you beat it," he scolded.

"You don't look like no cop!"

"That's it. I'm hauling your black ass in! Get in here," he said. The truth of the matter was that she'd seen his face, and he couldn't afford to be identified. He snatched her into the house and covered her mouth to stifle her screams. He dragged her into the kitchen and let her go. "If you scream, I will kill you," he said.

She whimpered softly and nodded her head in agreement. "How do I know you're not going to kill me anyway?" She'd started to cry softly, and for a brief moment, he felt sorry for her.

Then he realized that she was a dope user, a
person who would do or say just about anything to
get that next hit. He punched her violently in her
face, and blood spurted from her nose in gushing
waves. She slumped to the floor, asleep from the
knockout blow. He rummaged through a kitchen
drawer until he found a roll of duct tape. He taped
her hands, her feet, and finally her mouth. She
wouldn't be going anywhere until he could figure
out what to do with her.

He went to the living room, retrieved his meat
cleavers, and climbed the stairs quietly. Once at
the top he stopped and looked warily down the
long, narrow hallway leading to the back of the
house. To his left, he could hear Toot talking to his
young companion.

"Damn, baby, you got a pretty-ass pussy. You
gonna let me taste it or what?" Toot asked, licking
his thick lips greedily.

She didn't say a word. She opened her legs,
exposing her fleshy, wet pinkness. She placed
her finger in her mouth seductively and smiled at
Toot. He fumbled clumsily with the clasp on his
shorts and kicked out of his trousers. Toot pulled
his T-shirt over his head and stood stark naked in
front of the young girl. His penis was fully erect
and was unusually large for a man of his stature.

He never heard the tall figure creep up behind
him. The white man buried the first meat cleaver

in Toot's back between his shoulder blades. An ear-piercing, bloodcurdling scream escaped his lips. He shriveled to the ground in pain, afraid to move. Pretty Eyes leapt from the bed, put her foot on Toot's neck, and forced his face to the cold tile floor. She reached down and pulled the meat cleaver from his back, and he screamed again. She swung with as much power as she could muster and buried the cleaver deep within Toot's skull.

"Get dressed and meet me downstairs in the kitchen," the man said. He grabbed Toot by his feet and dragged him down the stairs.

As she got dressed, Pretty Eyes giggled at the sound of Toot's head thumping against the carpeted steps. She felt exhilarated and empowered from her kill. She descended the slippery stairs slowly, careful not to slip in Toot's blood. As she neared the kitchen, she heard a dull, repetitive thwack against the linoleum floor. Her face curled into a twisted grin of sinister satisfaction as she entered the kitchen. There, in the center of the floor, her partner was using the meat cleaver to hack through the cold flesh, bone, and gristle of Toot's neck. With one final tug, he ripped the head from Toot's shoulders and held it up toward Pretty Eyes as if he were dedicating an offering of human remains. She knelt before him and took the second cleaver into her hand. With one swift motion, she amputated Toot's arm at the shoulder.

Neither one of them paid attention to the blood filling the kitchen floor. They continued their grisly ritual until they had butchered Toot's body into six pieces. They tossed his head, his arms, his legs, and finally his torso into the rusted wheelbarrow with the flat tire.

The young dopefiend girl watched in stunned horror at the spectacle that had taken place in front of her. She had no idea that once they were finished with Toot's slaughter, she, too, would be hewn into six pieces. She would be next in their sadistic game of *Operation*.

Chapter 10

IF I GOT IT, YOU GOT IT

Chance Thimble walked along the boardwalk in Miami Beach, reeling with pain. He was tired of running, tired of hiding in dank, run-down, and seedy motels. He'd left Dallas in the middle of the night with a one-way ticket on Greyhound headed to Miami after seeing his face plastered across multiple news channels. Chance had a few problems. One of his biggest, though, was his love of women. Not that loving women was a bad thing, but his condition should have strictly forbidden his involvement with them. Too many loose nights of debauchery had cost Chance the rest of his life. He truly lived up to the name Chance. He'd pulled the trigger too many times in a game of sexual roulette, and he'd finally caught a slug. Chance Thimble had been diagnosed with the HIV virus, but he hadn't slowed down. No, he'd actually turned up the charm.

He continued to walk the boardwalk with his head held low and thought back to his diagnosis. He'd gone to his doctor after finding white splotchy spots on his tongue. Chance had thought that they were due to the pesky cold that he couldn't seem to shake, but after all the home diagnoses and home remedies, it still wouldn't go away. Waiting for his doctor to complete his blood work had been the longest and most nerve-racking two weeks of his life. And then he'd gotten the call.

"Chance, this is Dr. Petzel. We got your blood work back from the lab. I'd like to set up an appointment with you to discuss my findings as soon as possible."

He'd left work early, which he didn't mind because, at 25 years old, he barely made minimum wage as a stock boy at Walmart. He nervously entered the doctor's office and had been ushered into a private waiting area that looked more like an interrogation room than a waiting room. With its flat gunmetal gray walls, sparse stainless-steel furnishings, and dim lighting, the room seemed cold and impersonal.

Dr. Petzel entered the room carrying a cup of coffee in one hand and a single manila folder in the other. He had a stern but concerned look on his face. A single bead of sweat rested insouciantly on the doctor's brow, threatening to drop into his eye with one foul move.

"Chance, I won't keep you too long. After testing your blood, we've found the HIV virus in your blood work. There is medicine available as well as support groups if you find that you need them. I must warn you, though, I'm bound by law to report your condition to the CDC," he said.

Chance wanted to cry, but he couldn't. He wanted to lash out, he wanted to grab the doctor by his lapels and demand that he retest the blood, but he didn't. He simply stood and exited the doctor's office in dazed confusion. He'd foolishly believed that things like HIV and AIDS only happened to other people, not him, and now he was one of the "others." The night that he'd found out had been the longest, most restless night of his life, and after finally dozing off from utter exhaustion, he'd woken up in a cold sweat. He'd hoped that it was a dream, or rather a nightmare, but it wasn't. It was a slap in the face, a harsh, cold reality that Chance would have to face head-on.

The *knowing* was killing him. There was something about knowing that he was going to die that ate at Chance. He'd always believed that he'd die of old age, or at the very least be killed by the husband of one of the married women with whom he was sleeping. The more he thought about it, the angrier he became, until finally he reached his resolution. "If I'm going out, I'm taking as many of these bitches with me as I can."

And that was how it started. He was ferocious with his game. He found that women were open to a discreet extramarital affair if it was presented properly. He banked on infidelity, and married women were his preferred choice. He welcomed them all: black, white, fat, skinny, ugly, or pretty, it didn't matter to Chance. Cheating wives would be infected by him, who would then infect their unsuspecting husbands, who in turn, if they were cheating, would infect their mistresses, and so forth. Young girls were fun, too. They were so trusting, so naive, and so open to try new things. A lie here, a lie there, and he was in there.

By the time the Dallas Police Department issued the warrant for his arrest, he had transmitted the virus to eighty-seven women and girls. Chance Thimble had been charged with eighty-seven felony counts of criminal transmission of HIV. Thirty-nine of those cases also had additional charges of lewd and lascivious sexual battery of a minor. He'd knowingly transmitted his sickness to thirty-nine young girls who had yet to enjoy life. An all-out manhunt had been launched, and the news had called him a human epidemic. After the news broadcast, more people had come forward, both wives and husbands alike. After all was said and done, more than 200 people had been infected. Chance had effectively caused mass hysteria on the streets of Dallas, Texas.

He stopped walking and sat on a bench facing the beach. She was gorgeous, and not only was she gorgeous, but she was alone, and she was staring at him. Her jade green eyes burned through him, and then she smiled. She flashed her set of straight, perfectly white teeth in his direction and waved for him to join her.

He looked around in perplexed amazement. She couldn't possibly mean him. Chance knew that his game was tight, and he'd spent a majority of the money he'd saved on a new wardrobe as soon as he'd gotten to Florida, so he knew he looked good. But something about her eyes told him to pass her by. She had a look of hungry, wanton lust in her eyes, and he wanted her. He needed her for himself. Infection was inevitable, but if he gave her his sickness, then they would die together. He would spend the rest of his life trying to make her happy. In the short span of time that he'd been watching her, he'd found himself planning a future, however brief, with a woman he didn't even know.

Before he had the opportunity to snap out of his daydream, the woman with the gorgeous eyes approached him. "Hello, handsome, how are you?" she asked.

"Who . . . who me?" he stammered.

"Yes, you. What's your name?"

For a split second, he was so enamored with her that he almost gave her his real name, but then reality set in. For all he knew, she could have been a bounty hunter or a detective hot on his trail. "My name is Marcus Clements," he lied.

"Well, Marcus Clements, my name is Dawn Pope, and it's a pleasure to make your acquaintance," she said, extending her hand.

Chance took her hand into his own and felt his loins twitch. He let his eyes roam over her sensuous frame. Her coffee-colored skin blended effortlessly into the sunray yellow dyed two-piece bikini she wore. Her jet-black hair fell in large wet ringlets about her shoulders, and the beach water formed liquid pools of sexual moisture in her cleavage.

"Well, if you're only going to stare, I guess I was wrong about you and I'm just wasting my time," she said.

"What do you mean?"

"I mean I thought that you might be the type of man who could show me a good time, but—"

"No, no, I am that type, I just, I just . . ." he stuttered.

"You just what? Cat got your tongue, Marcus? Let's make this easy for you, shall we? What do you do for a living?" she asked, cutting him off in midsentence.

"I, uh, I'm a software engineer for Kinko's," he blurted out. *Shit, shit, shit.* As soon as the lie left his lips, he cursed himself. *Kinko's? Really? That's the dumbest lie you've ever told, dumbass,* he continued to scold himself.

"Oh, wow, that sounds fascinating. I own a small day spa down on Old Biscayne Boulevard. We do massage and acupuncture, you know, stuff like that," she said.

"Damn, Miss Independent, huh?"

"Yeah, I guess you could say that. We should go out tonight. I mean, if you want, I'd love to spend some time with you."

"That sounds good, but my paper isn't right just yet. I just moved to Miami, so I'm still trying to get my shit together," Chance said.

"Did I ask you about your finances, Marcus? No, I didn't. I said that I wanted to spend time with you. Listen, I know it seems like I'm being really forward, but I like your style. Most of these dudes down here in Miami are wearing dreads, a mouth-ful of gold teeth, and rocking Jordans. You're clean cut, and I need someone I can incorporate into every aspect of my life. All you have to do is keep it real with me and I got you, boo."

Chance didn't know what to think, but he knew that he didn't want to miss the opportunity to be with a woman who could finance his final mo-ments alive. "Okay, I'm convinced, Miss Pope. When and where?" he asked.

"If you want to walk me to my car, I'll give you the address and my phone number. You can meet me at the spa. I'll give you an awesome massage with a happy ending, and then I'll treat you to the best steak and lobster that Miami has to offer," she cooed.

Chance was all in. A massage, pussy, and dinner from a gorgeous woman? Yes indeed, he should have come to Miami a long time ago.

They walked to Dawn's cherry red Jaguar F-TYPE convertible in silence, mainly because he'd opted to walk a few steps behind her in an attempt to watch her walk. Her hips swayed seductively, and her buttocks bounced in rhythmic cadence with every step. His eyes followed the contours of her sinuous frame. From her shoulders to the natural arch in her back, she was rhythm manifested.

She leaned into her car, reached into the glove box, and removed a black business card. Dawn looked back at Chance and noticed his eyes trained on her butt. She smiled at him flirtatiously and handed him the card.

"Feel free to come by around seven p.m. I close at six thirty, so we'll have the place all to ourselves. See you soon, lover," she said. Dawn leaned in and kissed Chance on the cheek and let her hand slide along his arm. She got into her car and drove away slowly, teasing Chance through her rearview mirror.

He glanced down at the black card in his hand. It read:

Water Works Day Spa
We specialize in massage and Oriental-style acupuncture
Dawn Pope, Owner and Operator
305-555-1050

The red Jaguar pulled into the parking lot at the rear of Water Works Day Spa, and the pretty-eyed beachgoer climbed out and scurried through the back door of the parlor. Once inside, she surveyed her handiwork. Dawn Pope (the real Dawn Pope) lay crumpled in a bloody heap behind the front counter of the spa. Pretty Eyes lifted Dawn Pope's head by her long reddish brown hair and looked deep into her eyes. The cold stare of death ironically gave her life. She smiled psychotically and then dropped the dead woman's head, exposing the deep, crimson red laceration she'd made with her straight razor. The blood had coagulated around the wound and had crusted over her cold dead face.

"We're all born for a purpose, Mrs. Pope. It just so happens that the purpose you were born for is also the purpose you died for," she said.

She walked to the massage area and put out fresh towels and clean sheets. Next, she removed her bag of tools: a ball gag, a blindfold, and hand restraints. She swept and mopped the entire shop with the exception of the area where Dawn Pope's body lay. It was pure craftsmanship, her masterpiece, and she didn't want it disturbed. She dimmed the lights and lit candles. She turned on the stereo, and the soft sounds of running water filled the speakers throughout the spa.

The sun had just begun to fall over the streets of Miami, and a soft, steady mist of drizzling rain fell, beating a drum-like tempo across the asphalt. She heard a crackle and a buzz, and then the streetlight sprang to life with illumination. The luminescence of the overhead lights danced along the asphalt, turning the raindrops into a bejeweled runway of magnificent reds, yellows, and greens.

In the distance, she saw Chance Thimble approaching. He walked with his hands shoved deep into his pockets and his head held low as if that would somehow shield him from the impending storm.

"You look like you've seen better days, Mr. Clements. Maybe we should get you out of those wet clothes," she said.

Chance welcomed the warmth and shelter provided by the cozy spa. He'd walked back to his small, unimposing motel room to shower and change clothes and had gotten caught in the rain while walking back to the spa to meet his new ATM.

He could have just as easily had taken a cab, but cabbies talked too much and were too nosy. He didn't need some half-drunk cab driver talking his ear off, dropping him off, and then seeing his face on the news later, only to recall where he had picked him up and dropped him off.

They walked inside, and Chance smiled at her. She'd changed into a silk kimono-style garment of green and gold to match her smoldering eyes, and her lips shimmered from her glittery lip gloss. She led him to a room that was dimly lit except for the candles that burned and glowed softly against the walls. He heard the sound of running water and was immediately lulled into a sense of tranquility.

"Are you a freak, Marcus, and if so, how freaky are you?" she asked.

He wasn't sure how to quite answer the questions. That had always been one of his favorite lines, and now it was being used against him. So in return he used the line that he'd most enjoyed from one of his victims. "I guess I'll be as freaky as you need me to be," he whispered coyly.

"So what are you waiting for? Strip, handsome."

Something about the syrupy sexuality dripping from her voice coupled with the forcefulness of her orders aroused him. Even in his arousal, he felt a slight tinge of intimidation. Chance had always been the aggressor, but this woman, this gorgeous specimen of a woman, scared him, not because of the incredible sex he was anticipating, but because she seemed cold. Dripping with sexuality, yes, but cold, almost cold-blooded. When she looked at him, it felt more like she was looking through him. He undressed slowly, first his shoes, then his pants and boxers, and finally his tattered designer T-shirt. He stood butt naked in front of her. His erection curved upward, throbbing, seemingly begging his victim to take him.

"Lie down on the table on your back," she said.

Chance did as he was told and glanced over at Pretty Eyes, who was putting on latex gloves. She snapped the bands of the gloves playfully and smiled at Chance as she poured massage oil into her hand. She walked to him and began rubbing the oil on his chest in a circular motion. She let her hands follow the contours of his chest and midsection down to his throbbing manhood. She stroked it slowly and felt it pounding in the palm of her hand. Chance's eyes rolled to the back of his head, and his face contorted in a weird mask of sexual euphoria.

"You like that? How does that feel, baby?" she asked.

But Chance didn't answer. He was lost in a world that only freaks and perverts understood.

"Turn over," she ordered, and he did as he was told. He placed his face in the circular, cushioned doughnut of the massage table and stared at the terrazzo tile beneath him. He felt the warm, sweet wind of her breath as she whispered in his ear, "What do you think about bondage? Can I restrain you?"

"You can do whatever you want to do, baby, for real."

Pretty Eyes took five silk scarves from her little bag of tricks and tied his arms and legs tightly to the base of the massage table. She used the fifth scarf to tie his neck to the headrest of the table. Chance was totally immobile, completely at the mercy of the woman he had met only hours earlier. She knelt and whispered in his ear, "Are you comfortable, Chance?" She giggled as he struggled against his restraints. "Calm down. This will all be over soon," she said.

"I told you, my name is Marcus, Marcus Clements."

"Yeah, I know what you told me, but I know the truth! Let me explain how this is going to go, Chance!" she barked.

"Please, my name is Marcus! Just let me go. I promise you'll never see me again."

"You're not listening, Chance. I need you to be a good boy and listen," she said calmly.

Chance began to weep softly. He wasn't a good person, and he knew it. He'd done bad things and crossed a lot of the wrong people. He wasn't a crier either, but her bipolar-like personality really scared him. He could hear the click-clack of her heels against the cold tile. It sounded as though she'd left the room, but she returned seconds later and dropped a large leather bag in his line of sight.

"It's sad that it has to come to this, Chance. Why would you play God and sentence all those young girls to death?" she asked in a maternal tone.

"I don't know what you're talking about. Please, I'm begging you, let me go."

"Don't fucking lie to me, Chance!" she screamed with spittle escaping her shimmery lips. She pulled the straight razor from her bosom and slashed Chance across his back. He screamed, and his body went limp, maybe from the pain, maybe from shock, but he was afraid to move. "Now we're going to try this again, my love. Do you think that you're God, Chance? Do you think that you and you alone should be judge, jury, and executioner?" she asked.

He struggled to catch his breath. A searing pain rushed through his skin like hot lava. "No, no, I don't," he whispered hoarsely.

Her harsh and unfeeling laughter filled the small space and bounced from wall to wall. "You sound like you're in pain. Are you in pain, Chance?" she asked.

She didn't give him a chance to answer. She grabbed a candle and let the hot wax drip into the gash on Chance's back that she'd created with the razor. A shrill and horrific scream escaped from the bowels of Chance's tortured soul. The louder he screamed, the louder she laughed. She opened the bag beneath the table and removed bundles of razor-sharp crochet needles. There were over 200, a sharpened needle for each of the victims Chance had directly or indirectly infected with his thoughtless act. "Chance Thimble, I am appointed by God to bring you to justice for your crimes against humanity. My job is to make you suffer and to make you crave death. I decided to be artistic with your punishment. I thought long and hard about this, and since your last name is Thimble, I thought, why not see if he's really a thimble? Why not see if a thimble really, really protects against needles. You get it? What do you think?" she asked in a giddy voice.

"I think you're a psycho fucking bitch, that's what I think!"

"Now, now, Chance, shouting obscenities will only make me kill you slower," she cooed.

She tried to insert the ball gag into his mouth, but he clamped his lips together tightly, refusing her entry. Pretty Eyes jabbed one of the crochet needles into Chance's waxed-over wounds and he screamed again, this time with his teeth still clenched. "If you open up and let me gag you, I promise that your death will be quick and sweet," she promised.

Reluctantly, Chance opened his mouth. His entire body ached from fighting the urge to move. There was no escape, and he silently prayed that death would come a little quicker, but God had no answers for him. She inserted the sharpened needles one by one into his aching flesh until Chance looked more like a human pin cushion than a thimble. She removed the ball gag, and Chance whimpered softly, "Please, lady, please just kill me now."

"Just a little more torture and it'll all be done. Isn't this fun? Us bonding like this, I mean?" she asked as she inserted more needles.

There was very little skin left exposed on Chance's threadbare body. Blood leaked slowly from his puncture wounds, and his torturer had to step back to appraise her handiwork. *Just a couple more needles and he'll be perfect.* She walked to him and untied his neck, knelt in front of him, and smiled brightly. With her index finger and thumb, she forced his eye open and inserted a sharpened crochet needle into his eyeball. Chance opened his mouth to scream, but nothing came out, because as he opened his mouth, she jammed another needle into the fleshy part of his neck beneath his chin, pinning his tongue to the roof of his mouth. Her job had been done. Chance Thimble was on the downslope of life. Death would soon come in his black robe, wielding his sharpened sickle to claim Chance's wretched soul.

Chapter 11

THE SHOE

At the very same moment that Chance Thimble met his well-deserved but untimely demise, Alyssa Schumacher was ceremoniously downing shots of Fireball whiskey. She was perhaps the most sought-after and celebrated criminal defense attorney in New York City. Alyssa had foregone all the trappings of a mundane existence. She'd traded her apron for a briefcase, and she'd swapped adolescent soccer games and PTA meetings for murder cases and case studies. Alyssa Schumacher was a beast in the courtroom, and she knew it. She'd won so many cases that people half-seriously joked that she must've sold her soul to the devil.

Satan, however, had nothing to do with her wins. She was a shrewd attorney who had no compunction about breaking the law, and she would stoop as low as she needed to in order to win a case. Money was the motivation for Alyssa, and she earned hefty sums of it. Her latest case had

made her a superstar among her peers, a darling
in the media, and a pariah in the African American
community. She'd taken the case of a police officer
accused of killing an unarmed 14-year-old black
girl. According to eyewitnesses, the girl (a lesbian)
had just left the basketball court, parted ways with
her friends, and was headed home when the officer approached her with New York City's notorious
stop-and-frisk. She looked like a boy, dressed like
a boy, she even walked like a boy, but Trina Hayes
was no boy. He'd instructed her to get against the
wall so that he could frisk her. She, in turn, refused,
insisting that he call a female officer. The act of
defiance must have infuriated Franz Gottlieb, because he could be heard screaming racial epithets
at Trina. Moments later, witnesses said he shoved
her to the ground and fired two shots, one to her
head and one to her chest.

Not only did Franz Gottlieb have a history of violence within the NYPD, not only had he murdered
Trina Hayes in cold blood, but he'd been linked to
an American Nazi sympathizers group called the
National Socialists Movement. They saw themselves as the new arm of the Third Reich. Simply
put, Hitler's SS had been reborn. The community
had been outraged and a guilty plea should've been
inevitable, but there was no would've, could've, or
should've with Alyssa Schumacher. She'd not only
taken the case because Officer Gottlieb's family
was well off and had agreed to her excessive fees,
but she'd also taken it out of obligation.

After only two days of deliberations, a panel of all-white jurors had returned a verdict of not guilty unanimously. She'd successfully painted a picture of Trina Hayes as an aggressive wannabe who'd posed as a boy with unsuspecting female victims. She convinced the jury that the young girl was a bully who fought boys on a regular basis. She posed the question that if Trina Hayes had nothing to hide, then why not cooperate with Officer Gottlieb?

Upon hearing this, Trina's distraught mother stood and screamed, "Because she was a god-damned girl and she didn't want his fucking hands on her!"

The judge had had her removed from the court-room and Miss Schumacher had promptly used that to her advantage, stating that Trina was a product of violence. "Look at her mother's violent outburst," she'd said.

By the time the trial was over, anyone watching the proceedings would've believed that Franz Gottlieb was the victim. Franz had even managed a couple of tears and made it seem like, had it not been for God's grace and self-defense, he would have surely perished at the hands of the roguish teen, a girl, no less. Alyssa Schumacher had received so many death threats since the trial that she no longer took them seriously.

And now she was at Slattery's Midtown Pub celebrating with not only some of her closest peers, but Franz Gottlieb as well. He and his fellow brethren from the National Socialist Movement cheered and congratulated the young, seasoned attorney on a fight well fought.

Alyssa raised her glass and downed her ninth shot of whiskey and smiled broadly. She was feeling no pain as she stumbled to the bar for yet another round of shots for her and her "friends." She stood impatiently, waiting for the bartender to take her order. She tapped her fingers rhythmically against the Formica bar top, waiting. She looked around the bar for an available waitress, and then she saw him, a vision unlike anything she'd seen in New York City. He wasn't a tight-assed stiff neck like most of the well-to-do men in New York. No, she could tell by his swagger and his walk that he wasn't from around there. Even in the darkness of the German pub, he looked like money. From his Italian-cut suit to his Ferragamo loafers, he was the epitome of a well-dressed man.

He approached the bar and took a seat next to her. He smelled like money, too, a light, leathery scent with a hint of musk, a classy, manly smell. Alyssa had a bad habit of making assumptions and assessments of people upon their initial meetings. She had her preconceived notions drawn in her head that the tall, handsome stranger was quirky yet charismatic. He struck her as a social climber, obsessed with status and image, someone who, within a relatively short period of time, had risen from middle-class beginnings to the inner circle of whatever profession he'd chosen to pursue. She had no idea how wrong she was.

Mr. Handsome smiled cheerfully as he took the stool next to Alyssa, who anxiously returned the smile. "I'm celebrating," she slurred. "How about I buy the first round?"

He didn't answer. Instead, he stiffened and cocked his body to avoid her gaze and conversation. She wasn't exactly sure how she should take the rejection. On one hand, she felt disrespected and resentful of the slight. On the other hand, she felt determined to gain his attention. Nobody, absolutely nobody, had ever rejected Alyssa Schumacher, because not only was she driven and extremely successful in her field, but she was drop-dead gorgeous. She was not "model on the runway" gorgeous, but she had a timeless beauty that was reminiscent of an old twenties or thirties flick. It was a trait that had indeed helped more than it had hindered. With her porcelain skin, blue-black shoulder-length hair, and ice blue eyes, her features were decidedly German.

Alyssa excused herself and made her way to the ladies' room. Eager young gold-diggers anxious to find a financially stable doctor or lawyer primped and pranced around the bathroom chattering about dick, divorce, and their latest sexual conquests. Slattery's had turned into a meat factory where men came to play and women unknowingly got played.

Alyssa huffed under her breath. Their conversation was the main reason why she didn't have female friends. The shallowness and banality of their conversation threatened to drive her insane. Alyssa stepped to the wall-to-wall mirror, put her palms on the sink, and looked deep into her own reflection. "You look hammered," she said to the reflection staring back at her.

The trite females snickered and whispered some inside joke among each other and then left the restroom.

Alyssa leaned over the sink and put cold water on her face. The brisk, cold water sobered her up instantly. She freshened her makeup and breathed deep. The smell of expensive perfume and sanitized toilets invaded her nostrils, sobering her further. *Better, much better.*

As she exited the bathroom, she was relieved to see that he was still sitting at the bar. Alyssa sucked her teeth as she noticed one of the barracudas from the ladies' room in her seat trying to cozy up to Mr. Handsome. The look on his face said that he wasn't in the mood to be bothered, much like the look he had given her. She strolled casually across the bar until she was standing behind the woman but making eye contact with Mr. Handsome. His gaze blazed through the money-hungry women and came to rest on Alyssa. There was a "please rescue me" look in his eyes, and Alyssa smiled knowingly.

She tapped the young lady on her shoulder. "Excuse me, hon, I believe you're in my seat. Has my husband been boring you with his infamous war stories?"

"Oh, my! Oh, I'm sorry, he never said anything about being married," she said, looking Alyssa up and down. The gold-digger cut her eyes angrily at the man and got up slowly, cursing underneath her breath as she moved away.

"Nice save," he said.

"No problem. You looked like you needed help."

"I'm just not much on dealing with drunken females, you know?" he said.

"I'm sure. Well, we got off to a rough start earlier, so allow me to introduce myself properly. My name is Alyssa, Alyssa Schumacher, but my friends call me Shoe," she said, extending her hand.

"Pleased to meet you, Shoe. Now how about that drink that you promised me?"

"Of course. What's your poison?" she asked.

"A shot of Louis XIII."

"Hmmmm, a man with expensive tastes, I like that, Mr. . . . ." She let it linger, hoping that he would share his name. It wasn't lost on her that he hadn't given his name when she'd introduced herself.

"King. It's Mr. King. Now how about that drink?"

"Coming right up, Mr. King," she said.

Alyssa waved to the bartender, who seemed to almost run to take her order, not like before when she had purposely ignored Alyssa. Mr. Handsome had the female bartender running to gain his attention, just like half of the other women in the bar. She ordered their drinks: a shot of Louis XIII for him and a shot of Fireball for her.

"I'll be right back. I need to run to the little girl's room," she said flirtatiously.

Mr. King nodded and stood as a gesture of chivalry. Alyssa disappeared into the bathroom, and he looked around nervously. He removed a vial from the inner pocket of his Armani suit. The vial contained *gamma*-Hydroxybutyrate acid, or GHB, commonly known on the street as the date-rape drug. As soon as the bartender brought their drinks, Mr. King drank half of Alyssa's shot and mixed the remainder with GHB. It was colorless, odorless, and tasteless when mixed with a drink. GHB wouldn't hurt her. It would merely increase her sociability, heighten her attraction to him, and lower her inhibitions.

Mr. King put on his brightest smile as Alyssa approached the bar. "I thought you'd left me here to drink both of these shots alone," he gushed.

"No, of course not. That would only give these vultures a chance at you. I mean, look at you. You're gorgeous," she said.

"Well, thank you, pretty lady. Here's to new friendships," he said, raising his glass.

"To new and lasting friendships."

Their glasses clinked as they toasted and downed their drinks. Mr. King intentionally flirted with Alyssa to loosen her inhibitions, and by the time they finished their fifth shot, she was in love. His voice, his words, his eyes, his hands . . . oh God, his hands! Alyssa had studied the man, this Mr. King, until she felt like she knew him. She gently stroked his inner thigh, leaned in, and kissed him on the ear.

"You want to go back to my place?" she asked huskily.

He smiled his magical smile as Alyssa's hand found his crotch. "I would love to go back to your place. Did you feel what you were looking for? Does it meet with your approval?"

Alyssa's face blushed beet red. She wasn't used to being called out on her advances. For that matter, she rarely made advances. He took her hand and guided it to his man meat. His semi-erect penis was swollen, and Alyssa felt her panties moisten. They left Slattery's hand in hand, and she couldn't wait to have him inside of her.

She snuggled close to him as they walked toward her apartment building. The crisp fall wind of New York City was chilly and brisk, but not unbearable. Besides, Alyssa relished the opportunity to get close to her newfound friend. She giggled silently. This wasn't like her at all. She didn't meet random men at bars, and she most certainly didn't invite them back to her apartment. As a matter of fact, Alyssa Schumacher hadn't had sex in nearly four years, mostly by choice because she was allergic to the chemicals in condoms, so she didn't use them. Plus, she didn't want to run the risk of scraping the bottom of the genetic gene pool by procreating with one of the many cretins she'd encountered. She'd had her share of hot nights with her guilty pleasure, dim lights, a bottle of Moscato, and a black dildo that she affectionately called Tyrone, but no man had graced her inner sanctuary. She'd waited, albeit impatiently, and she had so much repressed sexual energy penned up inside that Mr. King was in for quite a night.

The doorman at her apartment building opened the door and ushered them into the beauty that was known simply as the Anthem. It was twenty-nine stories of sheer engineering genius, and Alyssa loved every square inch of it. She tugged Mr. King by his hand, anxious to get him up to her penthouse. He looked at her with an amused look on his face as she tried her best to kiss him, but he kept moving away. He wasn't much of a kisser, and he certainly didn't want to kiss Miss Schumacher.

The elevator came to a stop and dinged, and as soon as the doors opened, she started to undress. She kicked out of her expensive Manolo Blahnik heels first, and piece by piece, the rest of her clothing followed. She undressed until she was down to her bra, panties, and garter belt. She walked backward toward her apartment, teasing him, taunting him with lust-filled gestures and words.

Mr. King, however, wasn't moved. He kept a stern but inviting smirk on his face as he knelt and picked up each piece of clothing she dropped. Her apartment was immaculate. It was almost clinical with its stark white walls and snow-white leather furnishings. The hardwood floors seemed to go on forever and led out to a balcony that overlooked the city.

"Would you care for a drink, Mr. King?" Alyssa asked. She took a remote control from a nearby coffee table and clicked a button. The quiet hiss of gears could be heard as a wall slid open, exposing a fully stocked bar.

Mr. King's eyes were ablaze, not from the sight of the bar, but because of what the bar held. War photos, photos of swastikas, and war medals were aligned in a makeshift shrine. She noticed the strained look on his face and took his hand, leading him to the couch.

"I can understand your confusion with my pictures. Most people see the swastika and automatically think negatively about it, but—"

"Listen, you don't owe me any explanations. We're just having a good time, and besides, we just met," Mr. King said.

"No, no, I want to tell you though. I mean, I really like you, and I want you to know about me. If you're still interested after I'm done, then we can fuck each other's brains out. Deal?"

Reluctantly, he nodded. She was merely prolonging the inevitable, but whatever floated her boat was cool with him. She started at the beginning, telling Mr. King how her grandfather Kurt Schumacher had been an *obersturmfuhrer* (first lieutenant) in Hitler's Waffen SS army during World War II. She said that he'd been awarded the Knight's Cross of the Iron Cross for extreme battlefield bravery. That had been the medal that Mr. King saw displayed in the bar case. He'd died before she was born, of course, but his accomplishments had given her family a great sense of pride. She'd grown up wearing her heritage like a badge of honor, and according to her, she'd do anything within her power to make sure that the Fuhrer's dream of a pure society came to fruition.

"Even if that means letting killers go free?" he asked.

"That's part of my job, and I make no apologies for it. Sure, it's not all glamorous, but it pays the bills."

"Walk with me, Alyssa," he said.

He took her hand and led her to the balcony. The breeze was brisk, causing Alyssa's nipples to immediately harden. She hugged herself tightly, trying to put the discomfort of being outside in the cold in her lingerie out of her mind.

"Alyssa, I listened to your entire story, and the one thing that stood out to me is that you're a hate-monger. You spew hatred to your cronies, but you're afraid to publicly be who you are," Mr. King said.

"Wait a minute, I—" she began, but he smacked her violently.

"Shut the fuck up and listen! I knew a woman like you once, so full of hatred and self-loathing that she found it next to impossible to love the only son she had. That police officer you helped walk was a murderer—not just a murderer, but a murderer of children," he said. He turned his back to her and peered out across the night sky, reflectively lost in the lights that blanketed the city streets below.

"Who . . . who are you?" she asked, stammering as she stepped backward.

He turned toward her, his eyes ablaze with a burning hatred. "I'm your salvation. I'm here to cleanse you and make you whole again," he said, smiling. His smile wasn't genuine or friendly. It was the smile of death and deceit, a look that Alyssa Schumacher knew all too well.

"If you let me go now, I promise you'll never hear from me again. I won't tell anyone, I promise," she whined.

His cruel laughter bellowed and boomed through the blackened night sky. "I know you won't tell anyone. Dead people don't talk too good," he said.

Alyssa tried to run back inside of her apartment, but Mr. Handsome grabbed her by a handful of her hair before she made it inside. She kicked and screamed as he dragged her to the balcony, and the louder she screamed, the tighter his grip became entangled in her scalp.

"Stand up, bitch!" he spat.

She stumbled to her feet and faced him. For as long as she could remember, she had always been in a position of power. She'd played God on many occasions, saving those she felt deserved it and condemning those she deemed unworthy. And now she felt weak at the mercy of her desires because she had invited this demon, this monster, into her home.

He grabbed her by her throat, pulled her close, and whispered in her ear, "Don't fret, whore, it'll all be over soon. You're an important piece in this game." He laughed heartily again, licked her on her cheek, and then tossed her from the twenty-ninth-floor balcony. He smiled as her screams slowly faded and her body drifted ever so slowly toward her concrete grave below.

Chapter 12

PITY PARTY

Before she reached the steps, Monica could hear the high-pitched wails of Millicent's cries. She knocked lightly, but there was no answer. Monica knocked again, this time more forcefully. Bird threw open the door dressed only in grayish boxer shorts and a sagging T-shirt. He cradled Millicent, but she continued to scream. His features softened somewhat when he saw that it was Monica. "Oh, come in, Monkey. How are you?" he asked.

"I'm fine. Why is Millie crying like that?" Monica asked, reaching for the screaming child. The stench coming from the house caused Monica to heave. She tried desperately not to throw up from the sickly, pungent smell that slapped her in the face.

"I don't know, man. I fed her, I changed her, and I've been rocking her, and she still won't stop crying. This is some bullshit."

"She's probably crying because it smells like ass in here, Bird. Why don't you turn some damn lights on in here?"

As she entered the house, the smell grew stronger, and she tried to adjust her eyes to the darkness in search of the source of the foul odor. Monica walked to the plantation-style shutters covering the windows and opened them one by one. Light flooded the living room and dust particles swirled about the air, coming to rest on the Victorian furniture that adorned the space. Bird plopped down on the couch, and more dust began to dance about, prancing through the bright rays of sunlight.

And then Monica saw the source of the putrid odor. On the coffee table sat a glass of curdled milk, a rotten apple, and a half-eaten bowl of oatmeal. Monica handed the baby to Bird, and she immediately began to cry again. Monica gathered the dishes and trash and again had to fight the urge to hurl as she knelt to clean beneath the table. She grabbed an open bag from the floor, and as soon as she stood up, she dropped the bag. Along with the chips was a spoiled tuna sandwich, and from the looks of the molding bread, it had been there for days. The bag was crawling with maggots, and Monica all but ran to the kitchen to dump the mess.

She repeated her lighting ceremony in the kitchen, opening the blinds above the sink. She gasped in horror at the grotesque sight that invaded her eyes. In the corner of the kitchen where the refrigerator met the pantry was a large pile of soiled Pampers. Dishes were piled in the sink, along the countertops, and on the stove. Meat that had been left in the other side of the sink to thaw was now teeming with maggots. Flies and gnats buzzed around the kitchen as if they owned the place, coming to land on anything that even remotely seemed unclean.

This was a far cry from the Bird she'd met when she was assigned to the King Kochese case. His condo had been immaculate, and now he was living in squalor. She wasn't exactly sure how she should approach Bird about it, but something had to be done.

Monica walked to the living room trying to formulate her thoughts, trying to think over Millicent's incessant cries. She sat next to Bird, took the baby from his hands, and cradled her close to her bosom. She rocked back and forth slowly, and Millie's cries became whimpers until finally her whimpers became the mere pleasurable sounds of a sleeping baby who had been deprived of a restful slumber.

"What's going on with you, Bird?"

"Living, man, just living," Bird replied.

"I got a news flash for you, playboy—this ain't living. While I was in the kitchen, I pondered how to bring this shit to you, and I figured the only way to say it is to just say it. You know I love you, right?"

"Yeah, I know, so what's up?" he asked.

"Over the course of the Kochese case, you and I grew close, so I consider you my brother and my friend, but you're tripping, Bird. You're falling the fuck off!" Monica said sternly.

"Man, don't come up in my shit judging me!"

"I'm not judging you, nigga. Look around! As your friend, it's my job to give it to you straight. Look at this place, Bird! Bridgette worked hard to make this place a home, a place anyone would be proud to raise their children in. You got maggots and shit crawling around, dirty dishes and shitty Pampers all around. I remember when Bridgette was killed, you promised you'd die before you let her family take Millie away from you. That was three months ago, ninety fucking days, and look at you now, Bird. If Bridgette's people came in here and saw the conditions you have this baby living in, I wouldn't blame them one bit if they snatched her away," Monica scolded.

Bird doubled over as if in pain and began to sob. He hugged himself tightly, trying to escape the cold of a harsh truth.

"Look at her. Bird, look at your daughter!" she ordered. Reluctantly, Bird looked at the slumbering child with a contrite look in his eyes. Monica continued to drive her point home. "She has fifty percent of your DNA and fifty percent of her mother's. When I look at this gorgeous child, I see you both in her eyes, and she needs you, Bird. She needs you to love her and care for her. She needs to feel that same love she felt the very first time you held her in your arms."

"I don't know how, Monkey," he said between sobs. Bird had never lied to Monica, and she knew it. Maybe he didn't know how to love the baby. Maybe she was just another person to him. But if he didn't get it together, he would lose her. "I mean, I love her, you know that, but I don't know how to bounce back so that I can give her the best of me. Bridgette was my everything, Monkey, and when I lost her *and* my sister in the same day, it fucked me up. I find myself calling her from another room only to realize that she'll never answer, that she's never coming back. Can you imagine lying awake in bed and glancing into a dark bathroom, catching a glimpse of a ghost, of a person who meant everything to you? I'm afraid to walk into my own bedroom because it was her creation. I smell her, I feel her here, and it makes me sad, but at the same time, I'm afraid to leave the house because I fear losing the small connection that I have with her in this house," he cried.

"You have all the connection you'll ever need right here, Bird," she said softly, nodding at Millicent.

"And then what? What happens when she's old enough to understand that her mommy is gone and is never coming back? What happens when she wants to know why I didn't protect her mother? I can't explain that shit because I don't even know. I left the streets to escape the madness, but it found me. It found me and robbed me of my happiness and everything I've worked for."

"So you're just going to give up?"

"I'm not giving up. I just need time," he said.

"You don't get that fucking luxury, Bird. Millie needs you now! She's not a toy you can put on the shelf until you feel better, until you feel like being her daddy."

Bird took the baby from Monica's arms and nestled her close to his chest, nuzzling his nose close to her tiny head. He could smell the sweet aroma of her aloe-infused baby lotion. Her smell, her essence, shifted his mind to a simpler time when he knew nothing of death and the ill will of men. Millicent moved and cooed softly, and then it hit him: they were each other's salvation. God had plans, and He was never wrong. He sat staring at her, and it became clear that he'd been hiding from life, not living it. Had he and Bridgette been married and never given birth to Millicent, he would've just simply lost Bridgette, but he had a living, breathing part of her in the palm of his hands.

Bird stood and walked Millie to her crib and laid her on her side. She slept peacefully, her tiny hands cupped under her face. She had a smile on her face as if she and her father had shared the same revelation. Bird was mesmerized, almost transfixed, while watching his daughter, his heartstring, his only living connection to the woman who had forever changed his life.

Monica joined him next to her crib and took Bird's hand into her own. "You know why she's smiling, Bird? Because her mommy just told her that everything is going to be okay, that Daddy gets it," she said sweetly.

They sat facing one another in Bird's dining room. "Bird, I kind of wanted to give you an update. I know you wanted me to investigate Bridgette's murder, but I've been thrown into a hot case. Muldoon called me, and when I got to the crime scene, it was Drak."

"What do you mean it was Drak?"

"I mean someone killed him, Bird, but they didn't just kill him. They tortured him like they were trying to send a message. First your sister and Bridgette, and now Drak." Monica buried her head in her hands and shook her head.

"Damn, that's fucked up. Drak was cool as a muh'fucka. So do you think the murders are connected?"

"No, I don't believe so. It's a completely different MO from what I'm seeing, but you never know. Muldoon and my boss have me in charge of a task force to catch this sick bastard." Monica let out a guttural groan born strictly from exasperation.

"What's wrong, Monkey?"

"A few things, actually. First off, the guy directly underneath me is only a kid. I mean, he's smart, but he's a kid. He might be twenty-four or twenty-five. His name is Cody Roth, and the little fucker looks just like Harry Potter," she said, laughing.

"So what's the problem? What's so funny?"

"I'm just tripping on Harry Potter. He looks so Middle America, you know, Mr. Apple Pie, but he's from Park Row," she said.

"Oh, wow."

"Yeah, exactly. I'm meeting with him and the team when I leave here. Well, after I help you clean this pigsty," Monica teased.

"Monkey?"

"Yeah, Bird?"

"Thank you."

"You don't have to thank me. This place is filthy. If you want to thank me, help me clean up and then put on a pot of coffee," Monica said.

"I didn't mean for helping me clean, nerd. I meant for helping me call my mind back. You know, for helping me to realize what I have versus what I've lost. I almost lost my mind *and* my baby.

You made me see that Millie needs me, and for that, I'm forever grateful."

"Oh, boy, boo. That's what friends do. We tell each other the truth no matter how bad it hurts," she said.

"Straight up."

They put on music and began the daunting task of cleaning Bird's home. Monica took the living room, the bedrooms, and the dining room. She left the kitchen, bathrooms, and den to Bird. There was no way she was going back into that kitchen until it was clean after the atrocity she'd witnessed.

They talked and reminisced about their short past, from Baby Face's player ways to Drak's pretend loyalty. He'd been very convincing, and he'd fooled everyone, even King Kochese himself. The agency hadn't even let Monica in on the fact that Drak was undercover in King's organization. Monica's only regret was that Kochese would never serve time for Baby Face's murder.

They cleaned, scrubbed, and dusted until the house was spotless. By the time they'd finished cleaning, there were eight completely full bags of trash sitting idle on the side of the road. No longer did the house smell like rotting meat and wilted fruit. No, now it held the savory aromas of freshly brewed coffee and scented candles.

Bird took a sip of his coffee and joined Monica at the dining room table. He put his hand on top

of hers, leaned in, and kissed her on the cheek.
"You're a good friend, Monkey. By the way, how's
Jasmine?"

"Man, don't even get me started on her ass. She's
all googly-woogly over Kochese's brother Khalil.
This dude has her nose wide open," Monica hissed.

"Yeah, she's wide open because he's busting her
little guts up."

"Nah, let her tell it, they aren't even fucking yet."

"And he's got her like that? Damn, when he does
pop that little cherry, she's really gonna be sprung,"
Bird laughed.

"It's not funny, Bird! This dude creeps me out.
He's always popping up when we're out, and he
and Jazz are always huddled, whispering and shit.
I just don't trust him."

"As long as she's happy, you should be happy.
How's Mr. Mutt?" he asked.

"Don't call my baby a mutt, and he's fine, just
spoiled like a child. Speaking of Noisy Boy, I have
to go home and feed him before I meet with the
team."

Bird sipped his coffee and smiled at Monica.
She was absolutely right. Noisy Boy was spoiled
like a child, but it was all Monica's doing. She
would often take him to one of the many fancy pet
stores where patrons were allowed to bring their
pets inside and fill baskets with all the latest chew
toys and fancy collars.

"So what's the plan? You know, with the restaurants and bookstore?" Monica asked.

"I'm gonna hire some people to run them and just oversee the day-to-day from a distance, you feel me? It's too painful to be in there every day. Plus, that'll give me time to spend with the baby."

"Sounds good to me. I'll check on you guys later on. I love you, Bird, and always remember that we're family and you don't have to do this alone," Monica said.

"I really appreciate that, Monica. I think I'm going to take a shower, put some clothes on, and take Millicent to the park. Oh, yeah, and you know how you said friends always tell each other the truth?"

"Yeah, why?" she asked.

"Well, as your friend, I think it's my duty to tell you that you need to work out harder because your booty is spreading," Bird said, laughing.

Instinctively, Monica's hands went to her butt. "Ahhh, fuck you, Bird, you know you like this fat ass! You almost got me though. Asshole."

Chapter 13

TRAINING DAY

Jasmine and Khalil met in the baggage claim of DFW Airport. He embraced her and kissed her deeply. He nestled his nose into her neck and breathed deep. "Damn, I'm happy to see you! I really missed you, baby," he said.

"I missed you too. It's crazy, but the whole time that I was gone, I was wishing that we were together."

"Same here, baby, same here. Do you have any plans for today?" he asked.

"Not that I know of. Why, what's up?"

"I thought we could grab some lunch, talk about your weekend, and then head over to the track," Khalil said.

"The track?"

"Yeah, a motocross track, where they teach you how to ride four wheelers, dirt bikes, and motorcycles."

"That's different, baby. I've never ridden any of those before, and it sounds like fun."

Khalil slung Jasmine's bag over his shoulder and took her hand, headed for the parking garage. They had a lot of catching up to do. This had been the first weekend since they'd been involved that they hadn't spent together. He left DFW en route to Oak Cliff. He had a special treat for Jasmine that he was sure she'd enjoy.

In less than an hour, they pulled into the parking lot of Sweet Georgia Brown's. It was one of Dallas's most well-known soul food restaurants, and people came from miles around to taste their Southern soul delicacies.

"It smells really good in here, babe. How do you know about a soul food place? You don't strike me as the soul food type," Jasmine said.

"You'd be surprised at the things I know, baby girl."

The smell of meats and vegetables combined with the sweet smell of cakes and pies embedded itself in Jasmine's senses. The aroma was so deliciously thick that Jasmine could taste it just standing in line. Her eyes darted from dish to dish, and she felt the harsh sting of uncertainty. Khalil noticed the look in her eyes and moved closer to her.

"Are you okay, baby?" he asked.

"Everything looks so good I don't even know where to begin."

"How about I just order for you, honey?" he offered.

"Oh, my God, babe, that would be great! I'm getting fat just smelling it."

They both laughed as Khalil ordered their food: oxtails, black-eyed peas, cabbage, macaroni and cheese, and corn bread for Jasmine, smoked neck bones, collard greens, pinto beans, rice, and corn bread for him. They both took a slice of Sweet Georgia Brown's world-famous chess pie for dessert.

Over lunch, they discussed their weekend apart. Neither of them liked it, but it was necessary to ensure longevity in their relationship. It solidified what they both knew—that although they were okay apart, they were much more effective together. Jasmine ate until she couldn't take another bite. They continued to talk until the waitress, although nice about it, began to clear away their dishes as if asking them to leave.

Moments later, they were pulling into Metroplex Motocross. They went into the gift shop to get fitted for the track. After leaving, Jasmine felt like a stunt double. Her pink and white rider's suit was double insulated. She had pink elbow pads and kneepads, pink shin guards, and a pink helmet and goggles. Khalil chose the exact same outfit except his was a striking royal blue and black.

"Excuse me, but would you mind terribly if I troubled you to take a picture of my wife and me?" Khalil asked the fresh-faced young clerk.

She had to be at least 18 years old, but she looked much younger. She wasn't attractive in the least bit with her fire red hair, bulging blue eyes, and freckles. She looked like a female version of Howdy Doody.

Shock and love spread across Jasmine's face, and she clutched Khalil's hand tighter. She loved it when he called her his wife. There was something about the statement that felt so right, and every time he said it, it only served to make her fall deeper in love with him.

Their lesson went extremely well and quickly, all things considered, and by the end of the session, Jasmine was riding like a pro. Khalil waited with the instructor at the top of a large mound of red Texas clay, just beneath a huge sign that read FINISH. Jasmine was making her last pass. She jumped a hill and then came to a dusty halt, showering both Khalil and the instructor with dirt and gravel. Khalil smiled. The instructor, on the other hand, found nothing amusing about being sprayed with debris from the track. He huffed and walked away, leaving Khalil and Jasmine alone in her dusty cloud of glory.

"Did you enjoy yourself, Jazz?"

"Yes, I did. It was awesome!" she said excitedly. She sounded like a child coming off their first adrenaline-filled roller coaster ride.

Khalil's smile broadened. He loved watching Jasmine as she discovered new things. She had an almost childlike quality about her, and much like any other precocious kid, she took to new things she liked with an innocent ferociousness. She was an apt pupil, soaking in every tidbit of knowledge that Khalil had to offer. She had been created from strife and heartache and nurtured by pain.

Those days were long gone. They were working on new beginnings, and Khalil had committed himself to helping Jasmine learn to mask her pain and hone her emotions. He would teach her to use every ounce of grief in her body to her advantage.

Chapter 14

UNSTABLE VEXATION

Khalil and Jasmine sat in front of her building in his car, just talking. He put his hand on her knee and kissed her as if he'd never see her again. As they kissed, Jasmine let her hand glide to his crotch. Her breath caught in her throat. She had never consensually been with a man, but she knew enough to know that he was well-endowed. She continued to stroke it until it was fully erect.

"All right now, don't start anything that you can't or won't finish," Khalil said as he removed Jasmine's hand from his crotch.

"How do you know that I won't finish?"

"It's not time yet, Jasmine," he said.

"When will it be time? I'm ready, Khalil. I want you. I want to take this to the next level."

"Don't beg, Jasmine. It's not very becoming. When it's time, you'll know. We'll both know!" he barked.

The rejection caught her off guard, but more than anything, it bruised her tender ego. They'd been together for months, and although they seemed to be growing closer, Khalil still hadn't tried to bed her. She felt her blood boil, and her ears got hot. Her vision blurred, and she became agitated. She rubbed the palm of her hand against the fabric of her riding suit. Her green eyes met with his blue eyes, creating a cosmic shade of turquoise fury. And then she saw it: a slight smirk and a small hint of indignation. Was he laughing at her?

"You find something amusing about this shit? Am I funny to you?" she barked.

"Where did that come from?"

She ignored his question and continued her tirade. "You call me your wife, but you won't even make love to me! If I'm not getting it, somebody is getting it! Are you fucking that bitch Farrah? Or are you fucking that old rich bitch Madison from the boutique? Don't fucking play with me, Khalil!" she screamed.

"You need to go upstairs and calm down. I don't know what's wrong with you, but this is not okay."

The malevolence and rabid madness that had been in her eyes moments earlier now gave way to sadness and vexation. She pouted at first, but then her pouting gave way to uncontrollable and hysterical sobs. "I . . . I just love you, and I want to please you, and I don't want anyone else to have you. If you ever leave me or cheat on me, I don't know what I'll do. Yes, I do. I'd kill you! If I can't have you, then nobody can!" she cried. She sniffed and wiped her nose on the sleeve of her jacket. Jasmine smiled, flashing her perfectly straight teeth at Khalil. "You have the most beautiful eyes. Did you know that?" she cooed as if she hadn't just threatened to kill the man.

Khalil didn't know what to make of it. Within the span of two minutes, she'd gone through a full range of emotions. From their conversations, he'd learned that she was mentally unstable, but to see it firsthand was extraordinary.

Jasmine leaned over, kissed Khalil on his cheek, and gripped his penis. She smiled once again and purred softly, "This is mine, and I swear on my dead parents that I will kill you dead before I let you stick it in someone else." She exited the car, stepped onto the curb, and then stopped mid-stride. Jasmine turned back toward the car and tapped on the window with her flawlessly manicured fingernail, and Khalil lowered the glass.

"Yes, my love?" he asked.

"Do you still love me?"

"Of course I do," he said.

"You don't think I'm crazy, do you?"

"No, not in the least."

"Okay. Will you call me later?"

"Most definitely," he said.

"You promise?"

Khalil looked at Jasmine closely before answering. What he saw sent a cold chill down his spine, and he shivered. Jasmine leaned into the car, smiling her brightest smile, but her eyes weren't smiling. Her eyes were narrow slits of repudiation daring him to say no.

"Yes, baby, I promise," he said. He needed to distance himself from Jasmine, at least for the night. There was a quiet storm of murderous intent brewing inside of Jasmine Deitrich, and he knew it.

She blew Khalil a kiss and backed away from the car. Her eyes were still tapered incisions of green fire as she watched Khalil pull away from the curb and speed into the chilly Dallas night.

Chapter 15

FACE OFF

Monica jumped as Jasmine entered the house. It had been so long since she'd actually talked to her sister that she hadn't expected to see her at home. She was kneeling and pouring food into Noisy Boy's bowl when Jasmine walked in and slammed the door. As soon as she was inside, the interrogation began.

"Where have you been, Jasmine? I haven't seen you in weeks," Monica scolded.

"Man, I'm grown. Don't come for me unless I send for you."

"I just asked you a simple fucking question. Your professors have been calling saying that you haven't been to class in weeks. You're in danger of flunking out," Monica said.

"Okay, and?"

"And you need to answer my question. Where have you been? You been with your little boyfriend? Because he's certainly not a man if he'll let you jeopardize your education."

"Watch your fucking mouth, Monica. I'm warning you!" Jasmine shouted.

Noisy Boy instinctively barked. He'd never witnessed the sisters arguing. He circled the living room and came to rest between the two sisters. He whimpered softly and looked up at Jasmine with his ice blue puppy dog eyes.

"What are you going to do, Jasmine? What the fuck are you going to do if I keep talking about your precious Khalil?"

Jasmine's eyes flashed pure hatred. She'd never once considered hurting her sister, but looking at her now, she fantasized about shutting her up forever. She wondered how Monica would react if she slid a butcher's knife into the soft pit of her stomach. She pictured the satisfaction of hearing Monica scream, and she could only imagine the rush that it would bring to hear her sister apologize for disrespecting Khalil as she begged for her life.

As much as she hated Monica for blasphemy against Khalil's name, she would spare her sister. Jasmine threw her head back, and haughty laughter filled the room. She turned to walk away, and Monica grabbed her arm.

"Don't walk away from me when I'm talking to you, Jasmine!" Monica shouted.

Jasmine turned to face her sister with a calmness in her voice that startled the seasoned Monica. "If you don't take your hands off of me, I'm going to chop you up into micro-sized pieces and feed you to Noisy Boy," Jasmine whispered.

Monica released her arm and stared at her. She didn't know if Jasmine was serious, but she knew that her sister had problems. Khalil Cross had tainted her, and Monica wasn't sure whether she could get her back. "Jazzy Bell, what's wrong with you?"

"You don't get to call me that! Don't you ever call me that. You want to know what's wrong with me? I hate your fucking guts! You're no sister of mine. What I do with my life is my business. Now if you don't want me to smother you in your fucking sleep, then I would advise you to never touch me again!"

Monica knew then that Jasmine was too far gone to reach. She didn't like the fact that she and Khalil had gotten so close, but if he was the only person who could keep her sane and stable, then so be it.

As Jasmine walked toward her room, she was stopped in her tracks by the sound of Monica's voice. "Jasmine?"

"Yes, Monica?" she said without turning around.

"I have a meeting to go to, and I would appreciate it if you packed your shit and moved out before I get home."

"So you're abandoning me again? You're just going to put me out in the street?" Jasmine asked with her back still turned to Monica.

"For God's sake, you just talked about murdering me twice. I won't live in fear in my own house. I need you to leave."

Jasmine turned to face Monica, her lips curled into a menacing snarl, and then they just as quickly curled into a warm smile. "Yeah, Monica, no problem. I'll leave. You'll never have to worry about me again," she said, disappearing into her bedroom.

Monica watched Jasmine's door close. With her eyes still trained on the door, she kneeled and stroked Noisy Boy's snow-white coat. "I'll be back, baby. Keep an eye on things for me."

Noisy Boy raised his head and licked Monica's hand. He barked once, stood, walked to the door, and sat near it as if to tell Monica to handle her business and he would hold down the fort.

Jasmine had left Monica's in a huff. She hadn't taken many of her things because she didn't need them. She had more than enough money to buy a whole new wardrobe if she wanted it. Between the money she had left from her inheritance from Pop Pop and the money that Khalil had been funneling into her bank account, she was financially self-sufficient.

Her mind wasn't on those things, however. No, she was still angry at Monica for her blatant disrespect. After she'd left Jasmine inside the confines of the Buckner Youth Home for eleven-plus years, she'd had the audacity to treat her as if she owed her. In Jasmine's mind Monica only loved two things on God's green earth, and that was herself and Noisy Boy. Anyone outside of her immediate circle was expendable. Jasmine had no emotional connection to Monica, and if she felt that way, then it was only natural for Monica to feel the same way. Monica hadn't helped her with her hair, hadn't helped her fight off bullies or helped her pick out her dress for prom. Those things were nonexistent in Jasmine's world.

She shoved her hands into the pockets of her jacket to escape the late autumn chill. She closely watched the people who passed her. It was one of the many things Khalil had taught her. "You can never watch a man too closely, and if you look close enough, you can see his transgressions," Khalil had said during the course of one of their many conversations. People watching was her specialty.

She made eye contact with a man who seemed to be in deep thought. Shame washed across his face, and he dropped his head. More than likely, Jasmine surmised, he'd been arguing with his wife, probably about his infidelities, probably infidelities with a man. Men, when confronted by women, often found it hard to face other women. Men undoubtedly had their women-watching rituals, and the man never turned to look at her ass as she passed. That in itself told Jasmine that something was on his mind. She knew that there was something wrong with her way of thinking, but there was nothing to compare it to. She'd never really discussed her inner thoughts with anyone except Khalil, and he seemed to embrace every facet of her being.

She stopped walking and stood at the bus stop, contemplating her next move. Someone would have to pay for Monica's transgressions. Jasmine smiled to herself. She knew just how to make herself feel better. She dialed a number on her cell phone and waited.

"Are you home? Okay, good. Do you mind if I stop by? We need to talk," she said.

The bus squeaked and hissed to a halt, and the doors slid open. There was only one person ahead of her to board the bus, but he was taking an eternity. The elderly man climbed the steps of the bus slowly and one at a time. When he finally made it to the driver, he took forever to pay. Most elderly people who chose to ride the bus kept senior citizen bus passes, but not this man. He clumsily counted his fare out in pennies one by one. One, clink, clink. Two, clink, clink. Three, clink, clink. It went on like that until the bus driver, from sheer frustration, let the old man board the bus after inserting only forty-four cents.

Jasmine put the hood of her Multiple Hustles Couture jacket over her head and boarded the bus. She kept her head held low, staring at the floor to avoid the bus driver's gaze. Jasmine presented her day pass, shuffled to the back of the bus, and took a seat in the corner. She'd intentionally bought the pass so that after her deed was done, she could use the bus for a quick and inconspicuous getaway. She sat in the corner and closed her eyes, trying desperately to avoid the hodgepodge of passengers on the number sixty bus, bound for White Rock Lake. She would start to doze off only to be awakened by the familiar ding and then the sound of the compressed air from the brakes of the bus. At each stop, ding, whoosh, ding, whoosh until she finally saw the crystalline waters of White Rock Lake.

The reflection of the lights from the nearby houses and apartment buildings bounced carefree from wave to wave as Jasmine exited the bus. She stepped out into the cool brisk wind and shivered. It hadn't been that cold when she left North Dallas. *It must be the water.* Jasmine buried her hands deep in her pockets and tucked her head into her shoulders to avoid the aggressive nip. It was still a nice hike around the lake before she arrived at her destination. She adjusted the backpack on her back and continued the arduous trek.

Jasmine reached Winsted at White Rock and punched the security code into the keypad. The gate buzzed and clicked, and Jasmine ducked inside, careful not to be seen. She crossed the courtyard and ascended the stairs of building D two at a time until she reached the third floor. She knocked on the door of apartment D-357 timidly and waited. She could hear soft music playing through the door.

Farrah answered the door dressed only in red boy shorts and a Wonder Woman wife beater. She had a glass of red wine in one hand and a blunt in the other. "Hey, Jazz, what's going on? You said you needed to talk to me when we were on the phone, so what's up?" Farrah asked.

"Hi, Farrah, can I come in? It's cold out here."

Farrah didn't say a word. She took a toke from her blunt and blew out white ringlets of smoke. She stepped behind the door, giving Jasmine a clear path into her apartment. "What brings you out at this hour, baby girl?"

"Khalil and I got into a big-ass fight, and I just need someone to talk to," Jasmine said sadly. There was something in Farrah's eyes and tone of voice that angered Jasmine. There was a slight chuckle of merriment that belied her concern. Maybe Farrah was happy that Jasmine and Khalil were on the outs, or so she thought. There was a glimmer of imaginative hope in her eyes that

Khalil had somehow managed to wiggle out of Jasmine Deitrich's clutches.

"Come have a seat, girl, and tell me all about it," Farrah offered.

"Well, remember when we were in front of the school and you offered to have a threesome with us?"

"Yeah," Farrah said curiously.

"Khalil took you seriously, and now he wants to do it. I told him that I wasn't comfortable doing that because I'd never been with another woman, and he got mad. He gave me an ultimatum: either do it and enjoy it, or find another man," Jasmine said. She'd caught Farrah staring at her on more than one occasion, so she knew that she'd love to bury her head between her legs.

Farrah licked her lips lasciviously. Her one-dimensional mind registered only what she chose to hear. She couldn't believe her ears. Not only would she have a chance with Jasmine, but she would also have the opportunity to display her sexual prowess to Khalil. With a little luck and her miraculous lips, she would push Jasmine out of the picture altogether.

"I can't afford to lose him, Farrah. I love him too much," Jasmine said.

Farrah took Jasmine's hand and led her to her bedroom. She had the typical girl's room, a mixture of soft pinks, lavenders, and bold lime greens.

Jasmine took the backpack from her back and placed it upright on the nightstand next to the bed. She began to undress slowly until she was completely naked. She folded her clothes meticulously and placed them on the dresser on the opposite side of the room. Farrah eyeballed Jasmine salaciously, all the while rubbing her clitoris through her boy shorts. Jasmine scurried to the bed, jumped into it, and pulled the comforter up to her chin.

Farrah smiled mischievously. She loved the shy ones, the ones who weren't quite sure of their sexuality or were just downright curious. They were the easiest to turn out because she knew how to cater to their bodies. After all, who would know the right spots to touch and tease on a woman's body better than another woman?

Farrah peeled out of her red boy shorts and turned them inside out to let Jasmine see how soaked she was from anticipation. She unsnapped her bra, and her voluptuous breasts sprang free. Her pubic hair was cropped low and trimmed into the shape of a heart with a small tattoo above it that read, "Eat me." Farrah buried her fingers deep inside of her heated love box, and when she withdrew them, her fingers glistened from her own excitement. She licked her fingers one by one in an effort to tease Jasmine, who had her eyes trained on Farrah, watching her every move.

Farrah walked to the edge of the bed and snatched the blanket from Jasmine's body. Her erect eraser-sized chocolate nipples contrasted perfectly against her milky caramel-colored skin. Jasmine's nether regions were bald except for a one-inch-wide cropped strip of hair. A thin, fine trail of barely visible baby hair ran from her navel to her landing strip, and Farrah could barely contain herself.

Jasmine smiled as she noticed the anxiousness in Farrah's eyes. Jasmine opened her legs slightly, exposing the pink inside of her fleshy tightness. Farrah moved strangely, rubbing her knees together as if she would urinate on herself at any second. Jasmine looked at Farrah's thighs and saw the evidence of her orgasm. A clear bead of liquid had begun its sexual descent down Farrah's thigh, and Jasmine could no longer take it. She burst into a fit of laughter, breaking the awkward silence that plagued the intense encounter.

"What's so funny?"

"You look like you're doing the pee-pee dance," Jasmine teased.

"My pussy gets so wet it's unbelievable."

Farrah climbed onto the bed and positioned herself above Jasmine's body. Farrah tried to kiss her, but Jasmine moved her head, leaving only an exposed cheek to meet Farrah's wanton lips. She accepted the rejection and willfully moved on, leaving a trail of wet kisses in her wake as she made her way to Jasmine's snack pouch. Farrah gently massaged Jasmine's nipple with her right hand, tweaking it between her thumb and index finger. With her left hand, she inserted her index finger, and Jasmine moaned. She tried to insert two fingers, but another finger wouldn't fit. She continued to finger fuck Jasmine with her index finger until she felt her juices begin to flow freely.

Jasmine kept her eyes closed and was surprised that she was actually enjoying her lesbian encounter. She moaned and gyrated her hips in rhythm with Farrah's finger until sheer passion overtook her, and she erupted. A semi-clear liquid squirted onto Farrah's hand, and Jasmine whimpered softly from her euphoric orgasm. Farrah looked up and locked eyes with Jasmine, who had a dreamy, faraway look in her eyes.

"If you thought that was something, watch this!" Farrah said.

With her finger still inside Jasmine, she used the other hand to grip the girl's butt and squeezed softly. She licked Jasmine's throbbing clitoris and then sucked it gently in a circular motion. Jasmine looked down at Farrah. She had her eyes closed, completely lost in her task.

Jasmine carefully reached for the backpack and removed an eight-inch butcher's knife. Farrah began to suck Jasmine's clit ferociously, and Jasmine bucked and thrashed against Farrah's little pink sliver of heaven. Jasmine felt an insane rush of adrenaline surge through her body, and she felt the pressure mounting in her temples. She felt a wave of euphoric nirvana wash over her body, and at the precise moment that Jasmine's body released its orgasmic fluids, Jasmine raised her knife and buried it deep into the nape of Farrah's neck. She never uttered a sound, and with every ripple of orgasmic bliss, Jasmine let her knife fall deeper into her victim's neck. She grabbed Farrah by her freshly coiffed hair, pulled her head up, and placed her knife just above Farrah's clavicle. With one swift sweep of her blade, she severed Farrah's head from her body. She raised Farrah's head and looked at it with an amused look on her face.

"Now that's what you call a deadly piece of pussy!" Jasmine said.

Farrah seemed to be staring at Jasmine in confused horror. She was wide-eyed, and her tongue still jutted from her mouth, frozen in a permanent licking pose from beyond the darkness. Jasmine took Farrah's lifeless head, with its jagged neck meat, cartilage, and gore, and rubbed the tongue vigorously against her snatch. "You like that, huh, bitch?" she teased.

Jasmine tossed the head to the side, reached inside her backpack, and removed a fillet knife and a razor blade. She took the knife and Farrah's head and sat on the floor naked at the edge of the bed. Jasmine took the razor blade and started an outline at Farrah's forehead and cut down to the bone. She cut along the hairline, down around the jawline, underneath the chin, up to the fleshy part of skin between the ear and the temple until she'd finally made an incision around the entire circumference of Farrah's face.

"You know, Farrah, you're a goofy-looking bitch, now that I see your whole face," Jasmine said.

She took the head between her hands and popped the eyeballs from their sockets. They dangled from the openings, connected only by nerves and muscular tissue. Jasmine snipped both eyes from their restraints and tossed them to the side. "See what happens when you look at someone else's man? No-eye-having-ass bitch," she mused.

She held the head up once more, examining her incisions. When she found the opening that she was searching for, she slid the fillet knife in. With the skill of an expert fishmonger, Jasmine separated Farrah's face from her skull. She dropped the head and held Farrah's facial skin up against the light. She stared at it curiously, satisfied with her findings. She folded the facial skin neatly and put it at the bottom of the backpack. She then placed Farrah's severed head in the bookbag on top of her detached face. Jasmine stood and placed her hands on her hips and looked around, admiring her handiwork. She caught a glimpse of her naked, bloody body in the mirror that was attached to Farrah's dresser, and she smiled. It was not a smile of happiness, not even a smile of satisfaction, but more a smile of diabolical fulfillment.

Jasmine started walking toward the entrance to the bedroom and stopped suddenly. She whirled around in Farrah's direction. She still lay in a prone position on her stomach. Her once-school-girl-like smile was now replaced with a maniacal grimace. Jasmine ran toward the bed, scooping the butcher's knife up off the floor on her way. She turned Farrah's body over onto its back and jammed the knife deep into her chest, sawing and cutting in a downward motion until her innards were exposed down to her pelvis. She dropped the knife and began to root around in Farrah's insides with her hands. She pushed past the blood and organs, down past her intestines in search of her prize, but she never found it.

Jasmine stood up with blood dripping from her elbows to her fingertips. "They lied! They always said that the evil was inside, and they said that it could be taken out! Look what you made me do!" she screamed.

Jasmine walked to the shower in a daze. She left a trail of small blood drops along the carpet from the bedroom to the bathroom. She started the shower and stepped into the hot water. "You have to scrub the sins away, sins away, sins away, you have to scrub the sins away to make it into heaven," she sang in a preschool-style pitch as she washed Farrah's blood from her body.

When she was a child growing up in the Buckner Home, an abusive counselor named Mrs. Digsby would often sing the song while torturing the young girls. The smallest infraction was punishable by being made to stand in scalding hot water as Mrs. Digsby scrubbed the girls with a long-handled toilet brush while chanting the torturous ditty. She was eventually fired and brought up on charges by the State, but not before leaving a trail of broken and mentally abused young girls in her aftermath.

Jasmine stepped out of the shower and looked around as if confused by her surroundings. She entered the room and shrieked after the sight of what she'd done fully registered in her brain. She dressed quickly, not wanting to be in the room with the corpse any longer than she had to be. Jasmine tiptoed around the blood, careful not to get any on her Nike track shoes. She grabbed the backpack and headed toward the front door. Before leaving, she cracked the door to make sure that no one was in the breezeway. Once she was satisfied, she locked the bottom lock, pulled the door closed, and walked out into the still of a peculiarly cold and quiet night.

Chapter 16

LOVE IS LOVE

Jasmine exited the number sixty bus downtown and dialed Khalil's number, but it rang twice and went to voicemail. She tried again, and this time, Khalil picked up.

"Hello?"

"Hey, handsome, are you busy?" she asked.

"I'm never too busy for you. What's up?"

"I need a huge favor, my love."

"Anything, just name it," he said.

"Can I come and stay with you? Monica freaking put me out, babe!"

"What? Why? Where are you now?" he asked, concern clearly showing in his voice.

"She was being a bitch about how much time you and I spend together, and I checked her, so she told me to get my shit and get out," Jasmine said flatly.

"Wow, that's crazy! And yes, you can come and stay with me. Where are you?"

"I'm on the corner of Main and Ervay in front of Neiman Marcus," she said.

"Okay, baby, I'm not far away. I'll be there in less than ten minutes."

As soon as Jasmine hung up the phone with Khalil, Monica called, but Jasmine didn't answer. She was probably calling to apologize, but Jasmine wasn't trying to hear it. She was over Monica's attempt to play the protective big sister role, a role that Jasmine never asked her to play and one that she wasn't very good at anyway.

Within the short time period that it took Khalil to reach her, Monica had called seven times. Jasmine looked at her phone and switched it off. She didn't need another lecture. She didn't need any apologies, and she most certainly didn't need another interrogation about her love for Khalil. She was only interested in people being a part of her life who wanted to be there, and from the looks of it, Khalil was the only person she could count on.

Khalil pulled up and blew his horn. It pulled Jasmine from her reverie, but as she climbed into the car, she welcomed the coziness that the heater provided.

"So how do you feel, baby?" Khalil asked.

"Honestly, I'm over it. I mean, I've given her chance after chance, and Monica knows no boundaries. She operates with impunity and with no filter, and I'm sick of it."

"You want me to kill her?" Khalil asked seriously.

For a second, Jasmine just stared at him. It was hard to tell if he was serious, because his features masked his true thoughts. His face was stoic and unfeeling as he glared straight ahead, paying careful attention to the traffic. It was very late, and the streets of downtown Dallas were bare save a few club goers leaving various clubs. Khalil knew all too well the possibility of some drunken partier running a red light and ending both his and Jasmine's lives. There had been too many news reports of that exact thing happening in the city streets.

"Not yet," Jasmine whispered.

Khalil nodded. He understood her mindset. Sometimes the people closest to you were your worst enemies. Monica's time would come, and if he had anything to do with it, she would die by his hand and his hand alone.

They pulled into the parking garage of Billionaire's Row and parked. Jasmine loved the parking garage almost as much as she loved the condo. Where most parking garages were damp underground caverns with dim lighting and molding concrete walls, the garage at the Row, as she called it, was well-lit and homey. The walls were made of weathered stone, and the floors were slabs of marble with a pearl inlay. Everything about the building was next-level beautiful. Even the directory that hung from the walls was made from polished brass.

They entered the elevator and rode to Khalil's penthouse condo in silence, maybe because there wasn't much to talk about or maybe because Khalil silently wondered what could possibly be in the backpack that Jasmine clutched close to her chest. She had been through enough with her sister, and the last thing he wanted to do was to pry into her personal business. If she felt pressured, it could very well be the catalyst to push the young, fragile girl over the deep end.

The inside of Khalil's penthouse was toasty, to say the least. The fireplace burned bright flames of orange and dirty yellows, and the firewood crackled and hissed as the heat from its embers filled the opulent space. Jasmine placed the knapsack on the side of the couch and walked toward the bedroom. She still had clothes at Khalil's house from when he'd taken her shopping, and she wanted to change into something more comfortable.

When she emerged from the bedroom minutes later, Khalil had two king-sized down comforters stacked on top of one another in front of the fireplace, and pillows from the couch lined the blankets. Khalil had stripped down to his boxers and was pouring them both a glass of cognac when Jasmine entered the room. She felt overdressed in her flowered boy shorts and matching top but decided against going to change.

"What's all of this, babe?" she asked.

"I want to talk to you, get to know you. The *real* you."

Jasmine joined Khalil on the comforter and took a sip from her glass of cognac. The potent brown liquor burned her throat as it made its way down to her stomach. Between the heat from the fireplace and the heat that rushed through her veins, Jasmine felt like she was lying on a remote beach with the sun beaming on her skin. Khalil looked at her as if she were the only woman on earth. Never in a million years would he have guessed that he'd have fallen for Jasmine the way that he did. The glow from the fireplace cast an angelic aura over Jasmine, and Khalil smiled. She was his baby, his pupil, and someday she would be his wife and mother of his children. His past was his past, but if they were going to be together forever, he would need to tell her his deepest, darkest secrets.

"Jasmine, life as we know it is about to change, and I want you to know how much I love you before we go any further," Khalil said.

"I love you too, Khalil, more than you'll ever know."

"When I was growing up, I was miserable. My father had all the money in the world in my young mind, but I never wanted his money. I only wanted him to be my father, and he never had time for me. It's a fucked-up feeling to grow up and realize that no one loves you. I was invisible to my father, and my mother was too busy with her own habits and vices to see my misery," he said.

"Awww, that's so sad, baby. How could anyone not love you?" she asked.

"I'm sure that I must've had my issues. Maybe I cried too much or was a bad child. There had to be something about me to make my mom not want me, you know? Mothers don't really abandon their children unless that child has done something to run them away," he said reflectively.

"Is that what you think? You think it's your fault because your mom didn't love you? Nooooo, baby, no, it's not your fault. Some people just aren't meant to be parents," Jasmine said as she moved closer to Khalil. She took his face into her hands and kissed him softly and passionately. "I'm never going anywhere, babe. The fact that they didn't love you is just more motivation for me to love you the way you deserve to be loved."

"I just need you to know that life isn't always what it seems and people lie. I never want to be that person. I always want to be honest and up front with you," Khalil said.

"The more honest and open you are with me, the more in love I fall with you. You're so big and so strong, but you're so vulnerable, and I love that about you."

"There are some things about me that I really need to tell you, Jasmine. I really want to—" Khalil started.

But before he could finish his sentence, Jasmine had her hand in his boxer shorts. She stroked his manhood slowly until he was fully erect. "I don't care about anything right now except you, me, us at this very moment. I will never forsake you or leave you for anybody else, Khalil. You have my heart and everything in me," she said.

Jasmine lowered her head into Khalil's lap and took the head of his penis into her mouth. She'd listened to Farrah and the other girls at school preach that it was virtually impossible to keep a man if you didn't give him blowjobs from time to time. She didn't have a clue as to what she was doing, but she sucked it and licked it to some invisible medley playing in her head. She found her rhythm and made love to Khalil's phallus with her mouth.

Khalil himself was lost in some not-so-distant dream. He'd never known a woman quite like Jasmine. She was so eager to please, catering to Khalil, almost spoiling him at times. She was completely different from any woman he'd ever known. When she looked at him, she looked at him as if he were God manifested in the flesh. Her eyes burned through him, looking deep into his soul, pulling from him the very thing that he'd sworn off since his last love. Jasmine had been a game to him at first, a simple pawn in a game that was bigger than both of them. It hadn't worked out that way though. He'd fallen for Jasmine hard, and now she consumed him. He showed her love, of course, but he never let on that she was his everything. He couldn't. After all, they were bound in ways that he feared Jasmine could never understand.

He leaned on his elbows and threw his head back. He knew that she wasn't experienced in the sexual arts, but she was trying in earnest to give him pleasure, and he loved it. There was something about worldly women that turned Khalil off. Jasmine, however, was a beginner at best. Every few minutes she would look up at him as if to ask him if he was being pleasured correctly. She stroked his shaft and plopped his dick from her mouth.

"You like it? Am I doing it right, baby?" she asked shyly.

"Uh-huh, you're doing fantastic," Khalil huffed.

She lowered her head onto his meat again and took it into her mouth. It was beautiful, and Jasmine loved it. She imagined her and Khalil making a porno movie. The ones that she'd watched always had raunchy females in them who made far too much noise for her particular tastes. She preferred to be quiet and listen to Khalil's moans of pleasure. The more he got into it, the more she found herself making low and muffled moans of delight that for whatever reason seemed to make Khalil's dick throb. She could feel it throbbing against her lips. It turned her on, and she felt her pussy moisten.

Khalil reached around and grabbed her by her leg and guided her body to the sixty-nine position. He licked her clit softly and then stuck his whole tongue deep inside of her. Jasmine squealed in delight as Khalil wiggled his tongue inside of her. She tried to concentrate on her task, but she couldn't. She arched her back and began bucking, wilding, riding Khalil's tongue as if it were a penis. She completely lost her mind when he spread her butt cheeks and inserted his tongue inside of her anus. He withdrew it and flicked his tongue across her asshole, only to blow where he'd just licked. She shivered and giggled from the chilly sensation. He took her clitoris into his mouth and sucked firmly. Khalil flicked his tongue back and forth rapidly until Jasmine trembled and sprayed her hot, wet stickiness onto his chin.

He pushed her forward and scooted from beneath her. Khalil put the palm of his hand on the center of her back and pushed her chest to the soft covers. He entered her from the back, careful to only go as far as she could handle. He worked the head in slowly, taking small, steady strokes until he felt Jasmine's body relax. Little by little, inch by inch, he wiggled himself into her until his entire manhood was buried deep inside of her. She was so tight. Khalil couldn't believe how tight and wet she was. He spread her butt cheeks apart and gyrated his hips, giving her the full advantage of his manhood.

Jasmine clawed and scratched at the comforter. She bit into it, looking for a reprieve from Khalil's sexual admonishment. He hammered and stroked, gyrated and poked, arching his back and digging into her. Khalil put the flat part of his thumb against Jasmine's asshole and applied pressure. He never allowed his thumb to penetrate her, but he kept the pressure on it and made firm circular motions while he pumped into her for dear life. He could feel her muscles contracting as she reached yet another orgasm.

Khalil flipped her over to her back and looked deep into her eyes. The flames from the fireplace danced beautifully across her skin and set up shop in her jade green eyes. It only seemed to enhance an already-intense pair of eyes. A strange look had washed across her face. It was a look lost somewhere between pain and ecstasy. She wanted to cry, and she wanted to tell the world how this man had taken her from a girl to a full-fledged woman in less than an hour.

Tears began flowing freely from her eyes as he entered her. He put her feet against his chest and pushed himself deep inside of her. She felt like hot, wet silk on the inside, and Khalil never wanted it to end. He stroked gently but deeply. He wanted to feel every inch of her. If he had any doubts as to the extent of his love for Jasmine Deitrich, there was no doubt now. He would die before he let her go.

Jasmine stared back at Khalil from beneath him. She gripped his buttocks and encouraged him to pump harder, to go deeper. She pulled him close to her and kissed him. She let her tongue explore the confines of his mouth. Their tongues collided and twirled about each other, and the deeper they kissed, the more sensual the grind became until their bodies felt entwined with no sign of separation. She tried to keep Khalil's rhythm as he thrust in and out of her insatiably. She wanted to scream from the mountaintops to let the world know the wonders of this sexual wunderkind. She felt the familiar building of a monstrous climax and tried to brace herself, tried to hold it in, but her attempts were futile. She shuddered and shook. Her eyes rolled to the back of her head, and then it happened—the ultimate surge, an eruption of magnanimous proportions. She felt the rush of her fluids as she soaked Khalil's pelvis and the comforter beneath them.

"I can't hold it, baby!" she screamed.

"Me neither, baby, I'm cumming!" Khalil screamed.

They both came together, their juices mixing
and flowing between both of them. Khalil collapsed
on top of Jasmine, sweaty and out of breath. They
breathed in unison, Jasmine's inhale catching
Khalil's exhale. Khalil rolled off Jasmine and lay
on his back with his hands folded beneath his head.

"That was incredible, Jasmine," he said.

"Baby, that was more than incredible. It was in-
describable, like I don't have words for it," she said.
She propped herself up on her elbows and stared
at Khalil. He seemed to be far away as he gazed
into the darkness above him. He was extremely
quiet, and it worried Jasmine. She hadn't meant to
pressure him into making love to her, but she had
wanted it. "What are you thinking about, babe?"
Jasmine asked.

"Man, for the first time in my life I'm happy, you
know? I can see myself with you forever, baby girl.
I can see us walking through the park pushing
a stroller with our baby in it. It's crazy because
I've never considered even bringing a kid into
the world, but you make me want to invest in our
future, be a better man for you, and raise a family."

"Do you think that's possible for us? I mean, do
you think we would make good parents?" Jasmine
asked. She was completely lost in Khalil's conversation. She could smell the sincerity pouring

through his veins. She had never had a man talk to her that way, sharing his hopes and his dreams and, most importantly, including her in his future. In the past, she'd never understood how people could be so deeply in love that nothing else mattered. She understood now though. There was nothing on God's green earth that could keep her from Khalil, and in her eyes, he could do no wrong. For a split second she imagined her life without Khalil, and her heart sank. "It's just us, baby, remember? Until death do us part," Jasmine said.

"Even after I'm dead and gone, baby, I'll still love you. Heaven can't handle me, and hell can't hold me. Would you love me even if I weren't who you thought I was?" Khalil asked.

"Khalil, there is nothing that you could do, and I mean *nothing,* that could make me stop loving you. Like you said, baby, heaven can't handle me, and hell can't hold me."

Jasmine looked at Khalil, who'd quietly drifted off to sleep. His breathing was soft but labored, and the deeper he seemed to drift, the more his dick shrank. Jasmine chuckled silently. She'd put Khalil to sleep. She remembered Farrah saying on more than one occasion that if you didn't put them to sleep, then your pussy probably wasn't any good. As Jasmine looked at him, her mind drifted back to Farrah. Of course it had been Jasmine who'd told the lie in the first place, but silently she wondered if Khalil had indeed entertained Farrah's suggestion. She thought about how easy it would be to chop his dick off at this second and watch him bleed to death as he tried to figure out what had gone wrong. No man would ever toy with her. She had promised herself that while sitting in the courtyard during her freshman year of college. She watched the boys conquer and then discuss their conquests. For all she knew, Khalil Cross could be shooting her a line of malarkey and she'd fallen for it hook, line, and sinker. She reached out and touched his penis and then touched his face. He stirred slightly, but he didn't wake up.

Jasmine reached for the backpack and removed the knives and the razor. Then she removed Farrah's severed head and placed it on the marble hearth of the fireplace. She placed the knives next to the head and giggled. She removed the facial skin from the knapsack, stood, and unfolded it carefully. Jasmine looked for some way to hang it above the fireplace. On each end of the mantle were brass candleholders that were shaped like intertwined snakes with wings. She put a candleholder on two corners of Farrah's face and let it hang. It looked like a spooky Christmas stocking, except there would be no goodies in this stocking. Jasmine took the candles from the holders and lit them. She replaced the candles and then sat and waited.

Khalil wasn't sure how long he'd dozed off, but the smell of burning hair roused him from slumber. With his eyes still closed, he raised his nose to the air and sniffed. He wasn't dreaming. There was really something burning. He sprang up on his elbows and looked around. He saw Jasmine sitting in the glow of the fireplace, staring at him, watching him as he'd slept. The flame from the fireplace glimmered off something in the corner of his eye. He turned to look toward the fireplace, and he was petrified.

The flame had flickered from the blades resting on the base of the fireplace. Next to them was a severed head. The embers from the fire had popped and crackled and eventually come to settle in Farrah's hair. That had been the smell that had awakened him. He was at a loss for words. Why had she killed Farrah? He'd foolishly believed that they were friends, but evidently he'd been wrong. He couldn't speak. His mouth was frozen in question mode. He followed Jasmine's eyes to the mantle above the fireplace and froze. His eyes darted rapidly between the face and the skull. When she looked into his eyes, Jasmine saw her man buckle and show a weakness, but what she didn't know was that Khalil was an expert at masking his truest thoughts. No, it wasn't a look of weakness, but rather a look of pride and understanding.

Jasmine threw her head back, and her shrill but raucous and sinister laughter filled the room as Khalil smiled. "Heaven can't handle *us,* and hell can't hold *us,* and neither one of them want *us,* baby," he said, as he threw his head back and joined the love of his life in celebration.

Their rhythmic laughter echoed from wall to wall, and the flames frolicked to the sound of their voices, moving seductively in a ritualistic dance of sadistic sacrifice.

Chapter 17

BODY COUNT

Special Agent in Charge Monica Deitrich sat at a round table in a conference room of the J. Edgar Hoover Federal Building in downtown Dallas. "How many bodies so far, Agent Roth?" she asked.

"So far we've counted a total of sixteen bodies, ma'am."

"And of that sixteen, how many do you believe to be linked to the assassination of Agent Krutcher, also known as Drak?" she asked.

"So far we've counted zero, ma'am. We've yet to tie any of the victims to this case."

Agent Cody Roth stood and walked to the back of the room. He dimmed the lights and then started the projector at the front of the room. "Ma'am, the common thread among all of these people is that each of them has been in the news at one point or another. They have all had run-ins with the local police also, but Agent Krutcher was undercover, so his profile doesn't fit. As for Bridgette and Kimberly Bircher, ma'am, I can't seem to place them either."

"Okay, but you said local. So why are we here if Drak isn't a factor? He was a Fed. These other people were not," Monica said, confused.

"When I speak of local, I mean local in their respective locales. These bodies are spread across the continental United States with no clear pattern of operation. He could hit in Las Vegas, Nevada, next, or he could hit in Tupelo, Mississippi," Agent Roth said.

"So you don't really know if Drak and the Bircher women are tied to this?"

"All of my instincts say no, ma'am. The pieces just don't fit, Agent Deitrich," he said.

"We're not investigating your instincts, Agent Roth. We're investigating links and facts. So until you're one hundred percent sure, I need you to investigate all of these cases with vigor. I want the Krutcher and Bircher cases to receive the same attention that the other cases get, do you understand?" Monica asked.

Monica put her short, manicured blood red nails against the mahogany table and began to drum a rhythmic tap. *Sixteen bodies*. Was she dealing with a serial killer? Serial killers always had a method, a pattern in which they operated. She knew that. These were just bodies though. Nothing jumped out at her from what Agent Roth had shared with her. Some random maniac killing newsworthy victims was too farfetched to run with, but it was all they had. She studied the images on the screen as Agent Roth clicked through them one by one, explaining who they were and what they'd done.

"Do you have these images in a file?" she asked.

"Not yet, ma'am, but I can have a detailed case file on your desk by the a.m."

"Make it by the end of the day, Agent. This is a time-sensitive matter, and I have a feeling that until we find this killer, the bodies are going to keep piling up. I mean, just looking at these photos is exhausting. I agree with you that there is no clear path of murder here, but if—and that's a big if—if we're indeed dealing with a serial killer, then this person is a redemption killer," Monica said reflectively.

"Excuse me, ma'am, a redemption killer?"

"Yes, a redemption killer. He—or she, for that matter—feels they have an obligation to right some type of wrong. It's like they are pronouncing themselves the judge *and* jury over their victims. By killing them, he's cleansing them, so to speak. I mean, look," Monica said, walking to the screen. "Look at some of the crimes that these people committed. Pedophilia, drug dealing, et cetera, et cetera. This is our focus, people. We need to canvass the streets and get a feel for the people who were murdered."

"Excuse me, ma'am," Agent Roth said.

"Yes, Agent?"

"If we're canvasing the streets worrying about these victims, then how are we going to include Agent Krutcher and the Bircher women into our investigation?" he asked.

"Agent Cody Roth, you passed the agency with flying colors. I'm sure you're imaginative enough to get it done. Now I need that file. You're all dismissed," Monica said.

She took her seat and stared at the screen. She tried to lose herself in the victims, in their sorrow, hoping that one of them would speak to her from beyond the grave. Sixteen victims, and she didn't have one lead. It was frustrating, to say the least, but then again, that was why she'd transferred in the first place. She was a damn good profiler, and she knew it. It was only a matter of time before she put together a profile that would blow the case off its hinges.

She folded her hands and placed them underneath her chin. Nothing about the case stood out to her, but then again, Monica wasn't normal. Her epiphanies about cases generally came at odd hours of the night, waking her from a sound slumber at times. She loved being in the trenches, pistol drawn, going after the bad guys, and truth be told, she was bored but intrigued.

Her mind shifted to Jasmine. She'd tried to
call her multiple times, and she hadn't answered.
Monica eyed her phone. She wanted to call her but
decided against it. She would give Jasmine all the
time she needed, but it was hard.

She remembered how distraught she'd been
after the police had found Jasmine. For whatever
reason, Jasmine thought that Monica had abandoned her, but that couldn't have been further
from the truth. She'd cried almost every day, pining
for her sister, literally begging their grandfather
to bring her home. She would never be able to
make Jasmine understand the level of guilt she felt.
Tears streamed from Monica's eyes involuntarily,
and before she knew that she was crying, Muldoon
burst into the room and turned on the lights.

"Agent Deitrich, I'm glad you're still here. I have
some very important information to share with
you," he said.

Monica turned her back to Muldoon and wiped
the tears from her eyes quickly.

"Are you okay, Monica?" he asked.

"I'm fine, sir. What's this information that you
want to share with me?"

Agent Muldoon spread five eight-by-eleven photos out on the table in front of Monica. The first
photo had obviously been captured from a surveillance camera. It was a picture of a black Buick
Grand National with black tint parked inconspic-

uously near the intersection where Bridgette and
Kimberly Bircher had been murdered. The next
three photos were of the same car and the same
intersection, except these three photos were time-
lapse. Her eyes scanned the pictures hurriedly,
trying desperately to make a connection between
them, and then she saw it.

There was nothing in picture one, but in pictures
two and three, a bright orange halo came from
where the brake light in the rear window should
have been. The halo was a muzzle flash, probably
from a high-powered rifle, but it was definitely
a muzzle flash. The next picture was a mugshot,
that of a young black man with dreadlocks and
a mouthful of gold teeth. Oddly enough, he was
smiling in a photo that was normally reserved
for a far more solemn look. In the last photo, the
same young man was standing next to the Grand
National in profile. In his left hand he held a huge
chain, and on the end of that chain was an even
bigger Rottweiler. In his right hand he held an M14
sniper rifle. The rifle was generally used by the
US Marine Corps, so to see a common street thug
with a high-powered weapon of that caliber was
somewhat unsettling for Monica.

"Is this the piece of shit who killed Bird's wife
and sister? Where is he? I want to talk to him.
What's his name?" Monica shouted.

"His name was Jabari Coleman, and it's too late, Agent Deitrich. He's dead. We had him in custody, but he's dead."

"What? But how, sir?" she asked.

"Believe it or not, one of our fellow agents from the DEA did it. He says that Jabari was trying to escape, so he shot him, but it doesn't add up. The agent had a sudden surge in disposable income, so that lets us know that he was bought and paid for."

"What kind of surge, sir?"

"That's not important. What's important is the information that we gained from interrogating Mr. Coleman. We know that it was his car that was used in Bridgette's and Kimberly Bircher's deaths. This is also the murder weapon that was used," he said, pointing to the rifle in Jabari's hand. "But Mr. Coleman had an airtight alibi. He was in Minneapolis at his sister's wedding during the time of the killings. Mr. Coleman said that a white man in his twenties approached him and asked him if he wanted to sell his car. When he refused, the man offered him enough money to buy any car that he wanted. In addition to the car, the man also wanted a rifle. Mr. Coleman agreed, and the unsub gave him fifty thousand in hundred-dollar bills," Muldoon said.

"Forgive me if I sound naive, sir, but why would some random white guy want to harm Bridgette and Kim? The only viable explanation is that Bird is still in the life, and we both know that's bullshit, excuse my language."

"I don't know that, and neither do you, but what I do know is that whoever wanted the Bircher women dead is also responsible for Agent Krutcher's murder!" Muldoon said.

There was too much information coming at Monica. She tried to process the statement that her mentor had just made. "Wait, what? How can these murders be connected?"

"We canvassed the neighborhood where Agent Krutcher was doing his undercover work. A few witnesses came forward and said that they last saw Drak talking with a white man outside of a black Buick. At the time it didn't really make sense until we came across the Jabari Coleman thing. There are too many similar factors to be mere coincidence, Monica," Muldoon said.

Monica stood and paced the room in deep thought. Too many factors indeed. There was no connection between Drak and Bird, only her. Monica didn't like coincidences, and she most certainly didn't like not being in control. The whole scenario didn't make sense. Had Bird and Drak been murdered, then it would've made sense. Any number of people within King Kochese's organization could've done it in retaliation. The Bircher women, however, that was a conundrum that had Monica at a loss.

A light rap at the door pulled Monica from her thoughts. "Come in," she said, still pacing.

Agent Cody Roth entered the room sheepishly and presented Monica with a sealed manila envelope. "Everything that we've compiled so far is in that envelope, ma'am. Excuse my language, but I hope we catch this bastard soon. The things that he's done to these people are ghastly, to say the least," he said.

"You know what that means, Agent Roth?" Monica asked.

"What's that, ma'am?"

"It means get your head out of your ass and do your fucking job!" Monica spat.

Agent Roth nodded his understanding and dropped his head, and he exited the conference room.

Chapter 18

YOU SANK MY BATTLESHIP

John La Rue was feeling the familiar giddiness that he always felt just before his payday from Tran. He'd made a career from the US Navy, and after twenty-four years of enlistment, he'd landed his dream job. He was the port director for the entire port of Corpus Christi, Texas. Not only was he the director, but he wore an inspector's hat as well. He earned an incredible salary, but greed had a way of making a man believe that he had nothing when the world was at his feet. So it was no wonder that when he was approached by the sharply dressed Asian man known only as Tran, whose entire conversation was about his ability to change John's life financially, he was all ears.

Tran laid out a plan that involved John and his port. He wanted to use John's harbor as the point of entry for his business ventures. He assured John that for a few minutes of his time each month,

he'd be rewarded handsomely, with minimal risk.
Tran guaranteed John that every month he would
be paid the sum of $25,000 cash. All he had to do
was ensure that his cargo went untainted until his
men could unload the shipment. Tran couldn't tell
John what the load would be until the day of dock-
ing and unloading, but he could in all certainty
promise him that it had nothing to do with drugs.

In John's naivety he'd agreed and plunged head-
first into a full-fledged human trafficking ring. Just
as Tran had promised, every month for the last
year he'd been paid $25,000 cash for every ship-
ment. He'd made $300,000, and it was all socked
away waiting for his early, permanent retirement.
Tran had been a man of his word. The risk was
minimal, and even when US Customs stepped in
and investigated John La Rue, Tran had spared no
expense in making certain that the whole situation
went bye-bye.

But not before cameras flashed in his face and
reporters spewed accusations of him being on
the take. His face had been plastered on news
channels from Corpus Christi to Amarillo, Texas,
and that had only served to intensify an already
uncomfortable situation. John did, however, have
one thing working in his favor: he was in charge
of the entire port, and he was able to move with
absolute impunity.

John sat in his Port Authority vehicle and waited. Dusk had just settled over the docks, and darkness began to fall. Coming toward him was the familiar set of headlights that he'd grown to know. Tran's white limousine pulled up facing John and flashed the high-beam lights. As always, he got out of his vehicle and made his way to the car. He got in and sat across from Tran with a stupid grin plastered across his face.

"Why is it that every time I see you, Mr. La Rue, you have that idiotic smirk on your face?" Tran asked.

"A man should always smile when given large sums of money, Mr. Tran. Besides, I only have six more months before I have enough money to ride off into the sunset."

"Ride off into the sunset? Explain. I am not familiar with this term," Tran said, confused.

"I'm done. I'm out. I'm going to take my money and retire, maybe find a small villa in Costa Rica, and live life, you know?"

"Oooooh, maybe there's been some sort of mis-understanding. Were we not clear in our directive?" Tran asked.

"How do you mean?"

"My dear Mr. La Rue, there is no retirement in our line of work. We pay you a great deal of money to simply sit on your fat ass and open a gate for us. Do you honestly believe that the Yakuza would allow you to retire? No, Mr. La Rue, these immigrants will continue to come through these ports overseen by you," Tran said.

"What if I go to the authorities? What then?"

Tran reached into his inside blazer pocket, removed a photo, and passed it to John. Upon seeing the person in the picture, the blood drained from his face, and he began to sweat.

"Your daughter's name is Anna Beth. She's twenty years old, and she's a sophomore at Texas Women's University. She has a 3.2 grade point average. She speaks Cantonese, French, and Spanish. She's proficient in tennis and loves horseback riding. She goes to a Starbucks off campus every morning after she leaves LA Fitness, where she gets a double latte with extra foam. Her favorite food is Chinese, and her favorite color is orange. She likes to masturbate while watching rerun episodes of *That '70s Show* because she has a crush on Ashton Kutcher. Shall I go on? Are you getting the picture, Mr. La Rue?" Tran asked.

John searched, but there were no words. Tran knew too much. He would have rather not known about his daughter's masturbatory practices, but the rest of the information he was pretty well-versed in. There would be no early retirement for John La Rue. He wouldn't dare put his precious Anna Beth in danger, so he would continue to funnel the Asians through his port unfettered.

Tran tossed a stack of $100 bills into John's lap and tapped on the window lightly. The door opened, and John stepped out. He stood face-to-face with perhaps the largest Asian man he'd ever seen. He had to stand at least six foot eight, and he looked more like a sumo wrestler in a suit than a limousine driver. He stared at John menacingly and then returned to his car. As the limousine began to slowly roll away, Tran rolled his window down and spoke to John.

"Remember what I said, John, because I would hate to have to hurt such a beautiful young girl," he said. He snapped his finger, and the car stopped. "Wait, why hurt her when I can just have her smuggled into Japan? There are dignitaries there who would pay a small fortune to taste the nectar of a sweet, young American peach," Tran said. His cold, heartless laughter filled the air, and John could still hear remnants of his shrill cackle as the limousine sped away.

John counted the money slowly, exactly 250 $100 bills. He had made a nice ritual of banking his earnings, depositing $6,000 a week for four weeks and then celebrating with the odd $1,000. As long as he kept his deposits under $10,000, the authorities wouldn't be notified, and that was the last thing that he needed. John sighed heavily. He'd haphazardly made a deal with the devil with no foreseeable way out.

He dialed Anna Beth's number and waited for her to answer. The phone clicked, and he panicked. "Hello! Hello!" he screamed into the cellular.

"Hello, John, how are you?"

"Who is this? Where is Anna Beth?" John said.

"Anna Beth is the least of your worries tonight, Mr. La Rue. You're not a very good person. I don't think that you realize that slavery is illegal, John. It has been eradicated for quite some time now."

"Slavery? I don't know anything about slavery. What does that have to do with me?" he asked, honestly perplexed.

"Don't be naive, John. What do you think is going to happen to those girls you have locked away in that shipping container? Are you stupid enough to think that they are here for vacation?"

"I never really thought about it. I mean, I know that they aren't on vacation, I just . . . I mean, listen, what do you want from me? Where's my daughter?" John shouted. He was nervous and it showed. Anna Beth was his everything, and although he wasn't the best father, he'd tried his very best to give her the best of what he had. Her mother had died when Anna Beth was a sophomore in high school, and it had taken quite some time to get her back to normal, but through church and counseling, he'd gotten her turned around. She didn't deserve to be dragged into his mess, but John La Rue was at a crossroads. On one hand, he had the Yakuza threatening to harm Anna Beth if he didn't continue their work, and now he had this mystery woman threatening his darling daughter with the same fate if he carried out his orders from the Asians.

He heard Anna Beth's frightened, muffled voice on the other end of the phone. "Dad? Hello, Dad?"

"Anna Beth, are you okay, honey?" John asked.

"I'm scared, Daddy! Please do whatever they say, Dad, please."

"Where are you, Anna Beth? Has she harmed you?" John asked.

"I don't know where I am, Daddy. The last thing I remember is walking into the laundry room in the basement of my apartment building, and when I woke up I was blindfolded, but I—"

Then her captor was back on the phone. "Your daughter is perfectly fine, Mr. La Rue, and if you want her to stay that way, you will release those girls immediately. Let me ask you something: did you know that a lot of those girls are underage?" she asked.

"I don't know anything about those girls. I'm just the middleman here. Why are you targeting me? What about Tran and the Yakuza? They're the ones really responsible for all of this. If I release the girls, they will kill my daughter."

"If you *don't* release the girls, I am going to kill your daughter. As far as the Yakuza, a bigger target requires more preparation. They will get theirs, trust me, but you have my word that if you release those girls, we will make sure that she's kept safe."

"I don't have a key to the containers. I can't open them," John whined.

"You're a very resourceful and intelligent man, Mr. La Rue. I'm sure you can think of something. Now look toward the front gate. There should be a man walking toward you. Go with him, and he will escort you to the container. After he calls me to confirm that the girls are safe, I will release your daughter. You have my word."

"And then what? Where will they go?" John asked.

"That's not your concern. Do you see him yet?"

John looked toward the front gate. A tall, hooded figure walked in his direction, cloaked in the new darkness, and he carried something in his hand. His gait was upright and confident like that of a military man, a man who had been made to straighten his back and find his inner soldier, a walk that John knew all too well. "Yes, I see him. What should I say?" he asked.

"Nothing," she said, and then the phone went silent.

The hooded man wore dark glasses, too dark to have on at nighttime. John La Rue didn't utter a word. He stood stoically watching him as he stepped within inches of his face. He was so close, in fact, that John could smell his breath. It wasn't unpleasant, but it nevertheless made him feel uncomfortable. There was an eerily awkward quietness about the stranger, and John fidgeted nervously. He wanted to speak, he wanted answers, but his daughter's captor had instructed him to remain silent. Even from behind the dark shades, the man was studying him, he could tell, looking into his soul, searching for something that John wasn't sure he had.

He let his eyes fall to the man's hand. In it he held a satchel that resembled a doctor's bag. He had no idea what could be in the bag, but it couldn't be good, and it caused John's knees to buckle. After years of being enlisted in the military, he'd let himself go. No longer did he wake at the crack of dawn to jog his regimented five miles a day. There was a time when he was very cautious about the things that he ate, but being made to eat healthy food had caused a bit of a rebellious streak in John. Oreos were his favorite, and he'd been known to eat an entire three-row package of them in one sitting. Tran had called him fat earlier, and it had really bothered him. He rubbed his corpulent belly subconsciously and continued to wait.

Finally the man spoke, and his deep baritone boomed over the abandoned shipyard. "Take me to the girls," he said.

John obliged, silently leading the way to where the Asian girls awaited transport. "The men the girls belong to will be back in a few hours, and when they see that these girls are gone, they will kill us both," John said.

Loud, riotous laughter bellowed through the docks, bouncing from ship to ship, echoing across the water. Mr. Hooded didn't speak. His laughter had subsided, and all that remained was a slight snicker, as if he knew something that John La Rue didn't. He put his hand in the center of John's back and pushed him forward.

They reached a large CONEX shipping container, and John reached with shaking hands for the key ring attached to his belt loop. He'd lied to the lady on the phone, telling her that he didn't have the keys that stood between the young girls and their freedom. He unlocked the door and stepped back, giving his companion a full view into the metal box. Mr. Mysterious reached into his satchel and removed a flashlight, peering inside, and he was mortified by what he saw. Dozens of young Asian women ranging in age from 14 to 24 huddled in the far corners of the container, afraid of what might lie ahead. Some of them shielded their eyes from the light while the younger girls cowered behind the more seasoned women. Many of the women looked malnourished and beyond exhaustion. The container was a breeding ground for disease, and fecal matter and urine could be seen at their feet as he let his light shine about the box. There was a sickly odor permeating throughout the cargo box. It smelled like rotten fruit and death.

A majority of the girls seemed to gather around one particular woman. She was older than the rest and seemed to carry with her an aura of disdain, if not from being ogled by the two men, then perhaps from being seen in a state of dishevelment.

"Do any of you ladies speak English?" he asked with his flashlight trained on the Asian woman.

"Very little," she said.

"What is your name, sweetheart?"

"I am called Ling Woo," she said.

"Do you know where you are?"

"Judging by your dialect, I would say America," she said in broken English.

"How long have you been locked in here?"

"I and many of these girls were performing in the festival for *keira no hi* when we were kidnapped by the Yakuza, which takes place each year on the third Monday of September."

"Dear God, Thanksgiving is in two weeks. You've been at sea for nearly two months. How have you survived? What have you been eating?" he asked.

"We haven't eaten anything for the past couple of days. When the journey first started, they gave each of us rations, but it wasn't enough, so after it was gone, we survived on stale bread, orange peels, and apple cores. But soon, that was gone too."

"What did you eat after that?" he asked.

She turned to face the other women, "Move aside," she said in Japanese.

The frightened women parted, and at the back of the CONEX lay a pile of bones that had been picked clean. The lower half of a woman's body was still intact, as were her lower extremities for the most part. Except for a few bites from her legs, the lower body was untouched. Upon seeing the grotesque sight of the dead body, John turned on his heels and hurled.

"You need to see this shit! Turn your ass around!" the man barked. "This is what you condone," he added. He removed his 9 mm pistol from his waistband and pointed it at John's head. "Man the fuck up and look what you've done," he said.

John turned to face the women and fought the urge to vomit again.

"I know that you think that we are savages, but we had no choice. She fell ill on the journey, and we used what Buddha sent to us," she said.

The man turned to John La Rue with a fire blazing and raging in his eyes from a hatred long repressed. "Do you have money, John?" he screamed.

"W . . . what?"

"You heard me. Do you have any money?"

John reached into his pocket and removed nine crumpled $1 bills.

"Don't fucking play with me! I saw you meet with those men, and I know that they gave you money. Your life, your daughter's life, depends on your honesty. Now do you have money?" he asked through clenched teeth.

"I have twenty-five thousand dollars in my car."

"Get it now!"

Moments later, John returned with the stack of new $100 bills and handed them to him. Mr. Mysterious took one of the bills and held it against the flashlight. "At least they didn't play you and give you fake money," he said. He removed a second bill, then folded both bills and stuffed them into his pocket. He turned to the women. He could almost hear the rattle of their frail knees, maybe from fright or maybe from a debilitating need of food. "Take this money. It's not much, but it'll help get you and these girls to safety, maybe a hot shower, some clean clothes and something to eat, but whatever you decide to do, you may want to do it quickly."

"Thank you, sir. I don't know how I can ever repay you."

"No need for repayment. This piece of shit is going to repay your debt for you," he said. He turned to John La Rue, who had a sickened look on his face. The man grabbed him by the navy blue necktie that completed his ensemble and snatched him. "You come with me!" he barked and then added, "Is this vessel occupied?"

"No, it's out of service." John said. His legs felt like jelly, and he found it difficult to walk. "Wait, wait, I have more money. If you let me go, I'll give it to you, I promise," John whined.

The man stopped in his tracks and turned to face John. With a firm grip still on John's necktie, he pulled him close and slapped him at the same time. The momentum of his movement and the force of the blow caused John to stumble. It was in that instant that he knew that death was calling. He wasn't a good man, he wasn't a good father, and he had been a terrible husband. If nothing else, the military had taught him to fight. He lunged at the man, only to fall flat on his face. His brain told him to fight, but his body would not cooperate. His tormentor continued to drag him down the dock and up the gangplank until they reached the deck of the defunct ship. He snatched John by his necktie, causing him to stumble to the front of him. Once again he removed the pistol from his waist, all the while gripping the doctor's satchel tightly. This time he cocked the pistol, kicking a bullet into the chamber, and pointed it at his head.

"You're going to lead the way, and if you try anything funny, I'm going to put a bullet in the back of your head. Is there a place with a lot of mirrors on this ship?" he asked.

"I believe that there are mirrors in the gym."

"Take me there," he ordered.

They made their way through the gangways of the sea liner, and John felt another surge of confidence. He ducked and tried to run, but before he was barely fifty feet away, the goon leveled his pistol, aimed, and fired. The bullet ripped through John's calf, sending him tumbling to the ground. He lay prone, moaning and writhing in pain.

"Why are you trying me? Do you want your daughter to die, fool?" the attacker asked.

John shook his head no sheepishly and scrambled to his feet. They approached the gym, and just as John had said, there were mirrors everywhere. As they stepped through the door, the assailant struck John in the back of the head with the butt of his gun, knocking him unconscious.

John La Rue regained consciousness slowly. He opened his eyes in a foggy haze to blurred vision and a splitting headache. He wanted to move his hand to the spot where his head ached, but he couldn't move. He looked to his left and then to his right. Both of his hands had been bound with duct tape. He blinked rapidly as he looked straight ahead, trying desperately to focus. John could see himself in the mirror, and then panic set in. His aggressor was nowhere in sight. Maybe he'd left him there because he thought that John was already dead. He struggled against his restraints to no avail. John heard the sound of rickety wheels creaking down the hallway, and he struggled harder. The duct tape stretched and twisted, but it would not break. He fought until finally the sound was right up on him.

The mystery man still wore his hood and sunglasses as he entered the gym. It wasn't a small room, but it wasn't ostentatious either, just big enough for a serious fitness buff to really come in and do damage. "Ah, I see you're finally awake, Mr. La Rue," he said, removing his glasses and hood.

John stared at the man as if trying to recollect where he knew him from. Although a stunning shade of cold water blue, his eyes held pain, a pain that John could neither pinpoint nor care to discover.

"I hope you don't mind, but I took the liberty of borrowing a few things from the infirmary. As I walked through this ship, I started thinking. What kind of man, what kind of heartless moron, would help to smuggle defenseless women into the country to be used for God knows what?" he said. He went into his satchel and removed a huge syringe that resembled a turkey baster, filled with a clear liquid. "The funny thing," he said while thumping the syringe, "is that people like you don't think. See, if I ever have a daughter, it'll only

enhance my respect for women, and I looooooove
me some women," he said. John felt a stabbing
pain between his shoulder blades after the man
disappeared behind him. "But you, you have no
remorse for your actions. You're only motivated
by greed. I mean, does Anna Beth know that you
murdered her mother for the insurance money?"
he said as he buried the needle in John's lower
back. The look of surprised horror on John's face
from his startling revelation was enough to send
the torturer into a fit of hysterical laughter. He
moved to the front of John and loosened his tie
and carefully unbuttoned John's shirt. "Ohhhhhh,
you thought no one knew about that?" he asked.

Whereas before he'd flinched and jumped from
the pain of having the needle thrust into his spine,
John La Rue now felt no pain. The blue-eyed demon had injected him with an epidural anesthetic,
so although he was awake, he could feel nothing.

"You know, John, I'm a thinking man's man, and
you are not a thinker," he said. He made his way
back to his satchel, where he put on a black apron
that read "Kiss the Cook" on it. He tied it slowly,
keeping his eyes trained on John the entire time.

"What do you want from me? I haven't done
anything to you," John whimpered.

"See, that's where you're wrong, dumb ass," he
said as he slid his hands into heavy rubber gloves.
He removed a Stryker saw and clicked it on, and

it buzzed and whirred to life. The shrill whining of the skull saw shrieked ominously between the gunmetal gray walls of the *USS King's Cross*. He pulled a step stool across the cold metal floor. It screeched and clanked until it was positioned behind John's suspended body. John could no longer see what the man was doing, but the sound of the saw was close, very close. He took his footstool and stood in front of John, blocking what little view he had through the mirror. Again he heard the droning of the saw, and when he stepped down, John was finally able to see what he'd been doing. He had to squint his eyes to see it, but he nearly fainted when he saw the red incision extended across his forehead, but it couldn't have been too serious because he hadn't felt it. He reached into his bag again, this time removing a small chainsaw. He wasted little time with his work, and this time he didn't try to hide it. He cut both of John's legs off midway between his ankles and his knees.

John screamed from shock and horror more than anything else. The fact that he'd witnessed his legs being severed from his body and that he couldn't feel it terrified him. The man dropped the chainsaw, stepped back, and looked at John. The blue-eyed demon rested his hand on his chin, and his elbow rested on his other arm as if he was lost in deep thought. He snapped his fingers and went back to his bag of tricks and got a smooth-edged fillet knife. The blade on the knife was beyond sharp, so much so that he had no problem cutting away the forest of hair that covered the tattoo of a battleship on his chest. He cut into John's chest, digging around the tat until he was able to pull it from his body still attached to nerves and muscle tissue. As he moved to the side, John could see the fleshy hole, leaking his crimson red blood where his tattoo had once been. The man tossed John's tattooed flesh to the ground and retrieved his Stryker saw and a pair of rib shears. With one swift motion of his saw, he opened John's entire chest cavity, exposing his innards, but he was careful not to do internal damage. He took the rib shears and clipped his ribs away until he could see John's beating heart.

"John, what could have possibly been on your mind when you decided to do this? Did you think of the consequences at all? And I still have yet to hear you apologize," he said. John opened his mouth to speak, but the only thing that came out were clumps of blood plasma. "Now, now, John, no dying on me!" he said.

"Please, please, just kill me."

"Nooooooo, now why would I do that? I want to show you something," he said. He reached into his bag once more and removed a chisel and a rubber mallet. He climbed up on the footstool again and chiseled around John's skull. Once there was a slight separation all the way around, he used the chisel as a wedge to pop the crown of John's skull

off of the top of his head. He stepped off of the
stool and showed him the crown of his own skull.
"Look in the mirror, John. Can you see your own
thoughts?" he said.

"Please have mercy. Just fucking kill me!" John
pleaded.

"No, I won't. I've known people like you my
whole life: users who use people and pretend to
love them, and then when you're done with them,
you discard them like trash! No, the way this works
is that in another ten minutes the anesthetic will
begin to wear off. As it does, you will gradually
begin to feel the pain. Once it wears off completely,
you will feel every single thing that I've done to
you. That's if you don't bleed out first. You will
wish for death, but he won't come. You'll beg for
God's forgiveness, but He will not answer. And
finally, you'll remember . . . you'll remember
the night that you killed Margaret Ann. You'll
remember the girl's lives you ruined by helping the
Yakuza, and then, and only then, will death grant
you your sweet reprieve," he said. He removed the
apron and gloves and lifted his hoodie and then
placed his glasses over his cold, unfeeling eyes. He
reached into his pocket, removed the two crisp
$100 bills he'd gotten from the Asian women, and
placed them in the crown of John's skull. He then
placed the detached tattoo of the battleship on top
of the money and positioned it just beneath John's
feet so that it floated in his own blood.

Chapter 19

FREE PARKING

Anna Beth La Rue sat in the office of Senior Agent Muldoon, impatiently waiting for Monica and her team to arrive. When her kidnapper had mercifully released her, she'd tried to call her father. She'd tried numerous times to reach him, only to have his phone go to voicemail. Anna Beth felt it in her gut. She knew that something was wrong, and by the time the police contacted her about her father's murder, she was already prepared for the news. The Corpus Christi Police Department had been shut down by the NCIS, who in turn agreed to work with the FBI on the investigation.

She and her father had never really been close, but a wedge had really been drawn after the death of her mother. There were whispers and hushed conversations that her father had murdered her mother for the insurance money. When John had found out what people were saying, he'd isolated Anna Beth from the rest of her family. She was intelligent enough to realize that accidents happened, but the problem that she had with her mother's death was *how* she died.

John La Rue first laid eyes on Margaret Ann during his first tour of duty. As a young officer, he'd been extremely popular with the local ladies who swarmed the barracks on a regular basis. Margaret Ann was different. She was a professional female and highly motivated. It was extra incentive to John because, unlike most of the women he dealt with, Margaret Ann wasn't interested in his rank. She was, however, interested in the man underneath the machismo and bravado. After four months of courtship they were married, and a year later, Anna Beth was born. She'd heard the story of her conception so many times that it no longer embarrassed her.

Margaret Ann La Rue exceled in everything that she endeavored, hence Anna Beth's dilemma with her death. Her mother had been an avid swimmer, so much so that she volunteered to teach children and the elderly swimming at the local YMCA. She was also the head lifeguard. Her parents had gone on vacation, sans a then-13-year-old Anna Beth, to the Bimini Islands. According to her father they'd rented a yacht, rented some equipment, and gone snorkeling. Margaret Ann was diving into the water and misjudged the depth and must have hit her head on a shallow reef. It wasn't until he didn't see her surface in a timely fashion that he dove in to see where she was. The official report listed her death as an accident. They also listed the reason as blunt force trauma to the head. In everyone's mind, even Anna Beth's when she was angry with her father, that only meant that they didn't know whether she'd hit her head on a reef or if John had hit her across the head with something. At any rate, Anna Beth loved her father, but she wasn't his biggest fan.

The intercom in Muldoon's office crackled to life. "Excuse me, sir, Agents Deitrich and Roth are waiting for you in the conference room," the voice said.

"Thank you, Regina. If you'll follow me, Miss La Rue."

Muldoon escorted Anna Beth into the Roosevelt conference room and introduced her to Monica and Cody. "Miss La Rue, could you please tell these agents what you told the police? As I stated when we talked before, I am an agent in the DEA, so I have no jurisdiction in this case. However, as a courtesy to you, I will stay and listen."

Anna Beth nodded. She felt comfortable with him. Agent Muldoon reminded her of someone's grandfather. He was soft-spoken and very down-to-earth, and for whatever reason, he'd taken to the young girl.

"Take your time and try not to leave out any details please," Monica instructed.

Anna Beth started from the beginning, explaining to them how she'd walked to the laundry room, and the next thing she knew, she was blindfolded and tied up. "The lady who kidnapped me was actually really nice. She—"

"Wait, there was a woman?" Monica asked.

"Yeah, and her husband is the one who killed my father. Haven't you been listening?"

Monica looked at Cody warily, purposely ignoring Anna Beth's sarcastic question. As she recounted detail after detail, it became obvious that they weren't dealing with one person, but rather a duo. John La Rue's murder fit into their theory of the redemption killer, and they needed to find the macabre couple before another body hit the street.

"Is there anything else that you can think of that we need to know?" Cody Roth asked.

"Not really. I mean, she kept repeating this phrase, but I don't know if it's important," Anna Beth said.

"Anything that you can think of may be important. What is it?" Monica asked.

"It was random, but she said it a few times. She kept saying people aren't always who they appear to be, and sometimes the only way to stay in the game is by turning your weaknesses into strengths, or something like that."

Cody jotted down the phrase on a notepad, then asked, "What's that supposed to mean? Is there anything—and I mean anything—else that you can think of? Eye color, height, something."

"Look, mister, I told you everything I know. Jeez, can I go?" Anna Beth huffed as she crossed her arms like a frustrated child.

"I really appreciate you taking time out of your schedule to come and talk to us, Anna Beth. We'll be in touch if we need anything else from you," Monica said.

Anna Beth exited the room with Agent Muldoon in tow, and Monica turned to Cody with a dumb-founded look on her face. "What the fuck is going on? We have bodies dropping left and right, and we're not any closer to solving this case than we were when we found the first body," Monica said.

Cody scribbled some words on a piece of paper and shoved it into his pocket. "Ma'am, this is a dire dilemma. I mean, at the rate we're going, there will be a body in every state in the union."

Monica knew that he was right, but she was in the same position as Cody Roth. She had no clue where to start. For hours they talked, dissecting the case piece by piece until Monica could no longer think. She wanted a hot shower, a hot meal, and to fall asleep with Noisy Boy at the foot of her bed. Cody Roth disappeared and returned moments later with two cups of coffee in his hands.

"What are we doing here, Agent Roth?" Monica asked while stirring creamer and sugar into her coffee.

"I have no clue, ma'am. This isn't what I signed up for."

"What do you mean by that?" Monica asked.

"I'm just saying, ma'am, when I joined the FBI, I guess I had some grand illusions about what it would be like. I thought I'd be busting in on the bad guys like the real gang busters, like Elliot Ness did with Al Capone."

"I think we all had our illusions, Agent Roth. I thought that the connection I made with my last subject had prepared me for profiling. His unstable mental state gave me a love for the delicate mind, but this person or duo has me stumped."

"Just to break the ice, can I ask you a question?" Cody Roth asked shyly.

"Sure, shoot."

"Do you think there's a chance that maybe one day we can grab some dinner? You know, hang out outside of work?" he asked.

"I don't believe in dating anyone from work. It would be very conflicting, to say the least."

"I respect that, and I'll never ask again. Are you sure it's not because I look like a fourteen-year-old Harry Potter?" he asked with a sly smirk on his face.

Monica's face blushed beet red. She wasn't sure if anyone else had noticed his uncanny resemblance to the teen phenomenon, but to hear him mention it put her at ease.

Before she could rebut Agent Roth's accusation, Muldoon walked into the dim conference room. "Have we made any progress, Monica?" he asked.

"No, sir, not really. I'm at a loss, and I'm mentally exhausted. I actually feel like I'm regressing within this case."

"Okay, I think we need to start with the basics. What do we know?" Muldoon asked.

"From a profiling aspect, we know that we're looking for a male and a female. We also know that their MO is sadistic homicide. We know that they are only killing bad people or people who have been publicly accused of doing bad things," Cody Roth chimed in.

"So let's focus on what we have. I want you both to go home and get some rest. Start fresh in the morning. I want you two to pick these clues apart. There is something in here that will either lead us to these assholes or lead us to their next victims. I'll see you two in the morning. I have a date with a bottle of rum and a hot shower," Muldoon said.

Monica Deitrich and Cody Roth rode down the escalator in silence. It was a rather awkward

silence because, for one, he'd asked her out, and
two, they both felt like failures. Mr. Chadwick, a
spritely, graying, elderly black security guard
waved to them as they hit the ground floor.

"You two burning the midnight oil again, huh?"
he asked.

"Yes, something like that, sir. How have you
been?" Monica asked.

"Fair to middling, fair to middling. Nothing the
Lawd can't fix. Don't you worry yourself about
these here old bones. I'll be fine. Why you look
so sour, young man? You're healthy and in God's
favor. Besides, you're in the company of a beautiful woman, so you should be smiling from ear to
ear," Mr. Chadwick said with a huge smile on his
face. His bright smile and bouncy demeanor belied his 80-plus years. He'd been working for the
federal government since the early 1950s when a
black man was only allowed to mop floors and wait
tables. Now at 84 years old, he was eligible for retirement, but as he'd explained to his superiors, his
lovely Willean had long since passed on and there
wasn't much point in retiring. No, he'd rather work
and be of some use to somebody.

"I apologize, Mr. Chadwick. It's just that we're
at a standstill in this case. I guess my mind is just
preoccupied, sir. Please forgive my rudeness."

"No need to apologize, son. I've been here a
whole lot of years, and I'm more understanding

than people give me credit for. What kinda case are you working on, if you don't mind me asking?" Mr. Chadwick asked.

Monica had no problem sharing a few details with the elderly man. He was, after all, a government employee. So Monica and Cody explained to Mr. Chadwick where they were in the case and how they'd come to a complete stop. After a long silence, he raised his head and began to speak in his elderly, deep Southern dialect.

"Well, kids, it seems to me that you would need to find someone who has the financial means to move around the country with no problems. I think you're looking for a very manipulative man and a very vulnerable woman. I figure any woman who's driven to kill with a man is probably in love with that man. They're either married or very much in love. Look for people who have a reason and enough pain inside to kill and you'll find your murderers," Mr. Chadwick said.

Monica looked at him with a newfound respect. She'd always noticed him but had never really had the opportunity to speak with him. Everything that he'd just said made perfect sense. It was not only a starting point, but it may have been the focal point to break the case.

She and Agent Roth walked to the huge glass doors at the front of the building with Mr. Chadwick. Senior Agent Muldoon had just flicked a cigarette butt to the street and was making his way across the street to the parking lot adjacent to the building. Mr. Chadwick unlocked the doors, let them out, and bid them a good night.

Less than a block away, two people dressed in all black tied a long piece of piano wire to the handlebars of their black Dodge Tomahawk motorcycles. They were barely visible against the backdrop of the darkness covering the Dallas skyline. The pair both glanced at their watches and revved their engines as if signaling one another that they were in sync, and then they saw him.

Agent Muldoon stepped off the curb, headed toward the parking lot. The motorcycles were on opposite sides of the road, and they had agreed to ride the curb line until they reached their intended victim. As Agent Muldoon neared the middle of the street, he stopped. The assailants feared that they might lose their opportunity, but he was only waving good night to the two people exiting the building before he turned to continue toward the lot.

The cyclists nearly reached their top speed of 150 miles per hour by the time they reached him, and when the duo passed him in a black blur, the piano wire sliced him in half. He was still standing, frozen in place, when Monica yelled, "Slow down!" at the passing bikers.

It wasn't until she looked back in Senior Agent Muldoon's direction that she saw the top half of his body fall forward while his bottom half fell backward. His entrails plopped and splattered to the cold asphalt in a bloody and gooey mess. Agent Cody Roth's face turned pea green, and he lost not only the lunch he'd had earlier that day but also the coffee he'd just drunk.

Monica screamed as the grisly sight of what had just happened registered in her already-distressed brain. Agent Muldoon had been chopped in half like a scene from a D-list horror movie, right before their eyes. The FREE PARKING sign above Muldoon's severed body blinked ominously as his blood coated the downtown city streets.

Chapter 20

DO ME A SOLID

Monica couldn't believe it. She sat on her couch, balled up in a knot, scratching Noisy Boy's stomach. She was trying to process what had happened in her head, and it didn't make sense. Monica was sure that Muldoon had put in a lot of work, some clean, some not so much, but to be murdered in cold blood defied logic. By the time that she and Agent Roth finished giving their statements to their superiors about what they'd witnessed, she was drained.

Noisy Boy whimpered softly. He was her best friend, and he knew when there was something weighing heavily on her mind. He switched his body position and put his head underneath her hand. He loved it when she scratched his ear, and it seemed to calm her down.

Monica's mind shifted to Jasmine. She and Muldoon had grown extremely close since she'd

been home from Buckner. She was hesitant to call
and tell Jasmine what had happened because the
loss could send her into mental regression. She
would have to tell her though, because Jasmine
loved Muldoon. He'd filled a void for Jasmine that
she'd longed for since the death of Pop Pop, and if
Monica didn't tell her, it could have an even worse
effect on her delicate mind.

She grabbed her cell phone from the table and
dialed Jasmine's number, and much to her dis-
may, the number had been disconnected. Jasmine
couldn't be that mad, because the arguments
hadn't been that serious, or so she'd thought. If
Jasmine was still angry, then there was more to
it than Monica's questioning Jasmine's love for a
man she barely knew. She dialed Bird's number,
and he answered on the first ring.

"'Sup, Monkey?"

"Hey, Bird, are you busy?" she asked.

"Not really, just out and about with the baby. We
just left the restaurant, so now we're chilling. Ay, I
need to talk to you face-to-face, shawt."

"Yeah, same here. When would be a good time
for you?" Monica asked.

"It's whenever with me. You feel like meeting us
at the park by my house?"

"Okay, that's fine. I'll see you in a few," she said.

Monica pressed end and stuffed the cellular
deep into her pocket. She put Noisy Boy on his

leash and walked him to her car, but Noisy Boy pulled her to the nearest tree, cocked his leg up, and marked his territory. Maybe it was true that all men were dogs, because R. Kelly had been charged for pissing on some underage girl, probably in an effort to mark his territory or to assert his alpha male dominance. Just as quickly as the thought had crossed her mind, it was gone again. She was in her car in a flash and on her way to see Bird and her goddaughter.

Less than forty-five minutes later, she was pulling into the parking lot of the park. She spotted Bird sitting on a nearby bench. Millie was in her stroller, facing Bird, watching his every move as he studied a bundle of papers. Monica tiptoed up behind him and tapped his shoulders.

"Boo!" she said as he turned around.

He jumped, startled but not shaken. "Hey, Monkey, I see you love acting like a little monkey!" he said heatedly.

"Whatever, boy. Don't start, because I didn't come to see your ugly face anyways! I came to see Auntie's pwetty baby, yes, I did. I came to see my Millie Bean," Monica gushed. Millicent cooed and giggled at the sound of Monica's playful baby talk.

"So what's up, Monica?" Bird asked.

"You first," she said. She needed time to formulate a plan. Monica couldn't just go from cheerful to, "Oh, by the way, Muldoon was killed last night."

No, she would have to break it to Bird gently. Muldoon, along with Monica and Drak, had been instrumental in helping Bird get his life back, and of the three, he was closest to Monica. The last thing she wanted was for Bird to panic, thinking that either one of them was next on the hit list.

Noisy Boy circled the bench a couple of times and took a seat next to Millie's stroller. He allowed his eyes to roam the park freely in search of anything that seemed to be a threat to the small child.

"Well, I spent majority of the day with my attorney yesterday, and she started me thinking. I'm not getting any younger, and since you have a nigga permanently locked away in the friend zone, I need help from a *friend*. Just hear me out, okay? Promise me," he said.

Monica nodded. She wasn't sure where Bird was headed with it, but she would at least listen.

"Okay, so I'm living this square lifestyle and trying to be a good dad, but I've done my dirt. I've just been feeling like I need to get my affairs in order lately, you know?" Bird said.

"Stop talking like that, Bird. I think we're safe."

"We're never safe, Monica, and I'm not going to fool myself into believing that. There are still niggas out there who are sour and salty because they feel like I betrayed that fool King Kochese. They aren't eating, so guess who they're blaming? So if I live to see my baby graduate, go to college, get married, and have kids, great, but if not, I need to be prepared. I've made provisions just in case to make sure that my shit is straight," he said, riffling through the papers on his lap. He looked at Monica, trying to gauge her demeanor before continuing. "I've had the businesses put into Millie's name, and I've given you power of attorney. I've also taken out a half-million-dollar life insurance policy on myself and made you the beneficiary. And before you say anything, as her godmother, you have to take care of my baby if anything happens to me," Bird said in a somber tone.

"Bird, I don't know the first thing about raising a child, man."

"And neither did I, but a very good friend of mine, someone whom I respect very much, pulled my coattail and made me see that sometimes we don't have a choice. I need you, Monkey. Millie needs you."

"So you're just gonna use my own words against me, huh?"

"Pretty much, yeah," he said.

"Okay, you have my word. If anything happens to you, I will take care of her like she's my own."

"I just need you to sign here, here, and here," Bird said, flipping through the contents of the manila folder.

Monica scanned over the contents of the folder and signed quickly. After seeing the bodies of both

Drak and Muldoon, the last thing that she wanted to think about was Bird's death.

"So what's your news?" Bird asked.

"Remember I told you Jasmine had her head stuck up King's brother's ass? Well, this little hooker changed her number on me!" Monica barked.

"Wow."

"Yeah, wow is right. I swear, after the night I had, if I saw her right now, I'd probably snatch a mud hole in her ass," she said heatedly.

"Is it that bad? What kind of night did you have? Did one of your little boy toys cum too fast?" Bird laughed, trying to lighten the mood.

"Hell no. I wish! I need some, for real!"

Bird stood and faced Monica with outstretched arms, slapping his chest with a huge grin on his face. "Here you go, shawty, I got you covered. Candlelight and hard dick, that's what you need," Bird said.

"Eww, um, yeah, that's never going to happen, playa!" Monica said with a priceless scowl on her face.

"Yeah, whatever! Don't come begging when you wake up one morning and cobwebs done started growing on that thang."

"Yeah, I'm sure I won't. Seriously though, I need to tell you something serious."

"Okay, my bad. Go ahead," Bird said.

"Bird, Muldoon was murdered last night, right in front of me," Monica said.

Bird was speechless. He could only stare at Monica with his mouth open, disbelief pasted on his face. "W . . . what? How?" Bird stammered.

"You wouldn't believe me if I told you."

"Try me," he said.

Monica explained to him how the two suspects had cut him in half, and Bird's face went pale.

"See, man, and you wonder why I'm trying to get my shit together. First Drak, now Muldoon? It makes me wonder if that hit was for me and not for Bridgette and Kim. I'm telling you, somebody in King's court is gunning for me. Shit, they might be gunning for you!" Bird said nervously.

"Maybe, but we can't worry about that now. I need to figure out what's going on with my sister, and you need to take care of Millie."

"Use your head, Monica. What's the one common link?" Bird asked.

"What do you mean, common link?"

"I mean, if dude got her open like that, like King had you open, what's the one common link between the brothers?" he asked. He looked at Monica as if they were on a game show and he was trying to pry the answer from her.

"Hayden Cross!" Monica exclaimed.

"Exactly, Hayden Cross. Go to him. He's the source. Whatever drove the brothers undoubtedly came from their father," Bird said.

Monica walked into the ornate glass building of CrossTech. Her black patent leather heels clicked and clacked rhythmically against the polished terrazzo tile floor. She stepped to the security desk and tapped a perfectly manicured nail against the surface of the countertop.

"Excuse me," she said, but there was no reply from the young, rude security guard. He was preoccupied by something on his phone and never raised his head. "Excuse me!" Monica repeated, but the man kept tinkering with his phone, obviously ignoring her. Monica strode past the security desk. That must have caught his attention, because he sprang to his feet.

"You can't go out onto the property without a pass, man. You're gonna get me fired," he said, looking Monica up and down lasciviously.

"Well, you seemed like you were so busy, and I would hate to disturb your little *Candy Crush* or whatever has your attention," Monica snorted.

"Man, don't think 'cause you fine and shit that you're gonna play me. I'm the law 'round here, so if you wanna get past me, we gonna hafta exchange phone numbers or something!"

"Oh, okay, you want my number, daddy? Why didn't you just say that?" Monica asked.

"Hell yeah, I want your number! I get paid Friday. We can hit Red Lobster and shit."

Monica reached down to her waist, removed her badge, and shoved it in the man's face. "You still want my number?" she asked.

"No, ma'am, you're good. Welcome to CrossTech. How may I help you?"

"Wow, who knew you could be so well-mannered? Now let's start over. I'm here to see Mr. Hayden Cross," Monica said.

"Oh, shit! I'm really sorry, ma'am, I didn't know you were here for Mr. Cross. I need this job, so if I disrespected you, I'm sorry."

"No worries. Just tighten up, because you never know who you're talking to. So how about that pass?" Monica asked.

"Yes, ma'am. I just need your driver's license. Can I say something?" he asked while copying Monica's information onto a visitor's pass.

"Sure."

"If I wanted to take you out, would you actually go out with me? I mean, that offer to Red Lobster still stands," he said, blushing.

"I don't think so, sweetie. Just so you know, first impressions are the only impressions, and you came at me all wrong. Besides, Red Lobster isn't exactly my idea of high-class cuisine. So finish your shift in peace knowing that fucking with me, you're way above your pay grade, sweetheart," Monica said as she sashayed away.

The top-flight security guard watched Monica's sumptuous derriere twist away. The material of her executive dress slacks hugged her every curve while the jacket of her suit refused to cooperate, riding above the arch of her ass.

The elevator doors opened, and Monica stepped out into the lavish foyer of the executive floor. Emily, Hayden Cross's personal assistant, sat behind the receptionist's desk, filing the nails on her delicate and petite hands.

"Excuse me, ma'am, I need to speak with Mr. Cross," Monica said, flashing her badge.

Emily remembered the young agent from months earlier. She might have been elderly, but her memory was intact. "Greetings, Agent Deitrich. I remember you. Let me buzz him and let him know you're here. Have a seat, please."

Time seemed to stand still for Monica after she sat down. She'd heard Emily relay the message to Hayden, so she knew that he knew that she was there. She glanced at her watch repeatedly until Emily finally motioned for her to enter Mr. Cross's office.

When she stepped into his office, Hayden Cross was standing at the window with his arms folded behind his back. He didn't turn around to face Monica. He just continued to stare out over CrossTech's courtyard. He had spent decades building CrossTech into a powerhouse of cutting-edge military weaponry. Photos of him and some of the most influential men in Washington, DC, and abroad lined his walls, and Monica was impressed.

"Come in and make yourself comfortable, Miss Deitrich. Would you like a drink?" he said, motioning toward the bar.

"No, thank you. I really need to talk to you about your son, Khalil, and my sister."

"And what is it that you would like to know, Agent Deitrich?" Hayden said with his back still turned to her.

"I want to know how he has this hold on my sister. She's all but abandoned everything that she's worked for."

"I'm not sure how I can help you, but I'll try as much as I can," he said.

"I know that you don't know much about me. I'm sure all you know is that I was the agent who took your son down. However, I think it's important for you to know that somewhere along the road to conviction I fell in love with your son, and doing my job became more difficult by the day. My sister is twenty years old, and she's displaying the same signs that I displayed when I fell in love with Kochese."

"And somehow I am responsible for that? You took my son away from me, and now I'm supposed to help you break my other son's heart? So next week or the week after or next year, for that matter, you'll destroy my other son as well? I take it you won't be happy until you destroy the Cross men altogether?" Hayden admonished.

"Mr. Cross, let me be clear about something. When I was with Kochese, we talked regularly, and I know things about this man that people would pay money to learn. I know that he went to his grave hating your guts for what you did to him and his mother, a mother who was so damaged by you that she was unable to love her son because he reminded her of the man she could never have."

Hayden Cross glared at Monica. He wasn't used to being challenged, and he most certainly didn't like it. Her eyes ripped into his being, slicing away bits and pieces of his macho facade until he turned away in shame. He could see why Kochese had fallen for her. She was not only gorgeous, but she was fiery and courageous. Most people bowed under the pressure of his legend, under the weight from the man who had turned a loan into a billion-dollar corporation. To a certain extent, he resented Monica for reminding him of his humanity. He wasn't a saint, but he wasn't Lucifer either. Nobody knew the extent of his relationship with Kochese's mother, but for the sake of enlightenment, he would oblige Monica Deitrich.

"I want you to get comfortable, Miss Deitrich, and listen. I know that I've been vilified, but I need to explain some things to you, and perhaps by the time I'm done, you'll have a deeper understanding of Hayden Cross," he said.

Monica leaned back in the plush, high-backed leather chair as Hayden began to recount his experiences with Evelyn Mills.

"When I first met Effie, she was young and impressionable, you know? I didn't have a pot to piss in or a back door to throw it out of, but none of that mattered to her. She was infatuated with me as a person, so she overlooked my flaws and shortcomings. I was a different change of pace for Evelyn, you know? A white boy from the suburbs of Plano, Texas, I worked hard, and I played harder, and I never apologized for it. When I went to her and told her about my dreams and aspirations, she laughed at me and told me that it could never be done. She said that computers were stupid and that it would never work. Did it hurt me? Of course it did. But I just kept my disappointment bottled up inside. A little while later Effie came to me and said that she was pregnant, and I was both happy and crushed at the same time. I was happy because I would be having a child, someone whom I could love and who would love me. I was crushed because I felt like it would hinder my progress. Evelyn wanted me to forget about my fledgling business and concentrate on her and the baby, but my drive and determination wouldn't allow me to do that, so I scoffed at the idea. She gave me an ultimatum, and I've never been good with ultimatums, you know? She said it was either her and the baby, or my business.

"I swear, Agent Deitrich, I tried to make her understand that this business could make us rich beyond our wildest dreams. I told her that we could get married and raise the child together. But she didn't want that," Hayden said. His eyes welled up as if he was about to cry. He turned away from Monica and stared out the window before he continued speaking. "She was ashamed of our relationship. She looked me in my eyes and told me that there was no way that she could or would ever take a white boy home. She said that her family would never understand, and out of respect for her, I agreed, but I wasn't happy. I didn't want to be her little honky secret. I wanted the world to know that we were together and that we'd built our business from the ground up.

"We slowly started to drift apart, and the bigger her belly got, the more distant she became. I went to her with some things for the baby, and she told me that she'd been lying to me all along. She said that the baby belonged to someone else and that she never wanted to see me again. I begged her, Miss Deitrich, I pleaded with her to just let me be his father. She laughed in my face and said that she was pregnant by a black man, so how could a white boy help raise him, you know? I disappeared, but I still couldn't let her go, so I would watch her from a distance. She would never have the baby with her, and I assumed that his father had taken him from her because by this time she was on dope. Some of the places that I followed her to were seedy, to say the least. Real nasty places. I would try to call her from time to time, but I could never catch up with her, so I assumed that she had told me the truth. Even though I believed that her child wasn't mine, I still sent her money for him because I knew that she needed it. It wasn't until Kochese showed up at my door out of the blue years later that I knew that she'd lied," Hayden said.

"So why didn't you make it right when he showed up on your doorstep? You had to notice how much he looked like you."

"By the time he showed up, I'd already started my family. I was married, et cetera, and I couldn't process my thoughts fast enough to act. I had a bad habit back then of laughing when I got nervous or uncomfortable, so when he introduced himself, I started to laugh. I can only imagine what was going through his head, you know? I lived with the guilt of knowing that I abandoned my child on the word of his mother. She was sick, Monica, like she literally had mental problems and refused to get help. I worried that she would pass that trait on to our child, but as Effie said, he wasn't mine, so I put them both out of my head. Even as late as his trial my guilt was still strong, like new, and I tried to repay him the best way I could," Hayden said.

"Listen, I can appreciate you taking me on your trip down memory lane, but my major concern now is my sister's safety," Monica said.

"Yes, I know. That's what I've been trying to tell you. You're in danger, and your little sister is in grave danger, Miss Deitrich."

"What do you mean? Danger how though, Mr. Cross?" she asked.

"People aren't always who they appear to be, and sometimes the only way to stay in the game is by using your weaknesses as your strengths. You need to understand that the man you're dealing with, my son, Khalil Cross, is—" he started.

But before he could finish, Monica's cell phone rang. "Excuse me, Mr. Cross. I need to take this call," Monica said.

She listened intently as Cody Roth talked. Another body had been found, alive, the body of someone else Monica knew all too well. She needed to act fast if she was going to capitalize on a live victim. There was no time to waste because this could be just the break she needed for her case. She hung up the phone with Agent Roth and faced Hayden Cross.

"Mr. Cross, we will continue this conversation at a later time. Duty calls. Let's do lunch soon, and we'll continue to talk. I want to know more about your son Khalil."

As Monica rounded the corner leading to the foyer, she nearly collided with Khalil Cross. They locked eyes for a time, each of them searching the other's eyes. She searched for the meaning in his father's words, and he silently wondered when Jasmine would give him the okay to snap Monica's neck.

"How's my sister, Mr. Cross?" Monica asked.

"In good hands like Allstate, shawt."

Monica watched him as he walked away. *Shawt? No, not in a million years . . . couldn't be.*

Chapter 21

PRESSING BUSINESS

In a dark back alley between Market Center Boulevard and Dragon Street, just south of Oak Lawn Avenue, Monica met Agent Roth behind the Green House Tailor Shop of Dallas. It was in the heart of Dallas's Garment District, home to the Market Center and the World Trade Center. The entire alley had been sealed off with yellow tape, and someone had already alerted the media. Monica fought through the throng of reporters and onlookers and made her way to where Agent Roth was congregating with the other agents. Cody Roth hadn't given her many details over the phone. He'd only told her his location and the name of the victim.

The Honorable Judge Frederick T. Bachman had been murdered, but his wife, Alana Bachman, had lived. She was the district attorney for Dallas County and subsequently had teamed up with her

husband on many cases. She had chosen to be the
lead prosecutor during Kochese's trial, and Monica
had come to know her very well. Judge Bachman
had to be in his mid to late sixties, but Alana was
a beautiful and vibrant woman of maybe 40 years
old. She was a redheaded fireball, a hotshot attorney who had been considered a prodigy in the legal
arena. She'd risen fast and her portfolio had an im-
pressive 98 percent conviction rate attached to it.
She'd won so many cases that there were whispers
that Alana Bachman had sold her soul to the devil
much like Keanu Reeve's character in *The Devil's
Advocate*.

The truth of the matter was she had three very
key factors working in her favor. First, she knew
the law inside and out. Second, she was able to
appeal to the men on the average jury because she
was gorgeous and had a body most women would
kill to have. Lastly, she was able to get inside of
the female jurors' heads and have them somehow
live their lives vicariously through her. She was
perhaps one of the strongest women Monica had
ever had the pleasure of meeting, so to hear that
she was barely alive sent a ripple of fear coursing
through her body.

Frederick T. Bachman was another matter altogether. He was a hard-nosed judge who had made
far more enemies than friends, and it would be
hard for Monica to narrow down a motive or suspect, for that matter, in his murder.

"So what are we looking at Roth? How's DA Bachman?" Monica asked.

"She's not well, ma'am. They medevaced her to Parkland Memorial Hospital, and she's in critical condition. Judge Bachman, however, is an entirely different matter."

"What happened?" Monica asked, removing her notepad.

"Ma'am, it would probably serve us best if I just took you inside and showed you the crime scene versus trying to describe it. I don't think that I have an expansive enough vocabulary to explain the gruesomeness of what went on in there," Agent Roth said as he held the yellow tape up for Monica to pass into the warehouse.

As she entered the space, Monica fought the urge to throw up. The smell of burning flesh wafted through the air, invading her nostrils and causing her to wretch. There were rows of sewing stations lined up in the large space that resembled something from a CNBC news story on sweatshops. As they walked, their footsteps echoed against the walls of the Green House, and it gave Monica an uneasy feeling. They walked through a massive opening. It was not really a door, but rather a large shutter that was rolled or unrolled by a chain. The acrid odor was nauseating and sweet, almost like beef searing on a grill, but it was decidedly charred human flesh. The combination of scorched skin, charred muscle tissue, burned hair, and the iron-rich blood in Judge Bachman's body gave the smell permeating throughout the room a coppery, metallic component. As they neared the large industrial-sized garment presses, which also happened to be in neatly formed lines, the aroma grew stronger. At the base of a press near the back of the room, a forensics team gathered samples of the flesh that had melted to the floor beneath the press. Cameras flashed, and young agents eagerly scribbled on notepads in an effort to perhaps be the first to solve the case of the judge who had been murdered.

Monica gasped in horror as they stepped closer, and she witnessed firsthand the shockingly horrid sight before her. Judge Frederick T. Bachman's body had been pressed like a set of new sheets. The image terrified Monica. Someone had taken their time torturing the aging judge. They'd obviously duct taped him, because the tape had burned and melted into his skin. She covered her nose with the sleeve of her London Fog pea coat and stepped closer to examine the body. They'd laid his body flat and pressed his body, liquefying his skin, and then they'd folded his legs, breaking the bones in his knees and feet in the process. Finally they'd contorted his body, breaking his back and crushing his spine until his chest was pointed upward and pressed him again. The steam from the press had dissolved the aging flesh from his face and melted his eyeballs. The skin that hadn't fallen to the floor had been liquefied by the steam and lay in gooey puddles around his deformed corpse. It was a macabre scene, one that Monica was growing increasingly more accustomed to seeing.

"Agent Roth, what the fuck is going on? Is it me or are these murders becoming more grisly with each killing?" Monica asked.

"No, it's not just you, Agent Deitrich. I think we need to get down to the hospital and talk to Mrs. Bachman. We should be there when she wakes up. She may know something about the killer or killers, and if she says that there were two subjects, then we know that we are indeed dealing with a pair of murderers."

"Listen up!" she shouted. "I need all information processed and on my desk as soon as possible."

Agent Cody Roth pushed and shoved the paparazzi aside as he and Monica made their way to his unmarked black Chrysler 300. They sped to the hospital, sirens blaring. Cody Roth zipped in and out of traffic en route to the hospital. There was something connecting the murders, and Monica meant to find out what that connection was.

By the time they reached the hospital, Alana Bachman had been pronounced dead. She'd died from blunt force trauma, and according to Cody Roth, she'd been bludgeoned with a hot iron. They made the trek to the coroner's office, and Monica laughed at Agent Roth's corny observations.

"Why is it that the morgue is always in the basement? And why the hell is it always so cold and dark?" he asked.

The coroner was covering Alana's body with a white sheet when they stepped into the morgue. She lay on a cold stainless-steel slab, lifeless and unfeeling. Monica introduced herself, showed her credentials, and pulled the sheet back to examine Alana's body. She could see the large gash across her forehead and the imprint of an iron where the killer had held the steaming hot iron against her porcelain skin. Monica silently apologized to Mrs. Bachman for not being able to get to her and her husband in time. She found herself also apologizing to Jasmine for letting her down as well. She stared at the blistered, pus-filled print of the iron on the side of Alana's face, and for a second, she saw Jasmine lying there. As clear as day she saw her sister dead on the cold metal slab, and she shuddered. Hayden Cross had made reference to Jasmine being in grave danger. Why would he say that about his own son unless he knew *something*? Her mind ran in a million different directions, and then a frightening thought hit her. She whirled on her heels to face Agent Roth.

"Cody, I need you to follow Khalil Cross. Do not—I repeat, do not—let him out of your sight.

The last time I saw him he was at CrossTech. Start there. I have a few leads I want to follow up on myself. We may be breaking this case sooner than we think," Monica said.

Chapter 22

TO INHERIT THE THRONE

Khalil Cross paced aimlessly in his father's office, trying to process Hayden's actions. "What the fuck did you tell her?" Khalil screamed.

"I didn't tell her shit, I swear, son. You have to send the Deitrich girl home, son. Her sister won't rest until she's home."

"Jasmine isn't going anywhere, man. She loves me and I love her. Hell, even if I wanted her to leave, which I don't, but if I did, she wouldn't leave. Believe it or not, Hayden, it's not easy to walk out on real love," Khalil barked.

"This isn't a conversation that I'm going to have with you, son. You're going to always believe what you want to believe, and there's no changing that. I have done everything in my power to make you happy, and nothing seems to be good enough. I've made you rich beyond your wildest dreams, haven't I? When your brother turned up dead, I didn't hesitate to transfer his stock in CrossTech over to you, did I? Your sister denounced me as her father because of you, for God's sake."

"Bruh, fuck all of that bumping. Listen, I need you to be as honest as possible with me. Shit, you owe me that much. Now did you tell Monica Deitrich anything about me?" Khalil asked, moving closer to Hayden.

Hayden Cross backed up, stumbling over to his desk. "No, I didn't tell her shit, but she's not stupid. How long do you think that this can go on?"

Khalil didn't answer. He smiled sinisterly, showing perfectly white teeth. "Until she pays me."

Khalil exited CrossTech, trying to snuggle deep into the Louis Vuitton scarf wrapped around his neck. The harshly cold wind of the approaching winter whistled and whipped menacingly around his lean frame, threatening to topple him. He reached his white Phantom and ducked inside to escape the elements.

He sat for a long while, allowing the heat to kick in. While he waited, he dialed Jasmine's number. He couldn't believe that his father wanted him to give Jasmine up. She was by far the best thing that had ever happened to him, and he would never let her go. Hayden had made mention of his brother as if mentioning him would somehow evoke some type of emotion. His sister was another matter altogether, though. She'd been a tough cookie, but in the end, she'd ultimately met her demise the same way that his hardheaded brother had.

The truth of the matter was that with them out of the picture, Khalil stood to inherit everything. His father was worth upward of $3 billion, and he wanted it all. That money would finance a very nice lifestyle for him and Jasmine. As soon as Hayden was out of the picture and he received that check, he would give Jasmine half of it. In the event that anything ever happened to him, he wanted to make sure that she would always be taken care of.

"Hey, baby, what are you doing?" he asked.

"Nothing, just driving downtown to handle a little business. What are you doing?"

"Just finished arguing with my lame-ass dad. He's under the impression that I should send you home to your sister," Khalil said.

"I'm grown. Nobody can send me anywhere."

"Yeah, I told him as much. Anyway, what time do you think you'll be home?" he asked.

"Not sure yet. I guess it depends on how long it takes me to take care of my business."

"A'ight, bet. I love you," he said.

"Love you more."

Khalil was an evil man, and he knew it, but his love for Jasmine Deitrich was the real thing. He'd done things in his lifetime that he wasn't proud of, but they had all been necessary.

He put his car in drive and headed north from CrossTech. He drove for a long while. He had loose ends to tie up, and he knew exactly where he needed to start. He loved long drives. They afforded him the opportunity to think, something that he rarely got a chance to do. His next task would be simple and quick. Actually, the quicker the better. If he could make it fast, then he could be home waiting for Jasmine when she made it home.

He pulled up in front of 4651 NW Janette Avenue and parked. He looked around anxiously and ducked into his seat as a pair of headlights passed him slowly. After he was certain that they'd passed, he exited the car and made his way up the long driveway to the house.

The residence was unimposing and rather plain. It was well-lit in the front, but the sides of the house held darkened blind spots perfect for an unauthorized entry, if need be. He reached the front door and rang the doorbell. Minutes later, a middle-aged Spanish man answered the door.

"Well, Mr. Cross, what a pleasant surprise. Come in, come in," he said in perfect English.

Khalil entered the house, giving one last glance toward the road before closing the door behind him.

"What brings you out in this infernal cold, Mr. Cross? Are you having any problems?" he asked.

"Actually, I am, Dr. Carvalho, and I hope that you can help me with it."

"Anything that you need, my boy. Would you like some warm tea?" the doctor asked.

"No, sir, no, thank you. I actually don't have that kind of time. Could we perhaps speak for a minute, and then I'll leave you to finish your night?"

"Sure, let's go into the parlor. I'll have tea there if you don't mind," Dr. Carvalho said.

The sitting room was warm and inviting, but the furniture was hideous. It reminded Khalil of the furniture that one might see in an old movie. A large divan with deep curves and dark wood sat near the fireplace. Its print was the same pretentious white paisley print as the drapes and had begun to stain a moldy yellow due in part to the doctor's insistence of smoking his pipe inside of his home. The walls were covered with floral print wallpaper that did nothing for a room that already suffered from a lack of stylistic attention. Above the fireplace were the heads of animals that Khalil assumed were probably murdered in the name of big game hunting. In a far corner of the room was a large black bear that had undoubtedly met the same fate. The taxidermist had postured Yogi in the most menacing pose that he could muster, but it was clichéd with its outstretched arms, exaggerated claws, and threatening scowl.

"Dr. Carvalho, have you talked to anyone about me?" Khalil asked.

"Noooooo, I am a man of my word. I gave both you and your father my word. I rendered a service, so your medical records are protected."

Khalil stood, unbuttoned his overcoat, and removed a large nickel-plated .45-caliber pistol. He reached into his inside pocket and took out a silencer. Khalil screwed the silencer on the tip of his pistol slowly. "Doc, you have to forgive me if I don't believe you. I mean, men are prone to renege on their word when put under pressure. Would you agree?" he asked.

Dr. Carvalho stood and extended his hands in front of him as if his hands would somehow block the flurry of bullets coming his way if Khalil decided to shoot. "In certain instances, I suppose man's word is fallible, but I assure you that I am not one of those men. My word is as sound as my judgment, and my judgment says that you don't really want to shoot me," the doctor said in a hopeful tone.

Khalil fired a round into the doctor's thigh, and blood leapt from the wound. "Do you still trust your judgment, Doc?" Khalil asked.

Doctor Carvalho didn't respond. He prayed silently to God that this young man let him live. He'd been blessed enough to survive the Ifni War in the Spanish Sahara and Morocco. He was nobody's coward, and he would not beg the mestizo for his life. If he was going to kill him, then there was nothing that he could say to change his mind. "Young man, I've given you my word, and if that's not good enough, I apologize. I forgive you, son, and I want you to take this with you. The Lord is my salvation, and with my last breath, I want to use it to pray with you," Dr. Carvalho said.

"Doc, the Lord doesn't hear my prayers, but I can tell you this: Satan feeds on the souls of the naive and faint at heart," Khalil said.

Dr. Ruben Carvalho opened his mouth to speak in protest, but before he could form a word, Khalil had descended on him and buried his gun deep within his mouth, causing him to choke on his syllables. He pulled the trigger repeatedly until nothing was left of the doctor's face but a mask. The back of his head had been totally obliterated, and his blood and brain matter painted the back of the white couch with the ugly paisley pattern.

Junior Agent Cody Roth backed his black Chrysler into the neighbor's driveway across the street, turned off all his lights, and waited. Less than a half hour later, Khalil Cross emerged and headed toward his car. He didn't appear nervous or anxious. He strolled casually as if he'd just visited an old friend. He spent a few minutes still parked curbside before driving away into the night.

Cody waited until Khalil's taillights were well out of sight before he exited the car. He dashed across the street to the residence where Khalil had just fled. He knocked lightly on the front door and waited. After a short period with no answer, he knocked again, this time more forcefully, and much to his surprise, the door squeaked open a bit. Khalil hadn't secured the door when he'd left. His mistake was Cody's good fortune.

He pushed the door open and went inside. "Hello?" he said. Still no answer. He climbed the stairs just beyond the front door with his gun drawn. He had no idea what he was walking into, but he would be prepared for anything that transpired.

The house was older, maybe built in the sixties when house building was an art form and home builders actually took pride in their craft. The old wood on the stairs creaked and bowed underneath Cody's weight. He tried his best to adjust his eyes to the darkness of the stairway as he reached the top of the stairs. He went from room to room, whispering a nearly inaudible, "Hello," in search of any signs of life. He took the stairs two at a time on his way down.

Cody peeped into the kitchen and walked inside. As he made his way through the lavish kitchen, he was taken aback by the beauty of it. Even in the darkness, he could see the elaborate marble countertops and stainless-steel appliances. The cookware hung from hooks above the island in the middle of the expansive scullery. He was just about to step into the dining area when the sound of a loud screeching, screaming whistle startled him and stopped him in his tracks. He whipped around, gun pointed in the direction from which the sound originated.

The resident had obviously left a teapot on. Cody could feel his heart pounding, threatening to beat through the confines of his chest cavity. He continued his journey through the house until he happened upon a glow. He followed that glow until he reached the sitting room. The slightly graying man appeared to be asleep. The fireplace burned brightly, and he was covered with perhaps one of the ugliest quilts that Cody had ever come across. He tapped the man gently.

"Excuse me, sir? Sir, excuse me." He couldn't believe that anyone slept that hard, but he persisted and shook him harder. There was something wet on the quilt, and it pissed him off something fierce. "Sir!" he shouted.

But before he could get a drier grip, the man's body slumped forward. Cody Roth stumbled backward and fumbled around in the darkness for the nearest light switch. He reached for a lamp that sat on the end table and flicked the switch. Light flooded the room, and then he saw the horrific

sight of the sleeping man. He wasn't asleep at all.
Well, he was asleep, but more so in the eternal
sense. The back of his head was a hollow cavern of
bone fragments and oozed with what was left of his
brain. Cody Roth rummaged through his pocket
nervously in search of his cell phone. He dialed
Monica's number with shaking hands, but it went
to voicemail.

"Hello, you've reached Monica Deitrich. Sorry
that I missed your call. If you leave your name,
number, and a brief message, I'll be sure to get
back to you at my earliest convenience."

Cody's voice trembled as he hurriedly left
Monica a message. "Agent Deitrich, it's Agent
Roth. Listen, I followed Cross like you told me
to. I . . . I followed him to a house out in Highland
Park, and after he left, I went inside, and there's
another body, Monica. He literally blew the man's
brains out. Give me a call as soon as you get this,"
Cody said.

He sat on the divan across from the lifeless body
and stared at it. He placed another call, this time
to the Highland Park Police Department. "Hello,
this is Agent Cody Roth, identification number
7273203291. I'd like to report a homicide. I'm at . . .
hold on . . . I'm at 4651 North West Janette Avenue.
I don't know who did it. I'm following a possible
lead and stumbled upon the scene," he lied and
then added, "Just get your fucking asses out here
and can the bullshit questions!"

He paced the living room and tried to steady his hand enough to light his Marlboro Red cigarette. Once it was lit, he inhaled deeply. He leaned back on the sofa and blew out the semi-white ringlets of mental satisfaction.

Chapter 23

BAIT AND SWITCH

As Monica walked away from her car, her phone began to ring on the front seat. She considered going back to answer it, but she didn't want to lose sight of Jasmine. That was precisely the reason that she'd left her phone in the car in the first place. Jasmine knew her ring tone, and if she heard it, it would surely tip her off that Monica was tailing her.

Monica watched from a distance as Jasmine disappeared into a small boutique in the West End section of downtown Dallas. It was a little late at night to be shopping, but then again, nothing that Jasmine did was conventional. Monica took a seat on top of a newspaper machine directly across the street from the Image Boutique.

Jasmine was greeted by a tall, statuesque, tanned white woman. She was probably in her mid-forties, and she looked like money. She was probably the wife of some overly successful asshole who needed his wife out of the way so that he could play house with one of his daughter's college roommates. Monica laughed at her own prejudgment of the woman. As a profiler, it was her job to assess people, but she never passed judgment.

After a short period of time, Jasmine emerged from the boutique with the woman. They laughed and giggled like old friends, strolling arm in arm down the wide walkway. They headed in the direction away from Monica, but she still had an eye on them. For whatever reason, Jasmine turned quickly and looked in Monica's direction, but Monica dropped her head before Jasmine saw her, or at least she hoped she had. Spying on her little sister was so eighth grade, but she needed to know what was going on with her.

The pair stopped in front of Extreme Tan and Smoothies and went inside. Monica moved down the block to a perch in front of the tanning salon and waited.

She looked at her watch. They'd been inside for almost an hour. Monica walked back to her car and retrieved her phone. She listened to the first three voicemails, and the color drained from her face. If Khalil Cross was involved in a murder, then Jasmine was probably involved as well.

Monica drew her gun and ran toward the tanning salon. As she entered, she nearly slipped in a puddle of blood just beyond the door. There was a trail of blood from where she stood to behind the front counter. Monica followed the smeared crimson droplets to the other side of the counter. There she saw a young woman maybe in her early twenties with a pair of scissors jabbed into her head from beneath her jawline. From the looks of it, she'd tried to leave through the front door, had been stabbed, and then had been left to die behind the counter.

Monica moved stealthily through the salon in search of her sister, but there was no sign of Jasmine. She did, however, happen upon a familiar smell, an odor that was still pasted to her inner nostrils. It was the smell of burning flesh. Monica found the smell in a tanning room shimmering with the iridescent glow of the Sun Select 1400. A loud pop caused Monica to jump. The bulbs had begun to burst from too much power, and the room had started to fill with a thin layer of smoke. Monica covered her nose and searched for the plug to the tanning bed. After it was unplugged, she struggled to untie the shoelaces that someone had used to tie the lid to the base of the bed. It had been tied very securely, so much so that even if the person inside had been able to lift their legs to kick the lid, it would have been of little use. Being in a prone position had most definitely been a huge disadvantage.

Monica lifted the top of the bed and stepped back, fanning the steamy smoke in the process. There before her lay the woman she'd seen walk into the salon with Jasmine earlier. Her skin was burned and had begun to bubble and pus from overexposure to the UV lights. Her face was frozen into a grisly grimace of shocked terror, and a grayish smoky film covered what used to be a set of beautiful blue eyes. The palms of her hands were burned, and her fingerprints were all but nonexistent. She'd undoubtedly panicked and begun beating on the glass that housed the UV bulbs, not understanding that the glass was there as a layer of protection against the heat from the bulbs. Shards of glass were sprinkled on the bed, and some were embedded in her skin, and Monica surmised that she'd been trying to push her way out of the burning bed but to no avail.

Monica examined the contents of the woman's purse. Her name was Madison Keagan, and she was the owner of the boutique that she and Jasmine had come out of before heading to the salon. She examined the body closer and prepared to call the scene in to the authorities when she caught a glimpse of a moving figure from the corner of her eye. She stood and raised her pistol, inching toward the entrance of the room where she was. She stepped into the hallway just in time to see Jasmine burst through the rear exit of the building. Monica looked back toward the front entrance of the salon and then toward the back. For a split second she thought about calling it in, but she needed to speak with her sister first. She couldn't imagine her being interrogated by her higher-ups while she looked on in horror. There would be too many questions, and from experience she knew that she would also be under suspicion. They would want to know how long she had known that her sister was a murderer and if she had helped her in any of her capers.

Monica burst through the back door and looked anxiously up and down the dark alley. She caught sight of a nefarious figure disappearing into what appeared to be an abandoned building less than a block away, and she gave chase. Monica reached the door that Jasmine had fled into and opened it slowly. The broken chain on the door clattered loudly against the metal door, echoing throughout the empty building. Monica reached into the back pocket of her slacks and removed a small penlight. It wasn't much, but it was all that she had. It gave off just enough light for her not to fall and hurt herself.

"Jasmine," Monica whispered. "Jasmine, I know you're in here. Show yourself. We need to talk."

"Jazzy Bell, goddammit, let me help you!" Monica shouted. Her voice reverberated through-out the vacant building, but still there was no answer. She did, however, hear a faint stirring like someone was moving around. She crept forward, inching ever so slowly in the direction from where the sound came. Monica had her gun in one hand and her flashlight in the other. She was terrified of Jasmine, not in a physical sense, but rather in the sense that she wasn't sure what she was capable of. She'd threatened to kill Monica on two occasions, and Monica had taken those threats seriously. Her mind flashed back to her conversation with Mr. Chadwick, and what he'd said made perfect sense.

"Well, kids, it seems to me that you would need to find someone who has the financial means to move around the country with no problems. I think you're looking for a very manipulative man and a very vulnerable woman. I figure any woman who's driven to kill with a man is proba- bly in love with that man. They're either married or very much in love. Look for people who have a reason and enough pain inside to kill and you'll find your murderers,"

Those words kept playing over and over in her head until it threatened to drive her insane. Whatever Jasmine's reason for killing Mrs. Keagan, she saw no correlation between that murder and the redemption killings. Khalil Cross was another matter altogether. The messages that Cody had left her clearly implicated Khalil in a murder, and she had to get to Jasmine before she got back to Khalil.

Monica saw something moving in a corner just beneath an old workshop table. Monica shined her light in that direction and saw Jasmine's pink and white Air Max, with no shoestrings, hiding underneath some old, dirty pieces of cardboard. She'd obviously attempted to hide, but she'd neglected to cover her feet. "Come on out, Jasmine. It's over," Monica said.

But Jasmine didn't move. It was as if she believed that if she pretended not to hear Monica, she'd go away, like a child hiding underneath the covers trying to escape the bogeyman.

"Jasmine, get your ass out here!" Monica shouted before walking over and kicking her in the back. She kicked the cardboard away and froze in shocked disbelief.

Underneath the cardboard lay a homeless woman who reeked of urine and stale alcohol. "Heyyyy, what did I do, lady? I ain't did nuffin!" she slurred.

"Where did you get those shoes? Where the fuck did you get them from?" Monica barked.

"These are mine! A green-eyed angel gave them to me. She said I deserved 'em, and she let me have 'em. I ain't stole nuffin if that's what you thankin'," the old drunk said.

Monica was dumbfounded. She'd been too slow. With all her academy training, she'd been outsmarted by her kid sister. Jasmine had given the bum her shoes knowing that Monica would see them. Somehow she'd realized that it would slow her down enough for her to get away. Monica was angry but at the same time proud of her sister. She was the true definition of mixed emotions. She wanted to find her sister, she wanted justice to be served, but she couldn't help silently praising her, silently cheering her on.

Four blocks away, Jasmine Deitrich started the engine of the BMW 320i that Khalil had purchased for her. She had a clear view of the building that she'd exited, and she watched as Monica emerged from the uninhabited building and looked around in angst. Jasmine took out her cell phone and stared at the picture in her photo gallery. A wicked smile of depraved insanity spread across her beautiful face as she stared at the selfie that she'd taken with Madison Keagan's charred corpse. She went into her mailbox and found Khalil's last text to her and attached the photo. She laughed loudly as she looked at the photo that he'd sent to her. It was a picture of him with his arm around the dead doctor. It was an egregious and horrid photo, but in Jasmine's sick mind, it brought her and her lover closer together.

The street was abandoned save for Monica, who for whatever reason refused to move. The quietness of the night coupled with the steam that rose from beneath the Dallas streets gave off an almost unnerving quality. Jasmine put her car in drive, made a U-turn in the middle of the street, and drove in the opposite direction. She watched Monica through her rearview mirror as she sped off into the cold, dark night.

Chapter 24

PIECES

Monica walked into her apartment hours later and was greeted by an eager Noisy Boy. She was still confused about what had transpired. It made her question everything that she thought she knew about Jasmine. How could her sister take a life so effortlessly? Then again, maybe it wasn't Jasmine at all. Monica wasn't crazy though. She knew who it was. True, they were beautiful women, but their features weren't uniquely their own. It could have been Jasmine's Doppelgänger, her twin, but no, she knew who it was. She didn't want to believe that her little sister, the girl who had looked up to her, the girl who had followed her around so innocently and blindly when they were children, could be capable of committing such a despicable and heinous crime, but Monica knew who it was. Her innocence had been snatched from her at the tender age of 7, and the Buckner Home for Youth had changed her. No longer was she the young, beautiful little girl who loved to have tea parties and play *Monopoly*. No, Buckner had turned Jasmine into a monster, something unfathomable to Monica's comprehension.

Monica spread the folders that Cody Roth had given her out on her dining room table. She stared at the folders as if the details in each would somehow miraculously jump out at her. The folder read: "Victim #3: Samuel Alvarez."

Samuel Alvarez was a 49-year-old real estate mogul who'd made his money by standing on the backs of others. He'd amassed a huge fortune from the many houses and apartment buildings he owned throughout Dallas. Although he'd come from humble beginnings, those beginnings hadn't lasted long. Samuel started out with one ramshackle house on Pennsylvania Avenue when he was 29 years old, and by the eve of his second decade in business, he owned some 200 properties. As Monica read his file, she became more impressed by him. He was the son of an immigrant mother and father who'd sold stolen coffee from the mountains in Colombia. They stole it and sold it until they had enough money to send their only son to the US.

Samuel Alvarez had been investigated by the mayor and the Dallas Housing Authority concerning complaints of substandard living conditions in his properties. Of course Mr. Alvarez had fought tooth and nail, insisting that his properties were up to code. After an inspection from a less-than-reputable inspector and $25,000 in bribe money later, Samuel Alvarez walked out of his hearing fully exonerated and still in business. He was used to the complaints, but as he'd told one tenant, "You should feel fortunate to have a roof over your head. When I was young, we lived in the hills of Colombia with no roof and no running water. This is luxury!"

The most serious of any of the reports Monica noted was an incident in which tenants complained of hearing crackling noises coming from behind the walls of their apartments and the incessant smell of burning wires, complaints that went ignored and that subsequently cost a family of five their lives and displaced a dozen more. The condition of his properties was deplorable, and that was putting it mildly. Children were getting sick regularly because of mold and mildew, not to mention the fact that Mr. Alvarez insisted on using lead-based paint. Families who were no more than three days late with their rent were evicted immediately, sometimes coming home to find their belongings out on the curb. Samuel Alvarez ran a veritable revolving door of low-income, moderately educated tenants, who either didn't know any better or were too poor to hire legal representation.

Because of this, he continued to rake in the dough, living a lavish lifestyle at his tenants' expense.

He had very expensive tastes for a man from such meager beginnings, and for whatever reason he was fascinated with horses. He could often be seen tooling around Dallas in either a Mustang or a Ferrari, both of which had stallions as logos. He had a collection of some of the most expensive horses in the world. Andalusians, Clydesdales, and Arabian horses made up his stable. They were all housed at his ranch, the Bar-A-Ranch, paid for with money from his slums. His horses were his pride and joy, and Mr. Alvarez traded in his humanity in favor of equine devotion. It cost more to house and feed one horse monthly than it did to fix the most costly repair in one of his buildings.

Monica sighed. She hated judging people, but the truth of the matter was that he'd gotten what he deserved. She removed the crime scene photos in an attempt to study them, hoping to see a pattern, hoping to see something out of the norm.

The photos showed Samuel Alvarez hanging. He'd been hanged in the center of his stable of horses for Sea Biscuit and all of his equine friends to see, and as a reminder of his shady business dealings, the killer had sent a message. All of his pockets had been stuffed with rental receipts, all bearing the name of the family who had died in the electrical fire. They read, "Rogers family, no debt owed. Paid in full!"

Monica replaced the contents of the folder and tossed it to the side. She jotted down a few notes and moved to the next file: "Victim #8: Catarina Mulligan."

Reading over her file made Monica sick to her stomach. Mrs. Mulligan was indeed a terrible person. She hadn't stolen anything or murdered anyone, at least not according to the law. She was, however, a thief and a murderer. She was a self-proclaimed aristocrat who hobnobbed with the social elite regularly. Dinner parties and black-tie galas were a normal occurrence for Catarina, mostly due in part to her husband, a Republican senator for the state of Texas, Mitchell Mulligan. He'd afforded her a lifestyle not many women would ever enjoy. Mitchell Mulligan came from "old money," the kind of money that was sustainable for a lifetime.

Catarina Mulligan wasn't always her name though. She'd started life as Catherine Ann Salisbury. She was raised in a small town—a very small town, situated between Amarillo and Lubbock—called Muleshoe, Texas. With a population of fewer than 6,000 residents, Catherine knew that she couldn't live her life there. So at the tender age of 17, she left Muleshoe, leaving her alcoholic mother to raise the 2-year-old son she'd had with Wallaby Snyder. She'd left for the big city, changed her name to Catarina Strickland, and enrolled in nursing school.

Back then there were no cell phones, no Google, no Facebook, and no Instagram. There were none of the trappings of cyber celebrity that make anonymity next to impossible. When she left, her family assumed the worst, and why wouldn't they? She was a 17-year-old girl who had won the local Miss Sandhill Crane pageant for three consecutive years, and she had a beautiful baby boy. She worked at Lorna's Dry Goods part time, and she just happened to have a child by the star pitcher for Muleshoe High School. They figured, who would leave that life voluntarily? There were no massive manhunts in search of Catherine Ann Salisbury. She faded into obscurity, and over time, she faded from the hearts and minds of the local townspeople.

She worked hard and diligently as a candy striper, all the while continuing her education, and by the time she reached 30 years old, she was on the board of directors at Baylor Medical Center in Dallas.

The very first time that Catarina laid eyes on Mitchell Mulligan, she was in love. He wasn't a senator yet of course. He was a state representative who was known for throwing money at his problems rather than facing them head-on. When Mitchell's wealthy parents died, Baylor Medical Center erected a wing in their honor with some of the millions of dollars they'd donated over the years.

It was at the ribbon-cutting ceremony that Catarina first met Mitchell. Catarina saw him as a meal ticket, and Mitchell saw her as a trophy wife. It was a selfish match made in heaven. You see, it wasn't by chance that Catarina had won those pageants. No, she was by all accounts, and simply put, gorgeous. With her milky white skin, flaxen hair, and green catlike eyes, she was perfect for Mitchell's "good old boy next door" image. On one of their many encounters, Mitchell remarked that Catarina's name fit her perfectly because she looked like a cat, and he loved cats.

From that moment on, Catarina was enthralled by cats as well. It started gradually at first: a breast lift here, a tummy tuck there. But after a while, Mitchell's affection all but ceased, and Catarina devised the perfect scheme. Maybe if she looked like a cat, Mitchell would love her again.

And so it began. Catarina Mulligan slowly transformed her features to resemble a furry feline, and as her beauty dwindled, so did her humanity. The love that needed rekindling with Mitchell was irretrievably lost with every swipe of the scalpel and every silicone injection that she received. She had undergone the knife an astonishing forty-two times until she was no longer beautiful. When she looked in the mirror, she saw a deformed shell of a woman who had altered God's gift of beauty in the name of love. Her coworkers whispered about her deformity and silently laughed at the Cat Lady, as they called her.

Monica looked at Catarina's before and after photos and found it hard to believe that it was the same person. She'd most definitely destroyed herself. But Monica couldn't see a connection. Had she been killed because she abandoned her young son? True, it required redemption, but not murder. Monica flipped through the pages frantically in search of a reason.

She happened upon a list of names that Cody Roth had titled "Potential Suspects." Each name was of either a patient waiting for an organ donation or a parent of a child who was waiting. Apparently, according to the people on this list, they'd been deprioritized because of their financial status. Catarina had used her power on the board of directors to push her socialite pals to the front of the donors list. She'd done it for a multitude of reasons, ranging from money to continue her addiction to plastic surgery to gaining favor in the eyes of those who saw her as a grotesque freak. After all the accusations, she'd only been charged once, and the charge hadn't fit the crime.

Crishawn Barber was a beautiful and smart 10-year-old girl when her tiny heart failed, but after two years of being on the donors list, her parents were contacted, telling them that a heart was available. Crishawn's parents rushed her to the hospital, where she was prepped for surgery, but as she lay in the operating room, Catarina Mulligan came in and informed them that there had been a mistake and that there was no heart available. The Barber family begged and pleaded with her but to no avail. Crishawn Barber died a month and a half later on Christmas Day. As she opened her brand-new Easy-Bake Oven, she clutched her frail chest and stepped into the light.

Monica was in tears as she read story after story of families who had buried their children. In total, nineteen children had been approved and then were told that there had been a mistake. There were unconfirmed rumors from Catarina's colleagues that she was involved in an organ ring. She supplied organs to the rich for "revitalization." It was a new craze that allowed rich people the opportunity to be born again. Those who had squandered their lives with hard and fast living were granted a second chance by swapping all of their old organs for new ones supplied by a healthy, but dead, donor. Socialites called her a god, and the poor called her the devil. Catarina didn't care about the poor because she was loved by the rich, revered by the rich, and paid by the rich. A new life with brand-new organs cost upward of $5 million, and the super wealthy were more than willing to pay for the privilege of continuing their high-priced lifestyles. The names and ages of her victims had been included on Cody's list.

Crishawn Barber: 10 years old.

Akinde Myabi: 8 years old.

Morgan Linton: 13 years old.

Desmond Hillson: 17 years old.

Jacobi Paige: 22 years old.

Nyesha Denton: 14 years old.

Miguel Torrez: 11 years old.

And the list went on and on.

When Monica looked at the crime scene photos of Catarina's murder, she understood. She knew why the killer had chosen this method. Each one of Catarina's organs had been meticulously removed and placed on a stainless-steel table in the center of the SPCA building. Each organ had a stick pin in it with a name attached. Crishawn Barber's name was attached to her heart, Nyesha Denton's name was attached to her brain, and so forth and so on. To add insult to injury, the killers had cut out all of her implants and surgically removed the flesh that had been injected with silicone and dumped it into her empty carcass. Then they'd crudely sewn her body back together. After each organ was tagged, he released the feral felines housed in the SPCA building. By the time authorities reached Catarina's rotting corpse, the cats had begun to feast on her exposed organs. Monica read case after case until she was dizzy.

Superheroes & More comic book store owner Jody Dean had been bludgeoned to death with a metal green lantern. He'd been accused of molesting young boys who frequented his store.

Hakeem Jenkins had been accused of snatching purses from the elderly. He'd been skinned alive, and the killer had hot glued his skin over several purses.

L.D. Aryes, descendant of the legendary F.H. Aryes who had perfected the rocking horse that so many people had grown to love, was stuffed and mounted to a rocker. The killer had gone as far as to put a bridle in his mouth and a saddle on his back, turning him into a human rocking horse. He'd been sentenced to two years in federal prison after a jury found him guilty of running a fake charity for cancer-stricken children. He'd only been out of prison for four days when he was murdered.

The entire time that Monica was reading, she was jotting down notes, and she recognized a pattern. *Nah, it couldn't be.* She scanned the rest of the files, and the theory of a redemption killer no longer seemed plausible. The cases held one common thread that outweighed the need for redemption. Monica grabbed her cell phone and scrolled through it frantically until she reached Cody Roth's number.

"Hello."

"Hello, Cody, I need you to meet me at my house. Where are you?" Monica said excitedly.

"I just made it home. I can meet you, but wouldn't the office be closer?"

"Yes, it would, but I have everything right here. Just get here ASAP. And, Cody?"

"Yeah, boss?" he said warily.

"Don't tell anyone where you're going."

Chapter 25

MORE THAN LIFE

Khalil watched Jasmine as she slept peacefully on the massive California king-sized bed. She was nestled deep into the snow-white comforter that lined the huge bed. Khalil slid the covers back and watched the soft, rhythmic heave of her breathing. She was perfect in every way, from the soft contours of her body to the smoothness of her skin. Khalil bathed in her nakedness and breathed in her essence. He reveled in the wondrous love that he'd found in a woman who transcended everything that he expected in a woman. Her nature was loving toward him, she was intelligent, and her imagination knew no bounds. They had made love a total of five times, and each episode had been more intense than the last. He had awakened her inner freak, and Jasmine's sex drive was insatiable.

As he watched her sleep, he couldn't believe that moments earlier he was deep inside of her, stroking the very essence of her being. They'd established a connection, a bond that would never be broken. Jasmine had been on top of Khalil, riding him with her hands pressed firmly against his chest. Her back was arched, and her head was tilted back in sexual bliss. Her eyes rolled to the back of her head, and she shuddered from excitement as Khalil grabbed her waist and thrust into her vigorously. She'd taken his hands and pinned them to the bed, looked into his eyes, and kissed him deeply. Jasmine had bitten his lip until it bled, and when Khalil asked her why, she'd replied innocently, "Because I wanted to taste you." She'd looked into his eyes and asked him, "Am I your first, Khalil?"

"No, baby, unfortunately, you're not," he'd replied.

"Will I be your last, Khalil?" she asked, still riding his cock.

"Indeed, my love, there will never be another," he'd said.

He pulled her close and buried himself deep within her, and when she remarked how she could feel him swelling inside of her, he lost his mind. As he climaxed, so did she, spraying her love onto his pelvis and then almost immediately drifting off to sleep. They fit together like a hand and glove. His manhood filled her completely, and it only served to make him love her more. He'd broken her in, and she was all his, but before they went any further, Jasmine would need to know the truth.

Khalil roused Jasmine gently, but she merely stirred and shifted her lithe body.

"Hey, sleepyhead," he said, but again she shifted, this time raising her ass a bit, exposing the soft, wet pinkness of her juice box.

He knew exactly how to wake her up. He turned Jasmine over onto her back and kissed her gently. Khalil guided his stiffness to her moisture and stopped just short of thrusting it inside of her. He propped her legs into the folds of his arms and slid into her slowly. Jasmine gasped, and her eyes popped open. Even though she was still half asleep, she slid back and forth, meeting each of Khalil's thrusts until the friction of his pubic hair rubbing her clit and the sensation of magnificence plunging inside of her was too much to bear.

"Oh, my God, baby. I'm about . . . to . . . cum . . . already!" she screamed.

Just as her body began to quiver from her approaching orgasm, Khalil pulled out of Jasmine, rocked her legs back, and sucked her clitoris roughly. She screamed and tried to wiggle out of his clutches, but he was holding on too tight. He sucked until he could taste her orgasmic juices before finally burying his index finger inside of her tight hole. With every whimper and muscular clench, Jasmine released a gusher of seminal fluids. When Khalil finally freed her, she felt both dizzy and drained.

"Why do you do me like that, baby?" she asked.

"Because I'm your man, and I have to put my stamp on that pussy so that you know what it is."

"Sometimes when I hear you speak, it makes me think you're not white at all," she said jokingly.

"You'd be surprised. But seriously, I need you to know that I'll always be here for you no matter what, so between you lying there looking all sexy and me trying to show you how much I love you, it's easy to put in that work."

Jasmine had tears in her eyes, but not from sadness. After a lifetime of pain, she'd found someone who loved her unconditionally, someone who didn't judge and who actually embraced her inner flaws.

"I love you more than life, Khalil."

"I know, baby, I know, and I love you more. Now get up and get dressed. I want to show you something," he said, slapping her on her ass playfully.

An hour later they were on the road and headed toward Rockwall, Texas. As they drove across I-30 it began to rain, merely pelting the windshield at first and then building to a cataclysmic chorus of roaring deluge. Khalil and Jasmine did not speak, but rather they enjoyed the warm ambience of the fading sun. Between the gray skies and torrential rains, the raindrops cast a silvery glow over the fast-rising lake. The clouds hung low, threatening to expel yet another oversaturated downpour. Ironically, Tony! Toni! Toné! sang "It Never Rains (In Southern California)" across the radio airwaves.

Khalil exited I-30 and turned along what was usually a dusty gravel road. The rain, however, had turned the road into a gravelly mix of grayish white pasty mud. The ride was long, and it seemed that just as quickly as it had started, the rain had been stifled, giving way to the approaching dusk. Even with the durability of Khalil's Dodge pickup truck, they could both feel the bumpiness of the narrow road. Jasmine stared out of the tinted truck window and squinted as they approached a decrepit sign hanging on for dear life. They crossed a set of rickety railroad tracks, and Khalil heard Jasmine chuckle.

"What's so funny, baby?" he asked.

"That sign back there said, 'Short Line Railroad.'"

Khalil didn't reply, although he smiled gaily at Jasmine's childlike candor.

Thick canopies of trees lined the already-dark road, and as their destination drew near, twilight played peekaboo over the landscape of forestry and prairie. A thick blanket of steam lay across the marshlands leading to the road where Khalil's farmhouse sat situated beyond the woods. Darkness fell quickly as they turned onto the long road leading to his home. Jasmine lowered her window and allowed the crispness of the cold autumn wind to whip into the car and bathe her with its wintry chill. She breathed in deep, absorbing the smell of her autumn surroundings. The earthy, musty smell of falling leaves wafted through the air, hanging in her nostrils. Jasmine marveled at the plethora of smells that floated in the air. She leaned closer to the window and closed her eyes, trying to differentiate the many aromas that were comingling. There was the smell of slightly decaying leaves and rotting wood, and the sticky sweet smell of freezing sap from the nearby bigtooth maple trees mixed with the aromas of the prickly smell of Afghan pines, creating an almost festive smell of an encroaching winter. The earthen scent of packed undergrowth contrasted with the musky smell of wet leaves after a dark, sweet rain like a box of chocolates in the company of a pile of dirty laundry. As the winds of fall howled through the tall pines, the needles whipped against each other and released the heavenly scent of pine. The pungent smell of smoke came from piles of burning leaves, bonfires, or maybe an early fire in the fireplace from the sparse neighbors in the rural neighborhood. The acrid odor of chicken litter or cow manure that had been spread on plowed fields to enrich the soil drifted into the mix of smells and caused Jasmine to roll up her window.

In the clearing ahead of them sat an old house that had seen better days. It looked abandoned except for a dim light that bounced and flickered as they got closer. Khalil pulled into a barn that was off to the side of the house and parked.

"This place looks scary, babe. Where are we?" Jasmine asked nervously.

"You'll see. Follow me."

Khalil stepped out of the car and hurried to the passenger's side to open Jasmine's door. She loved that about Khalil. He was all about chivalry and good manners, an art that seemed to be long since lost on the average man. It was a stark contrast to the man she knew he *could* be. He led her to the center of the barn and lit a lantern. As the soft light flooded the room, a cold chill passed through Jasmine's body. Just beyond the iridescent light she saw something that startled her, but she was too mature to succumb to such childlike fears. She had always nurtured an image of herself, and in this image she was tough and resilient. Jasmine Deitrich had been tempered by terror at an early age, seasoned by grief, and qualified by experience to handle whatever fate threw at her.

Two bodies sat in what appeared to be antique thrones. A white man and woman who looked to be in their early to mid-twenties sat desiccated upon their perches. Behind them, flanking their shoulders, their bones had been loutishly fused back together in an attempt to create skeletal watchers. They'd been posed in such a way that they looked like guardians over their earthly flesh. Jasmine turned to Khalil. Her eyes searched his for answers to the many questions that flooded her mind. She opened her mouth to speak, but she didn't speak. She simply turned back to the corpses and stared. Khalil walked up behind her and slipped his arms around her waist.

"Baby, this is my brother, Malcolm Cross, and my sister, Christina Cross. Do you know why I've done this?" he asked.

"No, baby, I have no idea," she said, turning to face him. His hands rested on her firm backside as he gazed into her gorgeous green eyes.

"My brother and sister didn't accept me because we have different mothers. Their mother died some time ago, and they were set to inherit all that my father had worked for. I hated them for the way that they looked at me, like I was the outsider, like I was nobody. I deserve to be recognized as a Cross. It's my birthright!" he screamed. He took her hand and led her across the hundred-foot span of land that separated the barn from the house, and he unlocked the door. "Watch your step, baby girl," he said.

Silvery slivers of moonlight sliced their way through openings in the heavy drapes that lined the windows. Khalil flicked a light switch, and the house was immediately illuminated with bright lights. Jasmine looked around, not quite sure where she was. She could tell that the house was older, and the look of it reminded her of the log cabins she'd seen on television. Dark brown wood beams lined the ceiling and ran seamlessly into the wood paneled walls. Although meager, the furnishings in the home seemed antique but well taken care of. The couch was colossal, nearly stretching from one end of the living room to the other. The paintings that hung on the wall appeared oddly out of place considering the man Khalil Cross was. They were largely religious in nature, depicting the more famous scenes in the Bible. On the wall in front of her was a life-sized painting of a black Jesus Christ being tempted by a white Satan. There was also a life-sized painting of the betrayal of Jesus. It showed a black Jesus being kissed on the cheek by a white Judas, who, subsequently, just happened to be taking a bag of silver as he committed his betrayal.

Khalil kicked off his shoes and walked to the bar. "Would you like a drink, babe?" Khalil asked.

"No, I'm okay."

"Baby, I really think you need a drink. I need to talk to you about some things, and you'll probably need a drink by the time I'm finished," Khalil said.

"I don't want any liquor, but I will take hot tea if you have it."

He poured himself cognac over ice and put an old-style tea kettle on an open fire, and then he went outside and disappeared around the side of the house. Jasmine stood in the doorway, leaning against the doorjamb and waiting for Khalil to return. Behind her the tea kettle whistled and sputtered. Jasmine went into the kitchen and prepared a cup of warm tea. She sipped the auburn-colored liquid and instantly felt warmth deep in the pit of her bowels.

Khalil returned with his arms filled with small logs of precut firewood. Jasmine backed up and closed the door behind him. Again she sipped from her glass of the toasty libation and felt the rush of balminess take hold. Jasmine took a seat on the massive couch and covered herself with Khalil's jacket. She watched him intently as he tossed the wood into the fireplace and started the fire. The wood sizzled and crackled as it absorbed and evaporated the moisture caused by the midday showers. Beautiful shades of orange and yellows leapt and pranced about the inglenook. Khalil disappeared into a back room and then joined Jasmine on the couch. He took her into his arms and handed her a bundle of photos held together by a rubber band.

"What are these pictures of, baby?" Jasmine asked.

Khalil took the photos from Jasmine and spread them out across the table. "Baby, I'm not who you think I am."

"I don't care who you are, Khalil. I love you unconditionally, so nothing you've done matters to me."

"Look at the pictures, Jasmine," he said.

Jasmine took the photos and looked through them. The first picture was of a young black woman and a handsome white man. He looked a lot like Khalil. In the picture, the pair was on a lake, and they appeared to be happy. In the second picture, a tall young man with cornrows held a snow-white puppy in his arms. He was dressed in white and baby blue with a platinum chain on that read, "King." The third picture showed the same young man with a group of about twenty other people. They all surrounded him like he was their leader or something. Jasmine focused on the fourth picture. It was a photo of the young man, Bird, and Monica. Her head snapped toward Khalil and then back to the photo. The last few pictures were of the same guy dressed in a white linen pants set, standing next to Monica in a white sundress. They appeared to be on a yacht or a cruise ship, and they also looked like they'd just been married.

Jasmine was confused. She didn't understand why or how Khalil had pictures of Bird or her sister. "I . . . I don't understand, baby. What's going on?" Jasmine asked.

"I know you don't, and I'm going to try my best to explain the situation in its entirety." Khalil downed his drink and went to the bar to pour another. His back was still turned when he started to speak to Jasmine. "What I'm about to tell you is going to sound somewhat unbelievable, but I need you to know that I am being completely honest, and if you don't want to see me after I'm done, I'll understand. I wasn't always who I am now. I came from the slums, Jasmine. True, Hayden Cross is my father, but I'm a black man trapped in a white man's world."

"Stop being silly, baby. You're tanned, yeah, but you're a white boy. Accept that and move on," Jasmine said.

But Khalil ignored her comment and continued. "My mother was a black woman named Evelyn, and of course you know who my father is. He abandoned me and my mother when I was a kid, and I didn't see him again until I was older. Even then he laughed and slammed the door in my face when I told him who I was. I was a very bad person, but all of that changed when I met your sister. I loved her, Jasmine, I bared my soul to her, and she stepped on it. Bird did the exact same thing," he said reflectively.

"I'm confused. What the fuck do you mean, you loved my sister?"

"Does Monica ever talk to you about her cases? Did she ever tell you how she and Bird met or where she got Noisy Boy?" Khalil asked.

"No, she never talks about her cases. She says that she doesn't want to bring her work home, so I don't ask, and she doesn't talk about it."

"Everyone thought that I was dead, but I wasn't," he said.

"Babe, please tell me what the fuck is going on! I'm so lost and so confused right now that it's not even funny," Jasmine said.

"My name isn't Khalil Cross, baby. My name is Kochese Mills. I was a hustler on those Dallas streets for a long time until your sister came along. She made me fall in love with her, and then she busted me and tried to have me sent away forever," he said heatedly.

"My sister doesn't even like white boys."

"I told you before, I'm not a white boy. I am as black as you are, a product of a biracial relationship," he said.

"This doesn't make sense to me. If she busted you, then why aren't you in jail?"

"While I was in jail, my father came to me and gave me a gun. He told me to shoot myself, and at first I thought he was trying to be funny or something, but just before I went up on the stand, my lawyer whispered in my ear. He said that my father needed for it to look like a suicide and that if I could pull it off, I'd be a free man. So I did it. I shot myself in the chin, but I pointed the gun so that the bullet would exit. Damn near everyone in the courtroom was in on it, from my attorney to the bailiffs. They ushered me out of there into an ambulance that my father had hired. As far as the law and the world knew, Kochese Mills was dead and the case was over. My dad hired a top-notch plastic surgeon to change me into who you see," he said.

Jasmine's mind was blown, but it didn't change a thing. She loved Khalil or Kochese or whatever his name was, and she didn't give a damn who didn't like it. Maybe Monica knew that Khalil was really Kochese and that was the reason she was so adamant about her not seeing him. Maybe she wanted him back or wanted him all to herself. Whatever the case, she wouldn't leave him. She had made him a promise, and she intended to keep it. "How did he turn you into a white boy, though? Why wouldn't you choose to be black?" Jasmine asked out of curiosity.

"I asked my father the same thing, and his reply was that he needed me to blend in seamlessly and he wanted me to help him run CrossTech."

"So basically you used me? You used me to get back at my sister?" Jasmine asked. She felt her anger growing, and rage surged through her body.

"I'm not going to sit here and lie to you, baby. Come, let me show you something."

He took her hand and led her into the room where the surveillance monitors were.

"When I first met you, we met under false pretenses. I only wanted to keep an eye on Monica and make her life a living hell. I watched you two for a long time, you especially. Even when I met you in the park, I still had in my mind that I would just fuck you just to get back at Monica. That is, until I found out that we were just alike, two peas in a pod. We were both damaged goods, and I fell for you hard. I fell in love with every ounce of you. I tried to imagine my life without you in it, and it made my heart hurt. That's when I knew. I knew that this love was something that I never wanted to lose. So no, I didn't use you. I've helped you more than hurt you. Remember when you told me about those men who hurt you? I killed two of those men many, many years ago, baby. Michael Ross and Jappy died by my hand. Dirt Bag is still alive, and I'm saving him just for you," he said.

On the screen in front of them, Monica was opening the front door for Cody Roth. On another screen, Bird was in his living room, feeding Millie and watching television, and on yet another screen, Hayden Cross was sitting in his office, working on his computer and taking swigs from a Grey Goose bottle.

Jasmine focused her attention back on the monitor with Monica and Cody on it. "Can you turn up the volume on these or is it just pictures?" Jasmine asked.

Khalil flipped a switch, and Monica's voice flooded the small speakers.

"Come in, Cody. Let me grab my purse, and then we'll be on our way," Monica said.

"I thought what we needed was here, ma'am."

"It is, but we need to pay someone a visit. Then we'll come back, and I'll explain everything to you," she said.

Khalil flipped the switch off as Monica and Cody exited her place. Noisy Boy sat by the door looking at it as if Monica had unknowingly forgotten to take him with her.

"How did Monica make Noisy Boy so loyal to her? He was my best friend, you know?" he said.

"I'm your best friend now, baby, and I will never leave you. It's funny, but I don't even know what to call you now. I mean, it's obvious that Khalil isn't your name. What would you like me to call you?"

"You can call me Kochese, but I prefer King Kochese!"

"Okay, King Kochese it is. I love you, and I will die before I let anything happen to you. That's my word. Some women don't know a good thing when they have it, and some women know that they have a good thing and still abuse it, baby. Luckily, I'm neither one of those women," Jasmine said as she threw her arms around Kochese's neck and kissed him deeply.

They made love in front of the fireplace as their bodies meshed into a singular molecule of carnal fulfillment.

Chapter 26

WOODEN CROWN

"Make a right onto Oak Lawn," Monica said.

"Roger that, but could you tell me where we're headed?"

"It's late, but if I know Hayden Cross the way I think I do, he's still working. We need to get to CrossTech because I need answers, and for some strange reason, I think that Mr. Cross can help us," she said.

"It's your play. I'll follow your lead, boss. Can I ask you something?"

"Sure."

"Why did you ask me to come alone instead of assembling the entire team?" Cody asked inquisitively.

Monica thought for a long while before she could form the thoughts in her head to explain to him why she'd chosen that route. Growing up, she'd been told often by Pop Pop that honesty was the best policy, and she believed it, but she also didn't want to jeopardize her standing with the agency. Cody Roth was different though. She was almost certain that he wouldn't blow the whistle on her, so she would just have to take a chance. "Cody, listen, some of the things I found in those files have led me to believe that my sister might be involved."

Agent Roth stared at her for an eternity before blaring horns caused him to swerve and turn his attention back to the road. "Are you serious? When did you figure this out, Agent?"

"I'm not even sure yet, so I really haven't *figured* anything out yet. There is some crazy shit going on, and I'm not sure how to handle it. What I do know is that I don't want the Feds running down on my sister before I get a chance to talk to her if she is involved, you know?" Monica said.

Cody nodded and made the right turn onto Oak Lawn Avenue. Moments later, they were pulling into the parking lot of CrossTech. Cody parked close to the front entrance and turned the car off. He turned to Monica. "No matter what this guy says, ma'am, I'm still going to follow your lead."

Monica nodded. She really liked Agent Roth. He was thorough and loyal, two characteristics of a good agent. She removed her cell phone and dialed Hayden Cross's number, and he answered on the first ring.

"Hello, Agent Deitrich, how might I be of assistance?" he queried.

"I'm downstairs. I was wondering if we might continue our conversation. I have some questions that I really need you to clear up."

Monica's phone went silent. She feared that Hayden had perhaps ended their call as a way of telling her to get lost, but less than five minutes later, as Monica and Cody made their way back to his car, Hayden Cross appeared and opened the large glass doors of the CrossTech building. He ushered them inside and greeted them warmly. Rather than going up to his office, he showed them to the company auditorium that was affectionately called the Slaughterhouse. Their voices boomed and echoed from wall to wall in the large empty space, but Hayden wasn't worried. He'd long since sent all of his employees home for the night.

Even though they had complete privacy, Monica still tried her hardest to keep her voice at a minimum. "Mr. Cross, I need you to tell me everything that you can about your son Khalil. I have reason to believe that he and Jasmine are caught up in a very serious situation," Monica said.

"Agent Deitrich, I'm going to keep this short and sweet. I honestly believe that you're right. My son and Jasmine are two peas in a pod. What you need to know is that I believe that my son genuinely loves your sister."

"Yeah, I can believe that, but that doesn't give them any right to break the law," Monica said.

Agent Roth took a small notepad from the inside pocket of his blazer and flipped it open.

"I know that my time is near, Monica. May I call you Monica? I know my time is coming, and you'll more than likely arrest me, but I don't give a shit. I've led a nice life, and I tried to be a good person," he said. He watched Monica closely, trying to discern where her emotions were. He needed her to be an agent at that moment and not a concerned sister. "Monica, Khalil isn't who you think he is. He's my son, true, but his name isn't Khalil. Khalil is really Kochese."

"Yeah, right! Get the fuck out of here. I saw Kochese kill himself. I saw him lying on a cold slab in the morgue," Monica reasoned. She wasn't sure whether she was trying to convince Hayden or trying to convince herself, but she knew what she'd witnessed.

"What did you *really* see though, Monica? You saw Kochese shoot himself, not kill himself. Yes, you saw him lying on a cold table, true, but you were on the other side of the glass. Did you touch him? Did you feel his cold dead skin? No, you didn't, Monica. You see, it was all a ruse, a ploy to give my son a new life, a life that I denied him as a child."

Monica's head swam with questions and disbelief. She felt dizzy and sick to her stomach. Kochese was alive, and not only alive, but he was fucking her sister. She knew what he was capable of, and she knew how dangerous he was.

Wait a minute. "Hayden, how can Khalil and Kochese be one and the same? I've talked to Khalil. I've met him. He's a white boy, through and through, from his hair to his thin-ass lips. How do you explain that?"

"Agent Deitrich, I pride myself on being a man who covers all bases. I hired one of the best, if not *the* best, plastic surgeons in the world. Dr. Ruben Carvalho changed Kochese into what I wanted him to be, and that was a white man I could easily assimilate into my world. I'm a billionaire, for God's sake. Do you think that it would be hard for me to have or do anything that I freaking wanted? Do you have any idea what I do when I wake up in the mornings, Agent Deitrich?" Hayden asked.

"No, I don't, Mr. Cross. What do you do?"

"Any fucking thing that I want to do! That's another perk of being a billionaire," he said.

"Wait a minute. Did you say Dr. Ruben Carvalho? That's the name of the doctor killed by Khalil, the one that I was telling you about, Agent Deitrich," Agent Roth said.

"If that's the case, then that means Kochese is getting rid of all loose ends. Agent Deitrich, you were married to this lunatic, so you know how he thinks. He's my son, but I don't really know him. You have to find him before he hurts someone. If he hurts your sister, I'll never forgive myself," Hayden said.

"Why would you help him escape justice, Mr. Cross? He's a very dangerous man," Monica said.

"I know that now, but in all honesty, I thought that he'd change if given a second chance."

"Sounds to me like he has a chip on his shoulder and he's not going to rest until he spills the blood of everyone who knows his secret," Cody said.

"Yeah, it sounds that way, Cody. Mr. Cross, you once said that I would have to learn to use my weaknesses as my strengths to play the game. What did you mean by that?" Monica asked curiously.

"I meant it from a businessman's standpoint, but in your case, Kochese almost cost you your position in the DEA, and now Jasmine has you in emotional turmoil. Your loving nature is your weakness. It's also a strength, because the two people you seek also happen to be the two people you love the most. You will need to use that same love to beat them at their own game, because you perhaps know them better than they know themselves," Hayden said.

Chapter 27

TRUE 2 THE GAME

Monica thought about what Mr. Cross said. *A game*. But what kind of game? She had a hunch, but if she was wrong, then it had the potential to cost another life. She gazed from the window of the Chrysler, watching the blur of asphalt and city lights. She had to figure out a way to present her findings to Cody without him walking away thinking that she was completely insane.

A game.

What kind of game could they play that would allow such gruesome and grisly murders? And if it was a game, then what was the endgame?

The endgame.

If Jasmine and Kochese were indeed her pair of killers *and* if her hunch was right, then that would mean that Jasmine was in control, *not* Kochese. She was still lost in her thoughts when Cody informed her that they'd arrived at her place.

"Agent Roth, I know that your first loyalty is to the Bureau, but I'm asking for a little bit of that loyalty for myself. If we find my sister to be involved in this madness, I want you to promise me that you'll let me bring her in," Monica pleaded.

Agent Roth nodded his head in agreement. True, he was loyal to the Bureau first, but he had to take care of his partner. He chided himself, because for whatever reason, he was deathly afraid of letting Monica Deitrich down.

Once inside, Monica wasted little time diving into her theory. She was convinced that she was on to something. It was a matter of convincing Cody that worried her.

Unbeknownst to her, she and Cody weren't the only ones privy to their conversation. King Kochese and Jasmine sat quietly behind the surveillance screen of Kochese's lodge house.

"Agent Roth, what I'm about to tell you is going to seem farfetched and highly improbable, but hear me out. I really think I'm on to something here," Monica said. She handed Cody a case file and launched into her spiel. "The first murder that got us involved in this case was Agent Krutcher, aka Drak. He was murdered as a way of drawing us in."

"Yeah, but he wasn't first. Your friend Bird's wife and sister were first," Agent Roth interrupted her.

"For the sake of theory, hear me out. Let's say that he was first on a federal level, and the killers did it to draw us in," she said.

"Okay, I'm listening," Cody said attentively.

"He was murdered, and his body was drained into a top hat."

"Okay," Cody said, still not seeing a point.

Monica walked to a dry-erase board she'd set up in the open space of the living room and wrote the words "top hat." She tossed another file at him. "This slimeball Craig Jeffries, aka Toot, was killed, chopped up, and placed in a wheelbarrow," she said. On the dry-erase board, she wrote the word "wheelbarrow." File after file she tossed to Cody Roth. "Look at this guy's name, Chance Thimble," she said, and she wrote on her board "Chance, thimble." "Are you getting it yet?" she said excitedly.

Cody was still trying to make the connection, and Monica, feeling that she was on a roll, continued her barrage of information. "Jody Dean was killed with a lantern. Chance Thimble was killed at Water Works Day Spa, and large needles were stuck in his body like a thimble. Samuel Alvarez was hanged in a stable with horses. Catarina Mulligan, the Cat Lady, was placed in the SPCA with feral cats to feed on her body. The Bachmans were killed in the Green House with irons. Alyssa Schumacher, aka Shoe, was killed heinously. Hakeem Jenkins was skinned and turned into purses, and L.D. Aryes was turned into a human rocking horse. John La Rue was killed on a battleship, his battleship tattoo was cut off his body, and two hundred dollars was left in the crown of his skull. Get it? 'Do not pass Go. Do not collect two hundred dollars.' Let's not forget my friend and mentor Senior Agent Muldoon was killed in front of us, but more importantly in front of a sign that read, 'free parking,'" Monica said, winded.

She turned to the board and scribbled furiously, and by the time she was finished, she had her board sectioned into three columns.

> *Pieces: top hat, wheelbarrow, shoe, green house, battleship, iron, cat*
> *Cards/spaces: Chance, waterworks, free parking*
> *Streets: Atlantic Avenue*

Monica waited for Cody, but he still seemed to be clueless. "Remember Mr. Cross kept making mention of a game, the game, et cetera? Don't you see what all of these things have in common?" Monica urged. "All of these pieces fit, Cody. The iron, the purse, the top hat, they're all pieces from the game *Monopoly!*" she screamed.

"Yeah, I see the pieces, but I don't know if I buy the whole *Monopoly* theory," he said. "It's possible, but what happened to the dog? What happened to the car? Some of these pieces I've never seen in a *Monopoly* game."

"That's because you're not a *Monopoly* expert. Listen, I spent countless hours playing *Monopoly* with my family. Some of these pieces have been discontinued, some of them were added later, and some of them come only in deluxe sets. There is no game that my sister would rather play than *Monopoly,* and I'm willing to bet my life that she's behind this sadistic and twisted game of human-life *Monopoly,*" Monica barked.

"Okay, so let's suppose that your theory is true. What next?"

"Well, if they stay true to form, then we still have five pieces left. There's a sack of money, a cannon, a train, the racecar, and the dog. That's assuming that they're only using current pieces. Like I said, some of the pieces that they are using are retired pieces. That's what makes me think that Jasmine is involved. She knows that game better than anyone," Monica said.

"Okay, but what if they switch to more streets or cards or railroads or utilities? This crap could go on indefinitely, ma'am."

"Let's hope that we can catch them before it gets to that point, Cody, because if we don't find them, then God be with us all," Monica said.

Chapter 28

SNIPS AND SNAILS AND PUPPY DOG TAILS

Anna Beth La Rue had two loves: Starbucks coffee and her nine-month-old Scottie named Meatball. It was a gift from her ex-boyfriend Jason, and after a tumultuous breakup, they'd agreed that Meatball was better off with Anna Beth. She was still traumatized by the killing of her father, but she was trying desperately to pick up the pieces. Every day was a struggle, and she was always nervous because the green-eyed lady had warned her not to go to the authorities. But she hadn't listened. As soon as she'd been released, she'd gone directly to the authorities and spilled the beans.

Before she left her apartment, she checked through the peephole. While she was at the gym, she watched the doors, and walking down the street was virtually impossible because every few minutes she was looking over her shoulder. Her entire life was a nervous wreck, but Anna Beth had no idea how to reclaim her life.

She strolled along Pennsylvania Avenue after she'd finished her shift at Panera Bread, headed toward her apartment. The old DEA agent, Muldoon, whom she'd talked to when her father was murdered, had promised to keep her informed when they caught her father's killer, but she hadn't heard from him. She had no idea that Muldoon had been chopped into two pieces. Had she known, it would have really been cause for alarm.

Kochese and Jasmine sat inside Anna Beth's semi-plush apartment, waiting for her to arrive. One of the few arguments that Jasmine and Kochese had ever really had involved Anna Beth and Jasmine's reluctance to kill the young girl. She hadn't seen the need to kill Anna Beth because she didn't see her as a threat, but Kochese saw her as a loose end. Jasmine also argued that, from what they'd just heard, Monica was well aware of who the killers were, so why kill a young lady with her whole life ahead of her? Much to her chagrin, Kochese had totally disagreed. Anna Beth La Rue was disobedient, and even after she'd been warned not to, she still chose to go to the authorities. Therefore, she needed to be disciplined.

Kochese snatched a lamp from a nearby end table and ripped its cord from the base. He disappeared into the bathroom, started a bath, and returned a few seconds later. Jasmine watched him attentively as she listened to the slow, melodic drip of the running water. She fingered the long, stiletto-style knife that she had, playfully sticking the tip of her finger. As they waited, Jasmine could hear the water running over the side of the tub, splashing onto the tile floor. The overfill drain slurped thirstily, trying its hardest to drink the excess water, but to no avail. She leaned forward on the couch and craned her neck in the direction of the bathroom. She could see the water pouring out onto the floor, inching slowly toward the living room, where they waited. Jasmine looked at Kochese, who was lounging in the lush leather chair with his leg thrown over one arm of the chair. She was looking at him as if he should get up to stop the bath, but he didn't move. He continued to sit stoically, staring into outer space, twirling his chrome .45-caliber pistol much like a cowboy might in the Wild West.

Sensing Jasmine's irritation with the running water, Kochese stood, placed his gun on the seat, and went to turn the water off. Jasmine silently smiled a seal of approval. It seemed as though there was no limit to how far he would go to keep her happy. It was true that it was indeed the small things that counted the most. His small act of kindness, his miniscule gesture, made Jasmine want to give Kochese even more of herself. Jasmine's mind didn't work like most people's minds, and she was okay with that. In her mind, in order to give Kochese what he deserved for his extended gratitude, she would need to concede to his blood lust. "Baby, if you really want to kill her, you can," she said.

"Nah. You said she doesn't deserve it, so I'm good."

"No, really, I want you to. You're drained. You need to refuel, baby. Just kill her," Jasmine pleaded.

"Are you sure? Because I really want to."

"Yes, I'm sure. Enjoy it and savor it because I have a surprise for you when you're done," she teased.

"Really? What is it?"

"You'll have to wait to find out. If I told you, then it wouldn't be a surprise, would it?" she asked.

The sound of keys turning in the lock drew them from their revelry. Anna Beth stepped into her apartment and felt the urge to urinate. Her knees grew weak, and she buckled underneath the weight of Kochese and Jasmine's intrusive violation. Anna Beth subconsciously squeezed Meatball, and she continued to constrict the small terrier until he yipped from the pain. Before she had a chance to contest, Jasmine stood and snatched the puppy from her arms.

"Close the door, Anna Beth," Jasmine ordered.

Anna Beth did as she was told, and Jasmine noticed that her eyes darted from Jasmine's eyes to her precious pooch's eyes. "I won't hurt her as long as you do what you're told," Jasmine said.

"She is a he, and what the fuck are you doing in my place?" she demanded. They'd already killed her father, and she had gone to the authorities, true, but only after she'd gotten a call from NCIS. Anna Beth had been reluctant to tell them what she knew, but they'd convinced her. She was terrified, and it was plainly visible. "The Feds have already come to my place, threatening to throw me in jail if I don't cooperate. Made me feel like shit, like I was a bad person for letting my father's murderers go free. And you know what? I wholeheartedly agreed with them. So if you're going to kill me, go ahead and kill me! I hope you both burn in hell!" she screamed.

"Don't get slick, bitch! You're going to die soon enough, so why rush it?" Kochese spat incredulously.

Anna Beth's heart raced, thumping in her chest violently. She silently wondered whether they could hear the loud, hollow thump reverberating in her chest cavity. The man's eyes flashed blue fury. His words dripped hate-filled venom, and his eyes seethed with murderous intent.

"Anna Beth La Rue, you're going to die today because you're a liar and a disrespectful cunt. You gave Jasmine your fucking word that you wouldn't tell. You gave your word and lied, so that means your word ain't shit!"

"You people are crazy!" she screamed, and then added, turning to Jasmine, "You had to know that I would go to the police. What are you, fucking retarded or something?" Anna Beth screamed.

Jasmine's face contorted into a grimacing mask of anger and pain. Disappointment washed across her gorgeous features. "Anna Beth, you're being rude! That's a mean thing to say. Do you know that mentally ill people are the most misunderstood group on the planet? I have a registered IQ of one-sixty-seven, my college GPA was 3.9, and I have lucid dreams about murder. So I believe that eliminates me as a retard. Would you agree?" Jasmine snorted. Before Anna Beth had an opportunity to respond, she saw the lunacy in Jasmine's eyes manifest itself as she snapped Meatball's fragile neck. The tiny puppy yelped once and then went limp. His brown eyes stared out at Anna Beth, lifeless, cold, and unfeeling. He gazed into Anna Beth's eyes, begging her and beckoning to her to save him from beyond the veil. Meatball was her baby, her child until the eventual day that she decided to get married and have a child all her own.

"You fucking bitch! You killed my fucking dog!" Anna Beth cried.

Kochese knew that Anna Beth had gotten underneath Jasmine's skin. He tried futilely to defuse the situation, but Jasmine wasn't having it. "Heyyyyyyyy, there's no need for name-calling," he said.

"Did that strike you as retarded? No, bitch, try psychotic," Jasmine said. She used her stiletto knife to chop Meatball's lifeless body into pieces. Piece by piece Jasmine tossed his hairy body parts at Anna Beth's feet.

When Jasmine dropped his torso, Anna Beth lost it. She could no longer contain her anger, hurt, or resentment. Who were these people to come into her home and kill the last thing on earth that really loved her? She rushed toward Jasmine, but she was stopped short by the barrel of Kochese's .45-caliber.

"Slow your roll, bitch. Take a step back and peel out of your clothes," he said.

"Excuse me?" Anna Beth scoffed.

"You heard me. Strip butt-ass naked," he said, cocking his pistol.

Slowly she peeled layers of her winter clothes until she stood before them in all of her splendor. Kochese and Jasmine both stood looking at the young girl's taut body in utter disgust. Her body was gorgeous, and her perky nipples jutted forward from her corpulent breasts. The one flaw that caused such disdain from the couple was that as luscious as her body was, Anna Beth La Rue had a mound of auburn brown pubic hair between her legs. It wasn't shaped, it wasn't trimmed, it was just there, protruding from her pelvic area a whole half an inch. Her legs looked as if they hadn't been shaved in months.

"Follow me," Kochese instructed.

She was reluctant, but she complied because of the large pistol aimed at the center of her forehead. Slowly she followed Kochese into her bathroom. She had no idea why her tub was full of water or why her bathroom floor was covered in lukewarm water.

"Get into the tub and relax. It's going to be a long night," Kochese said.

Anna Beth climbed into the tub, which much to her surprise was rather warm, a stark contrast to the water that she'd stepped into on the floor. She leaned back and closed her eyes, trying to find some type of relaxation in the midst of turmoil. Anna Beth felt a tear drop from her eyes. She'd never been an overly emotional person, but she loved Meatball, and for them to kill him so violently hurt her heart. She opened her eyes just in time to see Kochese plug the cord that he'd snatched from the lamp into the wall at the base of the tub. He'd split the cord apart so that it looked like a serpent's tongue. He touched the two tips together and the lights flickered ominously from the sudden surge of energy. Kochese stepped up on the toilet seat and sat on its tank.

"You know, if you'd just kept your mouth shut, we wouldn't be going through this. You promised my baby you'd keep your mouth closed! You're a fucking liar!" Kochese spat.

"And you're a fucking murderer!" Anna Beth contested.

"Indeed," Kochese agreed calmly with a sinister smile on his face.

He dropped the exposed wires into the tub, and Anna Beth's body convulsed and flopped violently like a fish out of water. She attempted to stand, bracing herself against the tub, but the electricity surging through her body caused her muscles to seize. She fell back and floundered in the tub until her young heart could no longer take it. Her fingers were mangled and gnarled into a frozen, gripping position from trying to claw her way out of the tub. Her head hung over the side of the tub, rigid, motionless, and with an iced-over glaze in her eyes. Sure that she was dead, Kochese unplugged the fried cord. He stepped down onto the wet floor and checked Anna Beth's pulse. Jasmine came into the bathroom and knelt in the water on the floor and stared into Anna Beth La Rue's cold, lifeless eyes. She cocked her head to the side much like a curious puppy might.

"What are you looking at, baby?" Kochese asked.

"Nothing, it's just that death becomes her. Like she looks better dead than alive, you know?"

Kochese looked at Anna Beth's charred and deformed figure lying in the tub. Blood ran freely from her eyes and mouth and had begun to cloud the water left in the tub. Then he looked at Jasmine, who had a childlike smile of excited wonderment plastered across her beautiful face. Her mossy green eyes beamed and sparkled.

"Okay, baby, whatever you say. If you like it, I love it," Kochese said as he knelt beside his lover.

Chapter 29

DIAMOND LIFE

Kochese dialed Monica's cell phone number. He didn't bother to block his own cell number because she already knew that he and Jasmine were the murderers.

"Monica Deitrich," Monica's voice bellowed through the car from the hands-free device.

"Well, hello, shawt. Bet you never thought in a million years that you'd ever talk to me again, huh?" Kochese asked.

"It really surprised me, I can't lie. I mean, I thought you were dead, babe."

"Don't fucking 'babe' me, bitch! You left me for dead, not to mention the fact that you tried to have me put away," he snarled.

"Where is my sister, you piece of shit?"

"She's sitting right next to me, and I wish you could see the look on her face because you're disrespecting me," Kochese chuckled.

"Jasmine, you need to get away from him. He doesn't love you. He's using you to get back at me! Turn yourself in, and I may be able to help you," Monica pleaded.

"You're still the same selfish, arrogant bitch you were when we were kids, Moni. You think everything has to be about you, and it's not. It's a shame that you won't be around to see this love reach its full potential," Jasmine said.

"You see that, Monica? That's real love. Jasmine doesn't pretend with me. Her love is genuine, and I'll love her forever for that. You, my mom, and every other female who ever existed were just preparing me for this wonderfully magnificent woman," Kochese gushed.

"Whatever, Kochese! You're a fucking parasite, and when I find you, I'm going to put a bullet in your temple. I'll make sure that you're fucking dead this time," Monica said.

Loud, raucous laughter filled the car's enclosure. "You're funny, Monica. Let me explain to you how this is going to go. I have about, mmmmm, five or six more victims in mind. Let's see . . . you, my father, your partner, Bird, Dirt Bag, and a couple of other people you don't know. The question is, are you a good enough agent to stop us from killing these people while watching your own back?" Kochese said.

"Dirt Bag? What does he have to do with all of this?" Monica asked.

"That just lets me further know that you don't know shit about me, Monica, and you most certainly don't know shit about Kochese. If you come near us, I'll kill you!" Jasmine barked.

"You're going to choose this nigga over me?" Monica asked.

"No, I'm choosing the father of my unborn child over you! Family over everything, remember?" Jasmine said.

Both Monica and Kochese screamed an emphatic, "What?"

Jasmine smiled and nodded yes in Kochese's direction. He squeezed her leg and smiled brightly at her. She'd made him perhaps one of the happiest men on the planet.

"Ohhhhhh, shit, that completely changes the game, doesn't it, Monica?" Kochese teased.

She ignored Kochese's taunts. Instead, she addressed Jasmine directly. "Jasmine, do you think that's a good idea? How are you going to manage, considering the circumstances?" she asked.

"What circumstances?"

"How are you going to raise a child from a prison cell? You know me better than anyone, and you know I won't rest until you're locked away tight. I hope it's worth it, because one thing that I know about King Kochese Mills is that as soon as the heat is on, he's going to abandon you. He's going to trade you in for the next conquest, Jasmine. He only cares about one thing, and that's himself. Come home and let me help you, Jazzy Bell," Monica said.

There was a long, awkward silence, so long, in fact, that Monica feared Kochese and Jasmine had disconnected the call. "Hello?" she said.

"Yeah, we're here. Don't try to get into her head, Monica. It won't work. Just guard your neck," Kochese said and then disconnected the call.

He had timed his call perfectly, because as he pulled into the parking lot of CrossTech Industries, Hayden Cross was exiting the building. Kochese pulled up next to him and rolled down the passenger's side window. "What's good, old man?" Kochese asked.

"Don't speak to me like I'm one of your little corner thugs, Kochese. What do you want?"

"Did you ever take care of that little paperwork issue that we discussed?" Kochese asked.

"As a matter of fact, I did. Everything is a go, son. As of earlier today, you're a billionaire. I not only left the majority of my estate to you, but I transferred controlling interest of CrossTech over to you as well. Why are you in such a hurry, Kochese?" Hayden asked.

"No rush, just trying to make sure that your grandchild is taken care of!" Kochese beamed.

Hayden Cross looked at Jasmine and then at
Kochese. He leaned into the window and rubbed
Jasmine's stomach through her thick, goose-down
jacket. "Oh, my goodness. Seriously? Wow, we
need to celebrate. I'll ride with you guys. Head out
to the estate, Kochese," he said, climbing into the
back of Kochese's car.

He quickly sped away headed toward Bluffview.
It was the gated community where Hayden Cross's
seven-bedroom, 16,000-square-foot chateau was
located. The estate had cost him upwards of $10
million and had housing for a full staff. Hayden
hobnobbed with some of Dallas's wealthiest, and
his parties were legendary. On this night, there
would be no legendary party with the likes of
Trammell Crows or Mark Cubans. No, tonight
the grim reaper would be the only guest at this
party. Kochese pulled through the ten-foot-high
wrought iron gate, up the long one-hundred-yard
stone path leading to the estate, and around the
semicircular driveway. He parked in front of the
larger-than-life solid oak doors.

"You two go in and make yourselves comfortable.
I have a run to make, and I should be back shortly.
Remember, Jasmine, no drinking," Kochese said.

"Oh, come on, Kochese, one glass of wine to
celebrate won't hurt her," Hayden protested.

"Okay, one glass, under the condition that you
two wait until I come back. I have a surprise for
you both," he said.

They both agreed, exited the car, and disappeared inside the lavish manor.

Kochese drove slowly through the gravel. He'd learned a hard lesson about the loose gravel in his father's driveway. He drove full speed toward one of his familiar haunts. It had been quite some time since he'd last been to his old shopping plaza. The building that had once held his precious canines, King's Kennel, was now a flea market. It seemed that whoever had purchased the property had completely changed things around because it had a more Oriental feel to it. He pulled to the back of the plaza, parked his car, and climbed into a beat-up box truck.

Chapter 30

SKELETONS

Dirt Bag had tried to be a good father to Trina's son, De'Kovan. Next to being his father figure, being a good man to Trina was his ultimate purpose in life. He'd even managed to find a job that didn't hold his past against him. He was making decent money, plus Trina was working at the hobby shop, so their lives were finally starting to turn around, or so he thought.

You see, Dirt Bag had recently relapsed and backslid into the world of alcohol and illicit drug use. One night after celebrating with coworkers, Dirt Bag had come staggering drunk into the small, wood-framed house he shared with Trina and De'Kovan. The house was situated just across the railroad tracks from the hobby shop on a dead-end street in a community called Marvin Gardens. Each of the houses were small spaces, mostly two-bedroom flats with sketchy lawns and even

sketchier neighbors. The entire neighborhood
backed up on a wide creek that separated the small
community from the industrial area of Sherman,
Texas. Low-income blacks, whites, and Mexicans
all comingled in the neighborhood where the
median income was well below the poverty level.
It was, however, a far cry from some of the places
that Dirt Bag had had the displeasure of calling
home.

He'd come home drunk and in desperate need
of sleep when Trina set in on him about coming
home just before daybreak. They'd argued, and
Dirt Bag had called her unspeakable obscenities.
She lunged at him, and whether from his utter ine-
briation or by reflex, he'd allowed himself to strike
the only woman who had ever shown so much as
an ounce of faith in him. He'd promised Trina that
he'd never put his hands on her, and that promise
had been broken. Trina wasn't the average pretty
face though. She was able to give just as well as
she received, and they fought. Through the house
and into the front yard, Dirt Bag and Trina fought
until a concerned neighbor called the local police.
In the state of Texas, it's a well-known fact that
a majority of the time it's the man who faces jail
time in a domestic dispute unless the man calls the
police first. In this particular instance, however,
they received an officer with a significant amount
of empathy.

"What's going on?" the officer asked. The warring couple began to scream their explanation of events in unison, causing the cop to raise his hand in protest of the confusion. "Okay, you first, sir," he said to Dirt Bag. The sun had just begun to peek up over the shingled roofs of the houses, and thick fog blanketed the low-lying areas around the railroad tracks.

"I came in late. Well, early this morning. I was drunk, I admit that, I was drunk, but that don't give her cause to jump on me. She came at me, and I accidentally hit her," Dirt Bag said.

"Accidentally my ass!" Trina barked.

"Wait a minute, ma'am, you'll get your turn. I'm trying to resolve this issue without anyone going to jail."

"I ain't going to jail! Look at my eye!" Trina screamed.

"I see your eye, ma'am. I also see his eye and multiple scratches on his face and neck. If I had to guess, I would say that this guy got more than he bargained for. Let's make this simple. What is it that you want from this man?" the cop asked.

"I want him to get his shit and get out of my house!"

"*Your* house? Why should I leave? My name is on the lease too!" Dirt Bag shouted.

"Yeah, *my* house! You're not helping me. You spend your money on drinking and drugging!

Don't think I don't know you're dabbling again!"
Trina said sadly.

"Sir, let me give you a bit of advice. Don't be
selfish. If you don't think that you can do right by
this woman, then you should be man enough to
leave. Do you have children together?"

"He's not mine, but I love him like he's mine. I
know I have problems, but that little boy gives me
life. He's helping me atone for my past sins, and I
feel like he's given me a renewed sense of purpose.
That's why I don't wanna leave, Officer. That boy
and this woman are the only reason I'm still living,"
Dirt Bag cried.

Upon hearing this, Trina's heart and features
softened. She was mad at him for putting his
hands on her, but he wasn't a bad man. He had
always made sure that she and De'Kovan were
taken care of.

"This is what I can do for you, sir. My church
does community outreach, and if you're willing
to work hard, I'm sure that they can help you beat
your addiction. It's called the Community Chest,
and it's totally in-house. You can maintain your
current job and still attend daily meetings. I also
volunteer five nights a week, so at least you'll see a
familiar face," he said, handing Dirt Bag a business
card. He then turned to Trina. "Ma'am, I don't
know where your heart is, but if you love this man,
I suggest that you find a measure of forgiveness in

your heart. Our Lord and Savior has forgiven us countless times, and all He asks is that we follow His example and do the same. We've all fallen short, and sometimes it only takes those closest to us to say, 'Hey, I love you and I forgive you,'" the officer said.

Trina knew that he was right. She believed in God wholeheartedly, and for whatever reason, He'd used the officer as a vessel to bring them His word. "Dirty, I love you, and I want to make this work, maybe even one day be your wife, but it's me and De'Kovan, or the streets. There will be no in-between," she said.

"I promise, baby. Just don't give up on me. I'm willing to do whatever I have to do to keep you and Junior in my life."

"Well, now, it's settled then. Nobody needs to go to jail, and from the looks of it, someone is happy you've worked it out," the officer said, nodding toward the front door of their home where De'Kovan was standing, smiling.

Dirt Bag hadn't kept his promise though. Sure, there was no more physical violence, but he'd given in to the temptation and allure of crack cocaine. He'd given Trina the money for December's rent, but he knew where she kept it. He'd initially only meant to take $20, but Nuke had that good butter dope that he liked, and before he knew it, he'd taken half of the $800 he'd given her. The more worried he became, the more he smoked.

He sat in a dark corner of the old, abandoned warehouse that sat across the creek from his backyard. That was his favorite place to smoke his drugs. He felt invisible, like his sins were hidden from even God Himself.

Dirt Bag heard the crunch of gravel beneath heavy footsteps, and he readied himself for the barrage of curse words he was sure Trina would hurl his way. He stood and attempted to straighten his clothes. He ran his fingers through his kinky gray hair and wiped the sweat from his brow. "Baby, before you start, I got a little money coming from a side job I did. I done already called the landlord and let him know we're gonna be a little late with the rent, and he said cool," Dirt Bag lied.

He was ready to launch into even more lies when the figure finally emerged from the shadows. It wasn't Trina. It was some random white guy, probably someone who wanted to buy the building. It had been up for sale since they moved into the neighborhood. "Hey, I'm not trespassing, man. Me and the owner are good friends. He knows that I like to get away from my wife, come up here and think sometimes," he lied.

"Dirt Bag, I see you're still lying. I guess old habits die hard, huh?"

"Man, you don't know me. As a matter of fact, how do you know my fucking name?" Dirt Bag barked.

"I know you better than you know yourself, muh'fucka, trust. It smells like a musty-ass crackhouse in this bitch!" he said.

"Man, fuck you! I got enough problems, and I ain't gotta explain shit to you, white boy!" Dirt Bag spat.

"You might wanna watch your mouth. I'm here to collect a debt you owe."

"I don't owe nobody shit! You got your facts fucked up, homeboy! Who do I owe?" Dirt Bag asked skeptically. He knew that he didn't owe anyone because no one would extend credit to him.

"You owe King Ko-muh'fuckin'-chese, fuck boy!"

"Man, Kochese is dead, and my debt died with him," Dirt Bag snickered.

"Naw, nigga, see, that's where you're wrong. I'm alive and well. When you came to me and asked me to put you down, I told you I'd kill you if you fucked me over by getting high again. When that pussy nigga Silk tried to hire you to set me up, I met you at that fleabag hotel and gave you money to get outta town. You were with that fuck nigga Michael Ross and Jappy when y'all raped that little girl, and I let you live, nigga. Is that convincing enough for you, fool?" King growled.

Dirt Bag stumbled backward until his back was against the wall. He threw his hands up in front of him as if trying to ward off evil spirits. "King Kochese, man, I'm glad to see you, man. You look like one of them rich-ass peckerwoods, man. This little habit ain't shit, man. I can stop whenever I want to, man."

"Is that why I saw your girl and her son sitting on the front porch crying? You're a piece of shit, Dirt Bag, always have been, always will be," Kochese said.

"King, I've been doing dope so long that I don't know how to quit. Yeah, I might go a little while without smoking, but that shit always calls me back. I guess I'm worth more to my family dead than alive. Sometimes I be wishing that I just OD or something, so Trina and the boy can just collect the insurance money," Dirt Bag said.

He and Kochese had never been friends, and he knew that. Dirt Bag had only been a convenient nuisance to the kingpin. He wasn't quite sure if he was just high and imagining the whole thing, or if Kochese had actually come back from the dead. One thing that he knew for certain was the fact that King Kochese, no matter how mean and ruthless he was, still had a notoriously big heart for children. Dirt Bag considered asking him for the $400 he'd smoked up but thought better of it.

As if sensing that Dirt Bag was about to ask him for money, King went into his pocket and removed a wad of neatly folded $100 bills. "Give this to your girl and tell her Merry Christmas, but don't tell her where you got it from. Go handle that and meet me back here in fifteen minutes. I want to introduce you to someone. Dirt Bag, if I have to come and look for you, I'm going to be pissed. I'm going to kill that boy first, then I'm going to kill your bitch, and after you've watched me do it, I'll finally kill you to end your suffering, capisce?" Kochese said. He removed the .45-caliber pistol from his shoulder holster and cocked it for emphasis.

"Man, I'll be right back. Kochese, man, thank you, thank you, bro."

True to his word, ten minutes later Dirt Bag came running into the warehouse, winded. He doubled over, trying desperately to catch his breath. "Man, women ask too many damn questions," he panted.

Kochese didn't speak. He simply walked to the loading dock where he'd parked his box truck.

"C'mon, nigga, you're burning daylight," Kochese said.

Dirt Bag scurried through the warehouse until he was standing at Kochese's side. He drove the gravel roads leading away from the warehouse, avoiding the houses and all the major intersections, until he reached US 75 and headed south. An hour later, Kochese pulled into a run-down neighborhood just south of the North Dallas projects. He turned the truck off and shoved the keys deep into his pocket. "If you want to make sure that your girl and stepson have more money than they know what to do with, you'll be here when I get back," Kochese said.

He disappeared into a semi-dilapidated house
and emerged moments later with a huge grin on
his face. He patted the large bulge in his blazer
pocket and winked at Dirt Bag as he climbed
into the truck. "Yeeeaaaahhh, we're gonna party
tonight, Dirty!" Kochese said excitedly. He reached
into his jacket pocket and removed the quarter kilo
of rocked-up cocaine he'd just purchased.

Dirt Bag's eyes lit up, and he was barely able to
contain his excitement. He was almost salivating
as he watched Kochese chip off a piece about the
size of a pencil eraser and drop it into his hand.
"When we stop again, you can climb in the back and
try that out," Kochese said.

Dirt Bag nodded. He couldn't believe his luck.
He'd given Trina enough money for all the bills
and Christmas presents, with a little to spare.
Plus, Kochese had said something about Trina
and De'Kovan having more money than they knew
what to do with.

Kochese navigated his way expertly through
the streets of North Dallas until he came to the
University Park section of Dallas. Kochese drove
slowly along McFarlin Boulevard until he reached
his destination. He double-checked the GPS on his
cell phone and pulled up next to the intercom attached to the ten-foot-high stone gate. He pressed
the button and waited.

Seconds later, a woman's voice came over the
loudspeaker. "May I help you?" the voice said.

"Yes, ma'am, it's me, Khalil Cross. I need to speak with you about my father, Hayden Cross," Kochese lied.

The gate buzzed and whirred and slid open slowly. Kochese drove at a snail's pace along the travertine pavers leading to the house. The immoderate mansion was comparable to that of his father's with its profligate ornamentations and excessively abundant manicured shrubbery. Ms. Amanetto had indeed done very well for herself. Well, her late husband had done extremely well for both of them.

Her husband, Richard Amanetto, had been a shrewd businessman whose only goal was to help people who were too financially strapped to get by. He'd opened a string of check-cashing stores that charged well below the average check-cashing fees. He also offered advanced payday loans that charged a measly 10 percent of the dollar amount for payback. He'd been a saint in the small, less fortunate neighborhoods where he operated his shops, where a patron could borrow up to $1,000 for up to a month and only had to pay back $1,100. He'd managed to keep his business clean and clear of scandal the entire twenty-five years he was in business, and his wife hated it. She was beyond greedy, so when the Armenian crime syndicate approached her about partnering with her husband in his business, she was adamant that he join forces with them.

Richard had refused, and Patricia Amanetto had made sure to relay his refusal to the Armenians, who in turn murdered Richard, leaving Patricia as the sole benefactor of his check-cashing empire. The love that Richard Amanetto had amassed in the low-income sections of Dallas and Fort Worth quickly dissipated as Patricia and the Armenians drove up interest rates and used gestapo-type tactics to collect monies owed to the company.

Before the company went completely belly-up, Patricia Amanetto cashed out each one of her businesses and filed for bankruptcy. One by one, her buildings mysteriously caught fire, and she was never charged because the Armenians always provided her with an alibi: a vacation here, a charity ball there. She was never anywhere near the scene when a building went up in flames. It wasn't until one of those fires spread to an upstairs apartment, trapping and subsequently killing an elderly couple, that she actually caught backlash. Money talks, though, and Patricia Amanetto escaped with a two-year probation and one-year house arrest for her role.

As they pulled up to the front door, Patricia Amanetto opened the front door clad in a see-through satin teddy and six-inch stilettos. Kochese wasn't sure how she saw herself, but from the looks of it, she believed that she still had it. Maybe she had it back in the Stone Age, but her looks were a distant memory. Her beauty had faded from too many parties and loose living. Where her skin had once been taut and unblemished, it was now spotted and droopy. Although she'd paid for implants, her ample bosom had lost the fight with gravity, and wrinkles zigzagged through her overly tanned skin. She leaned against the frame of the large oak door seductively, holding a glass of champagne in one hand and a cigarette in the other.

"Dirt Bag, you stay here. Go ahead and climb in the back and take you a little hit. I'll be right back," Kochese said.

Dirt Bag scampered to the back of the box truck, not exchanging so much as a word with King Kochese. This was the moment he'd been waiting for, a chance to savor the sweet, undeniable taste of crack cocaine.

Kochese exited the truck and approached Ms. Amanetto.

"What can I do for you, Khalil?" she asked seductively.

"May I come in out of the cold, Ms. Amanetto?"

"Sure, you may *come* inside," she said with sexuality dripping from her lascivious tongue.

Kochese walked inside, purposely brushing against the horny nymph. She flicked her cigarette aside and closed the door, leaning against it with her arm above her head. Her pose caused Kochese to chuckle because she looked like a character from an old black-and-white movie. "I need a favor, Ms. Amanetto."

"I will do anything that you need me to do, Khalil. How is your father?" she asked.

"He's wonderful. That's why I'm here. My father doesn't know that I'm here, but he really needs you right now. We were talking, and he confided in me that CrossTech is on the verge of going belly-up. I told him if anyone could bail us out, it would be Ms. Amanetto. He protested, but my concern is saving a family dynasty, not saving his ego," Kochese lied.

"What is it that you need me to do?"

"Maybe take a ride to my father's home and help to convince him that you're the right person to invest in bringing CrossTech back from the dead," he said.

"Sure, why not? Follow me so that I can change into something more appropriate," she said. She climbed the stairs slowly, engaging Kochese in banal conversation along the way. "It's surprising that your father is in any real financial trouble because he's always been a very astute businessman. Why are you riding around in that jalopy? Well, if you want, we can take my car. I really wouldn't feel comfortable in that heap," she suggested.

"That's fine with me, as long as you don't mind a friend of mine riding with us. I'm really trying to help him kick a habit, you know?"

Patricia nodded yes. She'd caught a glimpse of his "friend," and he looked like an unsavory character.

They reached her room, and she undressed in front of Kochese. Her body was hideous. Every scar from her plastic surgery was visible. She was trying hard to entice Kochese, but he wouldn't bite.

Chapter 31

YOUR MOVE

They pulled into Hayden Cross's palatial estate approximately four hours after he'd originally left. Hayden Cross and Jasmine sat in his dining room laughing heartily when Kochese, Dirt Bag, and Patricia entered.

"Well, damn, son, I thought you'd gone AWOL on us. I was beginning to worry," Hayden said.

Jasmine ran to Kochese and threw her arms around his neck. "I missed you so much, baby. What's in the bag? Is it something for me?" she asked excitedly.

"Yeah, something like that," Kochese said, turning to Patricia and Dirt Bag. "You two have a seat and we can get started," he added.

Hayden looked warily from Dirt Bag to Patricia and then from Kochese to Jasmine. He knew that they both had problems, but the assembly was nerve-wrenching. "Is there some particular reason

why we've been assembled here today, son?" he
asked.

"As a matter of fact, there is, old man," Kochese
said, removing his pistol. He handed it to Jasmine
and winked. "If either of these fuckers move, I
want you to put a bullet in their heads, baby, you
understand?"

"Yes, my love, it would be my pleasure," she said.

Kochese removed a roll of duct tape from the
bag he was carrying. He instructed Hayden Cross
to put his hands at his side, and then he taped him
to his chair. He did the same to Patricia Amanetto,
but he did not tape Dirt Bag to his chair. No, he
had something special in store for him. Kochese
whispered in Jasmine's ear, who in turn walked
around the table and put the barrel of Kochese's
.45 against Dirt Bag's knee. She looked at Kochese
and pulled the trigger. A loud, thunderous crack
echoed throughout the dining room, and Dirt
Bag shrieked from the excruciating pain. Patricia
followed suit, screaming and crying until Kochese
buried his fist deep into her temple, silencing her
for the time being. Jasmine took aim at Dirt Bag's
other knee and popped off a round. He squirmed
and squealed in his chair and gripped the arm of
the chair until his caramel-colored knuckles were
almost white with tension. All the while Hayden
Cross looked on in dazed amazement. Kochese
slapped Patricia Amanetto lightly until she became
sentient.

"Wake up, old lady. Do you know what this is?" Kochese asked. He placed a white pillowcase, with a crudely drawn dollar sign on it, in front of her on the table.

"No, I have no idea." She pouted.

"Do you know what this is?" he said, placing a cardboard box on the table in front of her.

"It looks like a *Monopoly* game."

"Very good, very good. So we're going to play a game. Are you okay with that?" Kochese asked.

"I don't really have a choice, do I? Why are you doing this to me? I don't even know you people!" she screamed.

"Let me explain to you why you're going to die tonight."

"Die? Wait, I have money. I will give you my entire fortune of fifty million dollars. Just let me go. Please, dear God, I'm begging you," Patricia pleaded.

"You know, if I were still who I used to be, I probably would have gone for that. I mean, fifty million is a lot of bread. However, my daddy dearest has made me a billionaire, so fifty mill is kinda like punk money to me, so um, yeah, no, thanks," Kochese teased, then added, "I'm going to kill you tonight because you're an evil bitch, Patricia. You had your husband murdered for the sake of a dollar. Do you realize that those people in those run-down neighborhoods cherished your husband? Then along comes Miss Money Bags and completely disrupts the entire system. Those old people died because of your greed, and you were so smug that on the day of their funeral, you were vacationing in Jamaica!" Kochese barked.

"I'm sorry, I really am! I've changed, I swear."

"Your word means nothing to me, Patricia. Now I'm going to roll the dice for you since you're a little tied up. I'm going to shake the dice, and when you want me to roll them you just need to say now, okay?" Kochese said.

He set up the game board as if he were about to play a real game of *Monopoly*. On the table he also placed a leather tool holder that was folded and bound by a small strip of string. He untied the string and unrolled the leather. Inside was a vast assortment of knives: smooth blades, serrated edges, long knives, short knives, et cetera. Kochese rolled the dice, and it landed on double deuces. He took the fourth knife in the collection and made four small incisions into Patricia's skin. "Why would you betray your husband, Patty?" Kochese asked. He continued his game until he grew bored, and then he slit Patricia Amanetto's throat. King Kochese Mills opened the pillowcase, reached inside, and pulled out a handful of wrinkled $1 bills. He pulled her head back by her hair and shoved the bills deep into the laceration that he'd made in her neck. "Now the old bag is really full of money," he said, laughing boisterously.

He walked to Dirt Bag, who was writhing in pain. "Hey, nigga, wake yo' punk ass up. Do you know who this is?" Kochese asked, pointing to Jasmine.

Unable to speak, Dirt Bag simply shook his head no. He wasn't sure why Kochese had brought him to this house or who the rest of these people were, but what he did know was that he needed a hit. "Her name is Jasmine. This is the young girl that you, Michael Ross, and Jappy raped when she was only seven years old, you pedophilic piece of shit. I want you to die by her hand. We found each other, Dirt Bag, we found each other through the darkness, and we're here to cleanse you and send you home to your Maker," Kochese said softly.

"I've been waiting my whole life to ask you why, sir. I've always wanted to know, why me?" Jasmine said.

"I don't know. I was just a follower back then, young lady. I was following Michael Ross. I'm not making any excuses, but I was high on crack and stupid."

"You ruined my life. Y'all stole my childhood from me, and when I was supposed to be playing jacks and hopscotch, I was in a mental institution trying to not get raped by the perverted orderlies. I was a baby, and you ruined me!" Jasmine cried.

Kochese tossed the quarter key onto the table in front of Dirt Bag, and his eyes lit up.

"Smoke you a piece so that you can calm your nerves, playboy," Kochese said.

Dirt Bag reached into his pocket and removed his crack pipe. He chipped off a small piece of dope, placed it in his pipe, and sparked his lighter. His eyes widened, and the euphoric pleasure of the drug overtook his body. He put his straight shooter on the table and leaned back.

Jasmine climbed onto the table and sat in front of Dirt Bag. "I know you're not done. No, you're going to smoke until I tell you to stop," Jasmine said. She picked up his straight shooter and packed it with dope until the glass dick would hold no more. "Now smoke!" she screamed.

Dirt Bag did as he was told. He continued to inhale the milky white smoke until it felt as if his heart would leap from his chest. Again and again, she reloaded his crack pipe until Dirt Bag showed his first signs of an overdose. He scratched at the skin on his neck violently and picked at the wood on the table. He became agitated and began to sweat profusely. Dirt Bag felt his heart slow and then speed up and then slow down to a snail's pace. He trembled violently, coughed up black mucus, and then screamed, "I can't smoke any more dope, goddammit!"

"Oh, you're going to smoke or I'm going to blow your motherfucking head off," Jasmine said calmly.

All the while Hayden Cross sat transfixed, completely paralyzed with fear from the things that he'd witnessed. He could only imagine what they had in store for him.

"Just kill me now! If I smoke anymore, my heart will explode," Dirt Bag said. He'd begun to cry uncontrollably, and then his sadness turned to belligerence. "Bitch, if I could get up, I'd rip your fucking pussy hole out!" he shouted.

Jasmine took the pistol and jammed it into Dirt Bag's mouth, shattering his front teeth in the process. "You did that when I was seven years old, you piece of shit! You stole my soul, but King Kochese gave it back to me!" Jasmine said. She cocked the pistol and pulled the trigger. She giggled loudly as bone fragments and brain matter blew out the back of Dirt Bag's shattered skull. She looked at Kochese as if waiting for his blessing. He smiled warmly and nodded his approval of what she'd done.

"What now, Kochese? Are you going to kill your own father? Did my not being there cause you to hate me that much?" Hayden asked in a panic. He was terrified because he'd heard of mental illness, but he had never actually come in contact with anyone with mental issues. He'd accused Kochese's mother of being a crazy bitch, but she was nothing like this. She was stalker crazy. These

two were psychotic crazy, and he had no idea how
to handle it. He had no control over the situation,
and that scared him more than anything.

"Noooooooo, Daddy, I don't hate you at all. I just
don't like you very much. Do you realize that until
I met Jasmine, everyone in my life let me down?
My mother hated me because I was cursed with
your face!" Kochese said. He spread the *Monopoly*
board and put all its pieces in the proper place.
He then walked to Dirt Bag's exploded dome and
dug his hand deep into the back of his head until
his hand was saturated with blood. On the game
board, he scrawled in Dirt Bag's crimson red blood,
"Your move, bitch!"

"You see, Hayden . . . May I call you Hayden?
One thing that I know is murder," Kochese said
as he reached into his little bag of tricks. "When
they find your rotting corpse, they will know that
I did it, and I'm okay with that," he said. Kochese
placed a dead bird on the table and severed its
beak from its face. Then he placed a baby doll on
the table and drove a knife through its face. "Do
you have any idea why I am so determined to kill
you tonight, Hayden?" Kochese asked.

"I . . . I have no idea, son. I do know that I'm
not ready to die. You've already taken my other
children, Kochese. Please, I'm begging you to
spare my life," Hayden begged.

"Man, kill that humble pie shit! A child deserves for his parents to be together, you know? And since I can't bring my mother back, then the only way for you to be with her again is if I kill you and send you to heaven to meet her. Do you believe my mother is in heaven, Hayden?" Kochese asked with tears in his eyes.

"Yes, son, I believe she's in heaven. She was an angel."

Kochese slapped Hayden across the bridge of his nose with the butt of his pistol. Blood leapt from the wound and sprayed generously across the cherry wood table. "Don't patronize me, muh'fucka! You know as well as I know that my mother isn't in heaven. Why would God let a woman into heaven who had no love for her only son?" Kochese asked.

"You son of a bitch! You broke my fucking nose, you little prick! Maybe God let her into heaven because He knew that you were an evil little twit and He wanted to spare her the shame of raising a retard!" Hayden spit.

Kochese fell back into the table. Hayden's words had cut him deep, and he fought back tears.

"Nobody talks to King Kochese that way!" Jasmine screamed. She'd vowed to herself that she would be the only person to ever cause Kochese to shed a tear and they would only be tears of happiness. She reached into his leather sheath and removed a fillet knife. "Apologize, asshole, now!" she screamed.

"I'm not apologizing to this dumbass! I tried to atone, I tried to make him human, but there's no saving him. He's worthless!" Hayden said.

Kochese fell to his knees with his hands over his ears. He rocked back and forth with his eyes closed, trying desperately to shield himself from the berating of his father's harsh words.

Jasmine took the fillet knife, yanked Hayden Cross's head back, and cut his tongue from his head. He squirmed and mumbled as blood and spittle dripped from his mouth. Jasmine knelt next to Kochese and cradled him in her arms. "You're going to be a great father, baby. Hayden never deserved you as a son. He's heartless, baby, while you have a heart of gold," she said.

Kochese looked at Jasmine and smiled. She always knew how to make him feel better. He stood and then helped Jasmine to stand. "I love you, baby, I really do," Kochese said. He took Jasmine into his arms and kissed her deeply. He reached onto the table and grabbed a butcher's knife, all the while keeping his tongue buried deep in Jasmine's mouth. He cut his eyes at Hayden and buried the knife deep in his chest cavity. He pulled back from the wet, sensual kiss and whispered in Jasmine's ear, "Your turn."

"My pleasure, my love, my pleasure," she whispered. She pulled the butcher's knife from Hayden's chest, lifted his head by his chin gently, and slit his exposed throat.

Chapter 32

THE GAME DON'T WAIT

Monica was fuming. Kochese and Jasmine had gone too far. They continued their killing spree with a reckless disregard for the consequences. Monica had, however, devised a plan to smoke them out, to bring them out of the shadows, so to speak. She was about to step out on the front steps of the federal building and have Kochese's and Jasmine's faces plastered on every news outlet in the nation. The recent murders of Hayden Cross and Patricia Amanetto had garnered national headlines, and Monica feared the worst. If she made their identities public, at best it would drive them to come forward and turn themselves in, but worst-case scenario, some overzealous beat cop from Maine to Miami would use her pregnant sister and her crazed lover as target practice.

Monica stepped out onto the glazed marble platform of the federal building amid camera flashes and a barrage of questions. She held her hands up to silence the eager crowd.

"Ladies and gentlemen, for months we've been faced with a dire situation. We've narrowed our search down to a pair of ruthless serial killers with no regard for human life who've made a game out of their mounting body count. The method that they used was the game of *Monopoly*. They basically used pieces, property, and the like, to pick their victims. We now have names and faces to match our suspects. This is suspect number one, King Kochese Mills, aka Khalil Cross, the son of logistics mogul Hayden Cross. He was presumed dead but resurfaced with an assumed identity. He is armed and extremely dangerous," she said. Monica held up two photos, one of Kochese as she remembered him and the other of him as Khalil Cross.

"Agent Deitrich, are we to believe that this is the same man?" a reporter asked skeptically.

"You can believe what you want, but facts are facts, ma'am. This is the same person. You'd be surprised what a person can do with unlimited resources. Now this is the second suspect. Her name is Jasmine Deitrich, and she is also armed and dangerous," she said as she held up Jasmine's picture as well.

An uneasy hush fell over the crowd as the reporters scrambled to find the right words, and Monica sensed it immediately. "I know many of you are wondering if Miss Deitrich and I are related, and the answer is yes," she said.

A wave of whispers and muffled chatter washed over the growing crowd of reporters and onlookers.

"But I assure you . . ." she started, but she couldn't hear herself speak. "Ladies and gentlemen, please," she said, raising her hands to silence the crowd. "I assure you that I have no prejudice. Justice will be served. Jasmine Deitrich will be treated just as any other suspect would. I need to make mention that the FBI is offering a one-hundred-thousand-dollar reward to anyone who can offer information that leads to apprehending this duo dead or alive. Thank you," Monica said.

The throng of reporters went ballistic with questions. They came in quick flurries, a hailstorm of questions that Monica refused to answer. She turned on her heels and whispered into Agent Cody Roth's ear, "I want their pictures faxed to every police agency in the country. If we can't find them, we will bring them to us!" Monica turned back to the reporters. "Thank you all for coming and for all of your help and support."

Kochese lay awake in bed with Jasmine cradled snuggly in his arms. As he watched the news, he felt a pang of fury. Monica Deitrich had some nerve. She'd already caused him more damage than he needed or cared to remember, but now she had the audacity to bring her sister into it. It was bad enough that she'd left him for dead, tried to send him to prison for the rest of his life, and made a laughingstock of his street legacy, but she had essentially painted a bull's-eye on his and her sister's back. What kind of monster would sign a death warrant against her only sister, let alone a sister who was pregnant? He rewound the news broadcast to the beginning, paused it, and nudged Jasmine softly. "Jasmine, Jazzy Bell, wake up, mama," he whispered.

Jasmine's eyes blinked open, and she stared at Kochese lovingly. "Hey, my King, is everything okay?" she asked groggily.

"Not really. Your sister is on that bullshit. Why can't she just leave us alone?" Kochese shouted as he started the DVR.

Jasmine watched the press conference in dazed horror. It was as if Monica was saying fuck her, Kochese, and their unborn child. She kept rewinding it to Monica's voice. "Apprehending this duo dead or alive . . . dead or alive . . . dead or alive," Monica's voice resonated repeatedly. Jasmine let the DVR play while some pale-skinned reporter with dry hair and frumpy clothes did her best impression of Diane Sawyer.

"And there you have it, ladies and gentlemen. The FBI is offering a hundred thousand dollars—that's right, a hundred thousand dollars—to anyone with information that can lead to law enforcement apprehending who can only be called a modern-day Bonnie and Clyde. I'm Christine Sorensen reporting live in Dallas for WFAA Channel 8 news. Back to you, Jason," she said.

Jasmine clicked the TV off and looked at King. Soft moonlight flowed through the window, casting a sinister shadow over her child's father. "I don't know what to do, baby. She's my sister, but at the same time, she wants to hurt our baby," she said sadly.

"You and this child are all that matter to me. If you can't bring yourself to kill her, I will!" Kochese barked.

"She'll get hers, baby. We'll do it together. It's us against the world, right? 'Til death do us part?" Jasmine said.

"Damn skippy, 'til death do us part!"

Chapter 33

HARRY POTTY

Cody Roth bid Monica a good night and continued his work. She'd left because of utter exhaustion and frustration. It had been nearly seventy-two hours since their press conference aired, and there was still no word on Kochese and Jasmine's whereabouts. Cody was cross-referencing all of Hayden Cross's properties with power and sewer usage. Billionaire's Row had the highest concentrated usage, but that was to be expected from the amount of tenants. There was no way that Jasmine and Kochese would be able to come and go undetected to and from the condominium complex. There was, however, a property that stood out. It was a lodge-style home owned by Hayden Cross that was purportedly abandoned. In the last few months, however, it had gone from virtually no sewage or power usage to an overabundance of use. Cody printed his findings and circled them in red.

From the corner of his eye, he thought he saw movement, and he jumped from fright. The building was dark except for a few desk lamps that had been left on by agents who were overly eager to end their day. He had to laugh at himself. Of all the gruesome sights he'd witnessed associated with the bizarre case, the *Monopoly* board had spooked him the most. A dead bird with its beak sawed off, a baby doll with a knife through its forehead, and the *Monopoly* board with those ominous words written in blood had freaked him out more than the dead bodies. The thought of it made his stomach churn because he knew what it meant. Monica was in denial, but Cody Roth knew. He knew without a doubt that Jasmine and Kochese were going after Bird and his daughter Millicent.

Kochese sat next to his latest victim inside the old man's car. He hadn't particularly done anything wrong, but he was a means to an end. His sole purpose for killing the elderly man was to gain his security badge. He'd walked out with Monica, laughing and chatting, obviously to have a smoke, because he reached for his cigarette pack, but he crushed it upon realizing that it was empty. He and Monica parted ways, and he headed toward the parking lot. It was the same free parking lot where he and Jasmine had sliced Muldoon in half only weeks earlier.

Kochese caught the elderly man as he opened his car door. "Excuse me, sir, do you mind if I bum a smoke from you?" Kochese asked.

Mr. Chadwick looked the young man up and down. He wore a dirty mechanic's jumper, and his hands were filthy. He smelled normal, not nasty or musty and definitely not nice, but normal. Mr. Chadwick leaned inside his car, riffling through the center console in search of his cigarettes. Kochese shoved him inside, climbed in on top of him, and wrapped his strong hands around the scrawny man's neck. Mr. Chadwick tried futilely to fight back, but it was no use. Kochese snatched the ID from his jacket lapel and waited. He sat in the darkness of the old man's car waiting to see if he'd been seen, but nothing happened. He exited the car and scurried across the street to the federal building.

Kochese slid the ID card, and the LED light turned from red to green. The door lock clicked, and Kochese disappeared inside the building. He went to the building directory and scanned it until he saw what he was looking for: FBI 12TH FLOOR. He made it to the twelfth floor and walked the hall slowly and carefully, almost creeping, mindful to go undetected.

He saw Agent Cody Roth standing at a printer. He seemed to be talking to someone, maybe himself. Kochese considered running in on him, but

Cody may have been packing his agency-issued firearm. At the same time he was considering whether to kill him in the office, Cody stopped as if he'd heard Kochese's thoughts. Kochese ducked into the men's room just in the nick of time to keep his presence secret.

Cody sat at his desk doubled over in pain. He wasn't sure whether it was bad nerves or the triple beef and bean burrito he'd eaten from 7-Eleven earlier. He didn't like using public restrooms, but he knew from the gurgling in his stomach and the rectal cramps that he would never make it home in time. He farted and felt a hot, sticky wetness beneath his seat. Whenever Cody used the bathroom at home, he'd get completely naked and play the slots on his phone until his legs went to sleep, but in this particular situation there would be no time for games. He left his phone on his desk and headed for the toilet.

As he entered the bathroom, he had the strange feeling that he was being watched, like he wasn't alone. He got down on his hands and knees and scanned the floor of each stall. Nothing. He went to the last stall in the bathroom and laced the toilet with toilet paper. Cody fumbled with his zipper, clumsily trying to get his pants down.

"Ohhh, shit. Come on, man, damn! I'm gonna shit myself," he said to no one in particular. He tried to sit down on the toilet, but it felt like someone was jabbing a butcher's knife into his anus. He bent over as far as he could with no pain and slid onto the toilet sideways. As soon as he sat down, his bowels exploded in a brown fury. "Ahhhhhh," he said. He looked up, mostly from the satisfaction of relief, and noticed that the water and sewer lines ran overhead. He flushed the toilet in hopes of killing the putrid smell permeating from his insides and heard the water rush through the six-inch pipe. He silently wished that he'd brought his cell phone to pass the time as he emptied his bowels.

Meanwhile, two stalls down, Kochese got down on his stomach and shimmied to the stall next to Cody. He quietly stood on the toilet seat and removed a section of braided cable from his front pocket. It had enclosed loops on each end with a thick U-shaped slab of metal that encased the loops. Kochese slid one of the loops through the other and created a noose. To the other end he attached a sturdy and heavy-duty four-inch clamp. He slid the cable over the two pipes running the length of the bathroom. He looked over the top of the cubicle and lined his noose up with Cody's head. As soon as Cody sat straight and ripped a piece of toilet paper from its holder, Kochese let the noose fall over Cody's head and around his neck. Before Cody realized what was happening, Kochese yanked with all of his might. The more Cody struggled against the thin cable, the tighter the noose became. Kochese pulled tighter still until Cody was suspended in the air and he had enough slack to fix the four-inch clamp to the accessibility rail in the stall that he occupied. Cody kicked and fought, but it was no use. He had no footing, and had he been a tad more lucid, he would've thought to step up on the toilet, but Cody panicked, and that small misstep cost him his young life.

Kochese stepped out of his stall and opened Cody's stall door slowly. He could see the life draining from his eyes. "Goddamn, you's about a Harry Potter–looking muh'fucka, man," Kochese said. His rowdy laughter echoed throughout the posh government bathroom. He heard the raspy cough of Cody Roth taking his last breath, and he laughed again. Cody's pants were still around his ankles, and the tail of his Van Heusen dress shirt barely covered his man part as he swayed to and fro. Kochese stood next to him with a crazed smile spread across his lips and snapped a selfie with the dead agent. He scrolled through his phone and attached the picture to two recipients. The first was Jasmine, and the second was Agent Monica Deitrich, with a caption that read: Chilling with Harry Potter . . . or should I say Harry Potty?

Chapter 34

NOW OR NEVER

Monica stared at her phone in disbelief, unable to process the picture message that she'd just received. She felt directly responsible for the death of Agent Cody Roth. He was young and impressionable, and most of all, he looked up to Monica. Questions swirled in her head. The why's and the what-if's bombarded her already-fragile mind state. Would the outcome have been any different if she'd convinced Cody to leave with her instead of staying late to work? If she hadn't kicked Jasmine out of her house, would things have escalated to this point? She needed to contact Bird, because if the dead bird and baby doll meant what Cody Roth thought they meant, then Bird and Millicent were in danger.

She dialed Bird's number, but there was no answer. Monica sped through traffic en route to the federal building. By the time she pulled up, the Dallas Police Department and the local news were already on site. The building was crawling with Feds, and Monica felt a sudden rush of overwhelming anxiety. She showed her credentials and entered the building. She was immediately approached by bigwigs wanting answers.

"Agent Deitrich, come with us please," she was instructed.

She was led into the security room, where a half dozen senior agents waited. "Agent Deitrich, all things considered, how are you holding up?" an agent asked. His features belied his coarse gray hair, and he looked more like a Hollywood star than an FBI agent.

"I'm fine. What's going on?" she asked.

"We have surveillance footage that shows your sister waiting a block away from this building in a car registered to CrossTech Industries. Do you remember this?" he asked.

It was surveillance footage of her chatting with Mr. Chadwick just before his murder, but before she could speak, the next clip showed Mr. Chadwick being approached by Kochese. He made quick work of murdering the old man, and he was inside the federal building quickly. Clip by clip it showed Kochese's movements and his advancement toward Monica's office.

She felt dizzy, almost like she'd been doing drugs. She knew about Cody's death, and as fucked up as it was, she understood why he'd been killed. But Mr. Chadwick was an old man, a harmless old man. As the black-and-white clip rolled, it showed Kochese's blatant hatred and contempt for authority, because at one point he stopped, looked directly into the camera, and with both hands he gave the middle finger to the law and then gripped his balls. Seconds later he disappeared into the men's room, where shortly thereafter he was joined by an unsuspecting Cody Roth. The agent in charge clicked the surveillance footage off and sat on the desk facing Monica.

"No need to let the rest play. It basically shows the perp exiting the building and then joining your sister in the car parked up the block. What can you tell us about this man and your sister?" he asked.

Monica started at the beginning, bringing them up to speed on Jasmine's rape at 7 years old and her subsequent mental deterioration from the gang rape. She explained to them how she took King Kochese down and how everyone assumed that he was dead.

"How could you assume something of that magnitude without solid evidence, Agent?"

"Because his father bought and paid for the bailiffs, the EMTs, and the coroner. He bought everyone involved in Kochese Mills's phony suicide." She explained how Kochese and Jasmine met and how she came up with her *Monopoly* theory. She

laid it out for them piece by piece until they agreed
that she was indeed on the right track.

"Just so you know, Agent Deitrich, I've autho-
rized the increase of the reward to two hundred
thousand dollars. The fugitives are now on the
FBI's Ten Most Wanted list, and they've been
named public enemy number one!"

"Very well, sir," Monica said sadly. If the agency
got to Jasmine and Kochese first, there would be
no hesitation. They would be gunned down in the
name of vigilante justice for their fallen comrades.

"I have one more question before you leave,
Agent Deitrich," he said as Monica was preparing
to leave the room.

"Yes, sir?"

"Why are we just learning about your connection
to this case?" he asked.

Monica knew the answer to the question. She
also knew that it would land her in the proverbial
doghouse. She wanted to scream at the top of her
lungs because it was none of their motherfucking business, but she couldn't. She couldn't tell
them that she was trying to protect her sister. She
couldn't tell them that a part of her soul still held
love for Kochese Mills. She needed to take the high
road, so she gave them the most diplomatic answer
possible. Monica cleared her throat. "These devel-
opments are new with the exception of my sister's
mental state. Agent Roth and I were preparing a
file to present to the deputy director," she lied.

Monica exited the room and tried Bird's number again, but there was still no answer.

"Hey, you've reached Bird and Millie. We're unable to take your call at the moment, but if you leave a name, number, and a brief message, we'll be sure to return your call. Say hi, Millicent," Bird sang cheerfully in the outgoing voicemail message. An exuberant Millicent cooed and giggled on cue in the background and then beeeeeeeeeeep.

"Bird, this is Monkey. If you get this message, give me a call. I'm worried about you guys. Listen, I have reason to believe that Kochese—" But before she could finish her sentence, her phone beeped with another call. She looked at the phone, and Bird and Millicent's picture popped up. It was Bird returning her call. She clicked over.

"Hello? Bird?" she said.

He didn't answer. She heard only the sound of heavy breathing and Millicent's high-pitched and distressed wail.

"Hello, hello!" Monica screamed into the phone.

"Hello, Monica. Or should I still call you Monkey?" Kochese asked softly.

"Where the fuck is Bird? Why is Millie crying?"

"Bird is here, but he's a little tied up at the moment. The baby is probably crying because we're fucking her bitch-ass daddy up, man!" Kochese said with a chuckle.

"If you hurt her, I swear to God, I will hunt you down and make you pay with your life, Kochese."

"Yeah, yeah, yeah, whatever, toughie. Since you like to play games, I have a special game for you! Let's roll the dice. Pick a number between one and twelve," he said.

"I'm not going to play your little game, Kochese. Just let Bird and the baby go. This is between us. They don't have anything to do with this."

"That's where you're wrong. This is between all of us. Now pick a number, bitch, or so help me God, I'll kill this nigga right now!" Kochese barked.

Monica heard Bird scream in the background, and Millicent's cries became more frenzied.

"Okay, okay, four. I pick the number four," Monica said.

"Four. That's a good number. You have exactly four hours to figure out where we are. It's nine-oh-seven p.m. If you're not here by one-oh-seven a.m., I will kill them both, and Jasmine and I will disappear forever. You'll be left with their blood on your hands, Monica," Kochese said calmly.

"I'll be there, Kochese. Where's my sister?"

"Actually, as we speak, she's sharpening the knives we'll need to dissect Bird and his little bitch daughter," Kochese sneered.

"I'll find you in four hours, and when I do, I'm going to put a bullet in your forehead."

"Yeah, you can try, but remember that you have to bring ass to get ass. And, Monica?" he said.

"What?" she shouted.

"You'd better fucking come alone. If I so much as hear a caterpillar fart in the woods, I will kill these two, and you know I will, so don't fucking try me!" he said, and then added, "Are you willing to trade your life for snitch-ass Bird and your precious goddaughter? I guess that's the billion-dollar question. Get here, bitch! The sooner, the better," he said, and then Monica's phone went silent.

She ran to Cody Roth's office and riffled through his desk. She checked each drawer but found nothing. She sat at his desk. "Cody, you were a smart man. I know you came up with something. Help me, please. I know you can hear me. Help me," she said softly.

Cody's cell phone vibrated, and Monica picked it up, but it was just a notification for his email. Cody had a lock on his phone, so even if he had put the info in his cell phone, she wouldn't have been able to access it. She was in the process of putting his cell phone back when she noticed it. His cell phone had been lying on a sheet of paper he'd printed. She turned on Cody's desk lamp and read the paper. It was a reference page of properties owned by Hayden Cross, and he'd circled one of them in the long list of properties that he'd printed out.

121 Candlelite Trail, Rockwall, Texas.

"Cody Roth, you motherfucker, you! You're helping me from beyond the grave. Now that's some spooky shit! Thank you, thank you, thank you!" she shouted. Monica grabbed the paper and darted from his office. If she had guessed correctly, she could be in Rockwall in approximately an hour. She *could* be, but she needed to make a stop first. There was no way that she was walking into an ambush. She would need reinforcements.

Chapter 35

RACE THE CLOCK

10:46 p.m.

Monica drove along I-30 toward Lake Ray Hubbard, trying to digest what her night might come to be. The possibility of having to kill Kochese or Jasmine or both was very real, and it was something that she wasn't prepared for. She hadn't put out a call for backup because King Kochese had made his demands very clear. If Monica brought anyone with her, he wouldn't hesitate to kill both Bird *and* the baby. *Weaknesses and strengths, weaknesses and strengths . . .* Hayden Cross's words kept echoing in her head. She prayed that he was right, because if he wasn't, it could not only cost her life but also the lives of those she held dear.

She had no idea what she was stepping into, and the thought of the unknown terrified her. For all Monica knew, Jasmine and Kochese could be lying in wait, ready to ambush her as soon as she reached the property. Bird could already be dead, and they could've left Millie all alone, frightened and exposed to the frigid winter chill. Although Kochese had made it perfectly clear that she wasn't supposed to bring any backup, he hadn't said anything about bringing a friend. She glanced at the passenger's side of her vehicle, and they locked eyes. He looked away quickly as if to alert Monica that her exit was approaching and she needed to have her eyes on the road. Noisy Boy had been the only man in her life since King Kochese, and she felt safe with him. He panted heavily against the draft of the car's heater. She slid her hand along his shiny white coat and then scratched his belly.

"He might have had you first, but your loyalty belongs to me, huh, boy? Yeah, that's mama's baby," she said sweetly.

Jasmine was her weakness, and Noisy Boy was Kochese's weakness. Monica had cared for Noisy Boy since he was a puppy, and she'd sacrificed any type of love life. Bird used to scold her, saying that Noisy Boy was just a dog, but he wasn't just a dog to Monica. He was a part of her family, her child, and no man would ever stand between her and her child.

After King Kochese had shot himself in the courtroom, she'd taken Noisy Boy, partly because of guilt and partly because she'd grown attached to him. He'd been a friend when she was grieving for perhaps one of the most evil men to ever walk the streets of Dallas. It was Monica, not King, though, who'd nursed Noisy Boy back to health after he'd contracted parvo. The usually agile and energetic Noisy Boy had become lethargic and sickly, vomiting after each meal. He would lie around, whine and whimper for hours, and when he began to poop inside the house uncontrollably, Monica knew that something was wrong. She'd taken him to the vet, and after two weeks of sleepless nights and $900 in veterinary bills, her baby boy was well again. She loved Noisy Boy, so she had no doubt in her mind that he would protect her no matter the cost.

As she exited and turned down the long road leading to the Cross property, Monica rolled down the windows in her car so that she and Noisy Boy could enjoy the cold, crisp air of the wintry wind. According to Monica's GPS, she'd reach her destination in a quick thirteen minutes. She breathed in deep breaths and exhaled slowly, letting the icy air rush through her nostrils. Her pulse quickened, and even with the chill of the December night sky, she began to sweat. Her insides turned somersaults, and her tongue got wet. She heaved once and then again, forcing her to pull over on the dark, desolate road. She heaved again, and this time she felt her dinner fighting to escape the confines of her bowels. She threw her car into park, jumped out, and ran to the shoulder of the road. Monica doubled over and heaved once more, this time expelling the contents of her nausea-laden body. The queasiness would not subside, and she continued to vomit until there was nothing left inside but the clear liquid remnants of bile.

Monica stood slowly. She felt dizzy yet refreshed, and she climbed into her car with a new resolve. Kochese Mills had to die because he was not only a menace, but he was evil incarnate. She silently scolded herself for only bringing Noisy Boy, but if she'd told her superiors about her contact with Kochese, they would've wanted to assemble a tactical team, map out the area, et cetera, and she just didn't have that kind of time.

11:03 p.m.

Monica turned onto the long dirt road that led to the Cross property. Large trees formed a tight overhead canopy that inhibited any light from the full moon above. She drove fastidiously along the narrow road. It was only wide enough for a single vehicle, and the shoulder of the road on either side had deep declines with a four- or five-foot drop-off.

Monica crept to a halt, killed her lights, and exited her vehicle.

Ahead of her by approximately one hundred yards was a clearing, and in that clearing, barely visible, was a house with a single light on in a second-story window. She made her way to her trunk and put on her bulletproof vest marked FBI. Monica put on her gun belt, holstered her Kahr Arms CT9 9 mm pistol, and packed her belt with extra magazines. She shoved nearly an entire box of twelve-gauge shells packed with double-ought buck into the side pocket of her tactical cargo pants. Then she unbagged her favorite weapon: the Kel-Tec KSG twelve-gauge shotgun, which had once belonged to Agent Muldoon. She loaded it and cocked it just so it was ready in case shit got hectic. Monica strapped it to her shoulder and checked her penlight against the palm of her hand. She went back to the driver's side, opened the door, and knelt down.

"Come here, boy, come here," she said softly, patting her knee. Noisy Boy inched toward her, nuzzled his large head in her neck, and licked her chin. "Can I count on you to have my back, boy, huh, can I?" she asked.

Noisy Boy gave a high-pitched yelp, and Monica rubbed his stout nose.

"Okay, mama's baby, calm down. You can't bark when we get out here, okay? We can't let them know we're coming."

11:37 p.m.

Monica and Noisy Boy moved stealthily through the woods. The sounds of the forest were textured and caused Monica's heart to thump erratically. Convolving whispers in the wind, distant bird calls, crickets chirping, and the sound of flapping wings all gave rise to alarm. Monica had never been a country girl, and she wholeheartedly believed in things that went bump in the night. The wind wailed between distorted tree trunks, carrying the sickly stink of rotted wood. Monica moved quickly, ignoring the briars that caught at her pants. Noisy Boy kept a brisk pace, ignoring the critters that scurried around him. His eyes were planted straight ahead, and although he would occasionally wander off briefly to sniff the damp leaves and underbrush, he would quickly return to Monica's side.

When she reached the edge of the woods, Monica stopped, as did Noisy Boy. Ahead of them and to the right was a barn that had seen better days. With its faded and chipped fire truck red paint and termite-infested wood slats, it was barely standing.

Monica stood stoically, afraid to move. Against the darkness of the landscape, a lone light swayed ominously overhead in the barn. She couldn't make out whether there were people in the barn, but she didn't dare move.

The rustling of branches and leaves echoed against the empty night sky. The moon shone brightly, gleaming and bouncing from the rusty chrome of the abandoned pickup truck that happened to be the only barrier between the house and the barn. Monica removed her pistol and advanced slowly toward the barn with trepidation surging through her being with every step. She couldn't hear Bird's torturous pleas for help or Millie's sorrowful cries of discontent. No, she only heard nature's unsettling medley of night-loving varmints. She skulked to the corner of the barn, inched slowly to its open doors, and peered inside. Monica froze in shock and horror as she stepped into the doorway.

12:14 a.m.

There was no sign of Kochese or Jasmine, only Bird and Millicent. They'd hanged Bird by his neck, and he looked as though he'd been tortured. She could smell the stench of charred flesh, and when Monica scanned the room with her penlight, she saw exactly where the smell was coming from. In a corner of the barn, near a stable, a campfire had just been extinguished. The fire had been put out, but the logs still glowed a bright amber, and a branding iron lay across the cinders. Monica searched frantically with her penlight for any sign of Millicent. She was just to the left of where Bird hung, sound asleep. They'd swaddled her warmly in her baby blanket, placed her in a car seat on a workman's table, and placed her pacifier in her mouth.

Monica went to Bird's limp, lifeless body and felt for his pulse. There wasn't one. Kochese had jumped the gun and violated his word. Monica attempted to move toward Millicent, but as she did, the room was suddenly flooded with luminous light. It shone brilliantly, almost blinding Monica, and then she heard the voice of Satan himself.

"That's far enough, Monica. Drop the gun," Kochese said.

"I'm not dropping shit! You're a fucking liar! You said that I had until one-oh-seven a.m.!" Monica screamed.

"Well, I was gonna wait, but what my baby wants, my baby gets. You're in no position to call shots anyway, bitch. Now drop the fucking gun!"

A low, guttural growl began to grow in Noisy Boy's throat. "Easy, baby boy, easy. He's not worth it," Monica said softly. She turned and scanned the room, looking for Jasmine. "Where's my sister, asshole?"

The shrill screeching of metal on metal scraping invaded Monica's eardrums. Jasmine appeared from behind Kochese, rubbing two butcher's knives together blade to blade. "First of all, I'm not your fucking sister. You killed that shit the moment you decided to murder me and my family. Second of all, drop the fucking gun like King told you to, or I'm going to make a rib roast out of this fucking baby!" Jasmine barked.

Monica pointed her gun at Jasmine but kept her eyes trained on Kochese. "Jasmine, please don't make me do this. Drop the knives, please!" Monica ordered.

"You see, that's what I mean. You love this little bitch more than you love me!" Jasmine screamed. She made a move toward Millicent, and Monica let a shot ring out above Jasmine's head. The bullet ripped through the old wood of the barn, sending shards of splinters flying behind where Jasmine and Kochese stood. Jasmine stopped in her tracks, staring at Monica with a deranged look of confusion and angst in her eyes.

"Don't try me, Jasmine. The next one won't miss, I swear," Monica said.

"I told you, Jasmine. She doesn't love you. She loves everybody *but* you. I bet if she could have, she would have left you in Buckner."

"Shut up, Kochese!" Monica screamed.

"I bet she wishes that you were never born!"

"Shut the fuck up, Kochese!" Monica screamed again.

"I love you for real though, Jasmine! Who's always been here for you? Who taught you how to be who you are, taught you to love yourself? Who killed Michael Ross and Jappy on your behalf and then brought Dirt Bag to you to let you get revenge, baby?" Kochese asked.

"You did, baby," Jasmine cooed.

"I know you're not falling for this bullshit, Jasmine. Kochese is a killer. That's what killers do. They kill people. He's using you. Why can't you see that?" Monica said. She turned her attention to Jasmine.

Kochese seized the opportunity of Monica's distraction and whipped out his .45-caliber. Noisy Boy dropped his head low, bared his teeth, and began to growl.

"Over here, boy, come to daddy, come on, Noisy Boy, come to daddy," Kochese said.

Noisy Boy clambered to the center of the floor between Monica and Kochese, still growling, only now his growl was deeper, and his ice blue eyes were trained on Monica. She couldn't believe it. She'd naively believed that the brute beast understood loyalty, but he'd shown her different.

He was loyal to the alpha male who'd cared for him as a pup.

"You see, bitch, Noisy Boy knows what time it is. Since you love him so much, after I kill you, I'm going to chop your body up and feed you to Noisy for puppy chow," Kochese said harshly.

"Jasmine, why are you doing this? I can get you the help you need."

"What kind of help? Mental help? You think I'm crazy, Monica? If you really want to help, just let us go. Let us live our lives, Moni," Jasmine said sweetly.

"You know I can't do that. Between the two of you, there are at least twenty people dead. I'm sorry, Jazz, but I can't do that."

"Twenty bodies? You're short, big sister. Try close to sixty. And since you don't want to help me, then fuck you!" Jasmine snapped.

Her demeanor confused Monica. It was erratic, to say the least. At one point she'd be happy and angry the next. Her eyes were devoid of any feeling, yet Monica could see the hatred seething in her soul. Jasmine was dressed in an off-white nightgown and pink bunny slippers, and her hair was all over her head. She looked like a wild woman, and Monica could see the deterioration in Jasmine's mental state.

Monica removed her handcuffs and threw them at Jasmine. "No, I don't think you're crazy. I think you're lost and confused. Now put these on, and I will, like I said, get you the help you need. We can do it the easy way or the hard way. Either way, you're both going away for a very long time. Now put them on!" Monica said firmly.

Jasmine brought the knives up to her side and gripped them tightly, so tightly, in fact, that her knuckles turned white.

"Nobody's going to jail today, you fucking cunt, but you *are* going to die today!" Kochese shouted. He cocked his pistol and fired in Monica's direction.

She dove to the ground just in time to miss being hit by Kochese's wild bullet. The impact from hitting the ground knocked the wind from her, and she lay on the ground wriggling in pain. Noisy Boy barked and growled loudly, and just as Kochese made his move toward Monica to finish her off, Noisy Boy lunged at him. Kochese dropped his pistol in an attempt to ward off the snarling dog. His sharp canine teeth ripped into the right side of Kochese's face. He squirmed and screamed in agonizing pain as blood poured from the jagged wound along his jaw. His teeth were exposed where Noisy Boy had taken a chunk of meat from his cheek.

Jasmine picked up Kochese's gun and let off a round into the rabid pit bull. He yowled in pain and fell over to his side whimpering, trying desperately to lick the wound he'd sustained.

12:58 a.m.

Monica was still dazed, but not so much so that she didn't notice Jasmine standing over Noisy Boy, about to pump a second slug into his snow-white body. The hind quarter of his usually milky white mane was now beginning to turn a pinkish and crimson red. He moaned and whined and reminded Monica of when he was just a small puppy.

Noisy Boy lay helpless and unable to move. His head was cocked to one side, and his tongue was lapped over his teeth. Kochese, although in obvious pain, reached over and stroked the puppy's nose. True, he'd betrayed Kochese, but he still loved the dog. He'd had him since he was a week old, and he understood Noisy Boy's loyalty. Monica had taken care of him when Kochese was nowhere to be found. What Kochese couldn't understand was how Noisy Boy had known to pretend to switch sides in order to make Kochese lower his defenses. Kochese smiled to himself. *Maybe I taught him more than I thought I did.*

1:07 a.m.

Monica raised her pistol and, through blurred vision, took aim at Jasmine. She aimed at the arm that held the gun trained on Noisy Boy's body. Monica let a single shot fly in Jasmine's direction, striking her arm just below her elbow. She dropped the pistol and fell to her knees.

"You fucking shot me, Moni! I'm your sister, goddammit!"

"I know. That's why you're not dead, dummy. I can't believe you shot Noisy Boy!" Monica screamed.

"Noisy Boy? Noisy Boy? Is that all you care about, Noisy Boy?" Jasmine asked. Tears had begun to fall freely from her eyes, and she sobbed uncontrollably.

Kochese scrambled to his feet, trying to stop the bleeding with one hand, and he pulled Jasmine up with the other. She hugged him tightly and whispered something in his ear. Kochese looked into Jasmine's eyes with a sad look in his own and protested. Jasmine pushed Kochese aside and stood in front of him. "Go! Now, Kochese, goddammit!" she scolded.

Kochese began to back up toward the rear entrance of the barn. Monica took aim at Kochese, but Jasmine stepped into the line of fire. Upon seeing this, Kochese bolted from the back door.

Monica's heart dropped. She'd never seen that look in Kochese's eyes before. Not even when he told Monica that he loved her had she seen a look so loving. He'd always been heavily guarded with Monica, and even when he had opened up to her, his love was conditional. He looked at Jasmine with an unconditional love in his eyes, a look that said he'd rather die than be separated from her, and Monica felt a slight twinge of jealousy. She attempted to give chase, but Jasmine tackled her as she tried to pass.

"Let him go, Monica! Everything that he did, he did for me! Leave him be, bitch!" Jasmine spat as she struck her sister across the face. Jasmine kept her pinned to the floor for twenty minutes, and Kochese had too big of a head start for Monica to give chase.

Monica brought her 9 mm up to Jasmine's face and cocked it. "If you don't get the fuck off me, I swear on Pop Pop that I will blow your brains all over these barn walls. Now get off!" she said.

Jasmine didn't move. She sat on top of Monica and began to speak. "Remember when we were kids, and Mommy, Daddy, and Pop Pop would wake us up on Christmas morning after we'd dozed off waiting for Santa? I was thinking about those days a few weeks back, you know, wondering how life would be for my child," she said, rubbing her stomach gently, and then she continued. "That is, until Kochese and I went to the doctor last week and I found out that we were having twins. That's two girls or two boys, Monica, a family like we used to have, you know? When Kochese and I get married, we want to raise our children in one of those communities where everyone knows each other, you know? Where they bring you pie when you move in and stuff. I don't know if I want to do private school or just put them in public school like we went to. I still want you to be my maid of honor, too!" Jasmine said with a dazed look in her eyes.

Monica couldn't believe her ears. Her sister had lost all sense of reality. From the way she was speaking, one would never know that she was a serial killer, and it scared Monica.

She looked into Jasmine's eyes. She had a far-away look of peace and contentment. As much as Monica hated to burst Jasmine's bubble, she'd always been honest with her little sister.

"Jasmine, what makes you think that you're going to be a family? Kochese is in the wind. He left you here to take the fall. After spending more than eleven years in Buckner, you turn around and do some shit that could possibly land you in a mental institution for the rest of your life? You'll never be a family, Jasmine. When those kids are born, the State is going to take them from you, and you'll never see them again. Meanwhile, your little boo thang Kochese is going to be dodging the law if someone doesn't kill him first," Monica said.

"Kochese is a billionaire, Monica. Trust me when I tell you that wherever I end up, I won't be there long. My baby will make sure of that."

"Your baby? Listen to you! You think that grimy nigga gives a fuck about you? Well, he doesn't, you can believe that!" Monica spat.

Jasmine rolled off of her and lay on her back, staring up at the ceiling. "You sound jealous, Monica. Is it because he loves me and you can see it? He never looked at you like that, huh? When he looks at me, I can see the love in his eyes, I can feel the love pulsating in his every touch, and I feel good all over. So if I never have that feeling again, at least I was able to feel it once before I leave this earth. And you know what? I can accept that because it's something that I longed for my entire life, and Kochese, and Kochese alone, was the man who gave it to me."

"Jasmine, Kochese is the devil, but it's not my place to make you believe that. Earlier you said that there were almost sixty bodies. Where are they, Jasmine?" Monica asked.

Jasmine laughed riotously, and after all the gunfire and loud talking, Millicent still hadn't awakened. "Have you been in the house yet, Moni?" she asked.

"As a matter of fact, I haven't. Why?"

"Go to the house. You'll see. I'll watch the baby and your mutt," Jasmine sneered.

"Yeah, I bet you will. Stand your ass up, Jasmine."

Jasmine did as she was told, and Monica handcuffed her to a wooden beam in the center of the barn. She knelt next to Noisy Boy and felt his chest. His breathing was shallow and labored, but he would be okay until she was able to check out the inside of the house.

Chapter 36

GAME OVER

Monica approached the house with caution. She wasn't sure whether Kochese had left the property, and she wasn't taking any chances. She entered the house and moved from room to room slowly. She approached a room that glowed with the gray light of a black-and-white television. Monica entered the room and gasped in horror. There were pictures of some of Kochese and Jasmine's victims with the preplanned methods of their deaths scrawled on the paper in red Sharpie. The most alarming thing that spooked Monica was the monitors. It would have been different had there been surveillance cameras for the property, but Kochese had cameras spread around Dallas like the Feds. There were screens that showed the offices at CrossTech, screens of different street corners, and even one that showed the corner where Bird's restaurant had been. There were cameras placed strategically throughout her house, in her bathroom, in her bedroom, in the kitchen, even one in Jasmine's room, and Monica found herself wondering how long he'd been watching them.

She left the room and made her way upstairs toward the room with the light on. She thought back to her days undercover when she first realized that King Kochese was insane. Kochese had an underground crypt where he'd kept his mother's mummified body, refusing to, as he'd put it, let her soul rest until she saw his greatness. The memory made her skin crawl, and she shivered. Monica silently prayed that she wouldn't find anything even remotely close to that horrific scene. Nothing in her wildest imagination could have prepared her for what lay beyond the doors of that upstairs bedroom.

Monica ascended the stairs slowly, the aged wood giving way beneath her weight and squeaking with every step. The stairs were sandwiched between two narrow walls that made the tight corridor seem even more constricted. Monica opened the door guardedly. Creeeeak. Monica froze, unable to move, and her hand trembled uncontrollably.

The room had been turned into a giant chessboard, and it was even equipped with the pieces. Monica moved through the room to the center of the floor and examined the pieces more closely. Monica couldn't breathe, and her heart thumped in her chest so loud that she could have sworn that it could be heard by the dead. Boom-boom boom-boom boom-boom went her heart as she spun around the room, looking at the harrowing sight.

The chess pieces were the mummified bodies of their victims. Sixteen white men and women and sixteen black men and women had all been impaled on metal stakes that had been anchored to the wooden floor. As sick as it was, Monica had to admit that it was a work of art. Each victim had their chess piece embedded in their head like the horn of a unicorn, and Monica wondered what sick and sadistic game Kochese and Jasmine had been playing. True to her word, with the twenty-plus victims Monica knew about plus the thirty-two she'd just found, that brought their total to a little over fifty. There had to be more bodies, and if they were in the house, Monica would find them.

She eased through the house, but her mind wasn't really on dead bodies. With Bird dead, she would have to honor her word to him and care for Millicent, and she would have to have Jasmine committed if the courts would allow it. She silently prayed that they would because Jasmine's crimes were punishable by death.

Kochese Mills sat in the dining room of his old friend Nae, the lesbian he'd employed during his lucrative drug operation. She was the only person he knew who would possibly have his back. "Nae, man, I really appreciate this shit. Yo, I need to use your computer," he said.

"Yeah, fool, whatever you need. I still can't believe it's you. Shit, if it weren't for the fact that you knew a bunch of shit that only you and I knew, I still wouldn't believe it was you in the flesh, man, straight up."

Nae brought Kochese the computer and left him to do his business. Kochese looked over his shoulder to make sure that he was alone and logged into his bank account. As much as he tried to fathom it, he still couldn't wrap his head around the fact that he was a billionaire, but he was working against the clock. It wouldn't be long before Monica and the Feds took the notion to freeze all of his accounts.

Kochese took out his cell phone and placed an international call to Barclays Capital of Zurich. He set up an account and then transferred the $2.3 billion his father had transferred into his account before he murdered him. King Kochese still had friends in low places, friends he never mentioned to anyone but who happened to be the type of people a man in his unique position could use in times like these. Manny Contreras was one of those people., Manny was a mastermind, and if he was going to disappear, he would need Manny's help. In the old days, when Kochese was just starting out, he and Manny had become fast friends. They shared money, resources, and even women from time to time, but as Kochese ascended to the ranks of street legend and kingpin, Manny sank deep into the underworld as a fixer. There was no aspect of illegality that Manny wasn't a part of.

He placed a call to Manny. He hadn't expected him to answer the phone, but much to his surprise, Manny answered on the first ring.

"*Bueno,*" Manny said.

"Manny, what's up, brother?"

"Excuse me, *papi,* but who is this?" he asked.

"It's King Kochese, playa. Damn, don't you recognize my voice?"

"Voice means nothing, *baba.* The King I knew is dead and gone, so you're going to have to do better than that," Manny scoffed.

"Manny, seriously, brother, it's me. I've known you since the Michael Ross days. I was at your wedding to Cecilia. I was there when Mateo was born, man."

"That's shit that you can find out over a game of checkers, *baba,* so forgive me if I call bullshit," Manny snickered.

"Okay, ask me something that only you and King Kochese would know, chief. I don't have all night. I'm kind of pressed for time."

"Let's see. I celebrated my twenty-fifth birthday with some of my closest associates, including King Kochese, in the Dominican Republic. Something happened on that trip that only me and King know happened. What is it?" Manny asked.

Kochese was getting irritated. He adjusted the blood-soaked bandage on his cheek and sighed heavily. "We said we would never speak on it again, but if it'll convince you so that we can get on with this shit, so be it. We were in the DR kicking it for your birthday, and we got fucked up. Everybody else had passed out, and it was only you and I awake, so we went out. You met a little bitch named Natalia and took her back to the villa. We were gonna run a train on her, but when we got her in the room and got her undressed, the *she* was a *he*. We chopped his dick off, killed that *maricon*, and buried him behind the villa, and we vowed to never speak on it again," King Kochese said.

Manny laughed ruthlessly. "Okay, King, I believe it's you, *baba*. What do you need?"

"Yo, bro, I need to disappear for a while. I need a whole new identity, Manny: ID, social security number, shit, fingerprints if I can get them. I even want a new face," Kochese said.

"I got you covered, *baba*. I got you covered. A whole new face, huh?"

"Yeah, dawg, I want to change my entire face. Well, not everything. The doctor can leave the scar as a reminder to never trust again, neither man nor beast."